The Vanishing Season

The
Vanishing
Season

Joanna Schaffhausen

Minotaur Books
New York

THE VANISHING SEASON. Copyright © 2017 by Joanna Schaffhausen. All rights reserved. Printed in the United States of America. For information, address St. Martin's Press, 175 Fifth Avenue, New York, N.Y. 10010.

www.minotaurbooks.com

The Library of Congress Cataloging-in-Publication Data is available upon request.

ISBN 978-1-250-12604-7 (hardcover)
ISBN 978-1-250-12605-4 (ebook)

Our books may be purchased in bulk for promotional, educational, or business use. Please contact your local bookseller or the Macmillan Corporate and Premium Sales Department at 1-800-221-7945, extension 5442, or by email at MacmillanSpecialMarkets@macmillan.com.

First Edition: December 2017

10 9 8 7 6 5 4 3 2 1

To my mother and father,
who raised me in a house full of great books

Acknowledgments

Many thanks to the Mystery Writers of America and St. Martin's Press, for sponsoring the First Crime Novel Award, and for taking a chance on this book. Thanks also to Publishing Director Kelley Ragland, for answering dozens of questions from a clueless newbie, and to my intrepid editor, Elizabeth Lacks, for her sure, guiding hand. Huge thanks as well to my agent, Jill Marsal, for invaluable advice, input, and support.

It turns out that if I don't have readers to hold me accountable, the words stay firmly in my head. Thank you to my badass beta team, for making me do the work. I am grateful for your enthusiasm, your thoughtful criticism, and your helpful questions: Julie Kline Benamati, Katie Bradley, Stacie Brooks, Rony Camille, Ethan Cusick, Rayshell Reddick Daniels, Michelle Farley, Jason Grenier, Suzanne Holliday, Shannon Howl, Katie Hull, Jaconda Kearse, Robbie McGraw, Kimberly Moore, Tali Kastner, Michelle Kiefer, Rebecca Gullotti LeBlanc, Jill Svihovec, Dawn Volkart, Michelle Weger, and Paula Woolman. #TeamBump forever.

My unending gratitude and appreciation to Amanda Wilde, who's been my friend and partner in imagined crime for nigh on twenty years now, and who is the only person to have edited all versions of this particular story. You are a rare gem, my dear.

Special thanks to Team Grandparents, who helped me carve out time to write: Brian and Stephanie Schaffhausen, and Larry and Cherry Rooney.

Lastly, my heartfelt thanks to the good-humored humans who live with me: my rock, my love, and the only one of my readers who can nag me in bed at night, Garrett Rooney, and our precocious, hilarious daughter, Eleanor, who has a greater passion for justice than most grownups I know.

The Vanishing Season

Fourteen Years Ago

I t's too dark to go out but too hot to sleep. I hear summer night sounds through my open window: teenagers laughing, a ball slapping against the pavement. Sirens wail far away. I am spread like Jesus on the cross, no body parts touching, but still my skin burns into the sheets. I get up and creep down the stairs, outside into the dead air. The city has stored up the sun all day long, and now heat is radiating back off the concrete.

I prowl around the neighborhood, but no one I know is out. Fans spin in the windows over my head, and I catch snatches of arguments, of television shows wafting out into the night. Jack and Lindsay Bierenbaum are getting it on. I am standing underneath their window in the shadows when I first see her, the girl on the bike. She's wearing short shorts, and her long hair flows behind her in a ponytail as she pedals toward the illumination in the park across the street.

She's almost there when a car pulls up next to her. They are lit by the streetlamp above as if they were on a stage, and so I become the audience. There's a man inside the car and he says something I can't hear. He's gesturing, asking for directions, maybe. She hops off the bike and points down the road, but he doesn't drive away. He gets out of the car. I can see he has a cloth in his hand, and I guess it's a handkerchief to wipe away his sweat.

I am wrong.

She struggles briefly when he puts the cloth over her mouth, then goes limp in his arms. He stuffs her into the back of the car so fast I think I must have imagined it. I am wooden, transfixed. He sees me when he loads her bike into his trunk; our eyes meet across the street. Still I cannot move.

He stares hard at me for a long moment and then raises a finger to his lips.

The slam of the car door makes me jump. He drives away and I don't see his face again until much later, on the news, next to faces of more young girls who disappeared.

Until then, since then, I see his face in my mind, his finger pressed to his lips. I see her rag doll body shoved into his car. *Shhh. Don't tell anyone.*

I never have.

I

Ellery Hathaway emerged from the steamy bathroom, toweling her hair dry, dressed again and ready to leave, but Sam still lay sprawled in the motel bed with its squeaky mattress and scratchy sheets. Always he wanted to stay just a little bit longer, kiss her just one more time. It was one of the things she hated about him. "It's almost midnight," she said as she laid the damp towel over the back of a cheap motel chair. The room was swimming in shadows, just like always, because she never let him see her all the way naked. It was a practical concern more than a manipulative one, but the more she held back, the more he wanted. She definitely had his attention now.

He rolled to the nightstand to put his watch back on but made no other move to get dressed. "It's July already. Seems like we just had Memorial Day."

She went to the window and looked out at the oppressive summer night. It was black as pitch and filled with trees. The motel gravel went about ten feet back, and then there was nothing but dense woods and the invisible creatures hiding within them. "He'll take another one soon," she said. "Just like last year, and we've done nothing to stop it."

"Christ, Ellie. Not this again." He sat up and tugged on his pants. "I thought you agreed to let this go."

She rested her forehead against the glass, which vibrated in time to the churning of the antiquated air-conditioning unit below it, and she felt the hum penetrate to her veins. "Three people are dead," she said, more to herself than to Sam. Lord knew he'd heard the words from her enough times that she need not repeat them now. The last time they'd had this conversation was more than six months ago, back when he was just the chief and she was a junior patrol officer. He had not listened to her then, but maybe now was different, now that she had something he wanted.

He came half naked to the window, long limbs moving in easy grace. It was one of the things she loved about him. "We have no proof of any murder," he said. "You know that as well as I do. We don't even know these people are dead."

"They're dead." The first one, nineteen-year-old Bea Nesbit, disappeared three years ago somewhere between Woodbury and Boston, where she went to school. Back then, the State Police had gotten involved in the search, and Ellery had been happy to let them. She'd been on the job only seven months at that point and did not know the Nesbit family. Ten days later, Bea was still missing and Ellery had received the first card in her mailbox.

Sam touched her hunched shoulder, pushing it back down with gentle fingers. "People leave their lives all the time and don't look back."

She jerked away from his hand. No one needed to explain to her the urge to disappear, not when she hadn't seen her natural hair color in more than a decade. Lately, she'd been dying it a dark chestnut brown, a no-nonsense shade whose remnants resembled the color of dried blood as it washed down the drain of her white porcelain sink.

Sam's hair was an honest salt-and-pepper black. He was twenty-two years older and had worked his way up through the ranks in Boston before taking the small town position in Woodbury as chief of police, where he'd become accustomed to being the smartest cop in the room. Ellery was the only female officer in the department, not that this was a great accomplishment on a squad of eight people, but it meant that, for all his depth of knowledge, there were certain experiences she had that Sam lacked.

"Bea Nesbit, Mark Roy, and Shannon Blessing are dead," she reminded him, turning around so she could look into his eyes as she said it. "In the next two weeks, unless we do something, another name will be added to that list. We'll have another grieving family and no answers to give them. Is that what you want?"

"What would you have me do? These cases have already been investigated by our department and others. We have no bodies, no evidence, no suggestion that a crime even took place. I'm not ignoring you, Ellie, but I have to have something to go on here besides your gut feeling."

Her cheeks burned hot and she looked away. At least he hadn't actually called it women's intuition. The only evidence she had, besides what little was contained in the official files, was locked at home in her bedroom drawer, in an envelope where she didn't have to see the birthday cards unless she specifically went looking for them. Not that there was much to see. She could picture the baffled expression on Sam's face if she brought them in and tried to explain what they meant.

This isn't evidence of anything but the fact that you're another

*year older. Congratulations, Officer Hathaway. You're aging just
like the rest of us.*

Maybe if she told him about her other birthday, the one from
years ago, then he would understand. He would have to act. Or
maybe he would just look at her with pity and horror. Either way,
once she told him, she could never take it back.

"You could reinvestigate the cases," she said to Sam, trying
to keep her voice steady. "Take a fresh look. If we can figure out
what the relationship is between the victims, we might be able to
stop him from taking another one."

"You're the only one who thinks there is a relationship."

"So then give me the cases." She raised her chin, challenging
him to deny her. They had one detective on the force, and she
sure as hell wasn't it.

Frustration flashed in Sam's eyes, and then, worse, sympathy.
He shook his head almost imperceptibly. "You know I can't do
that."

"Fine. Right. Just don't blame me when you've got another
one missing." She crossed the room to put on her boots.

"And what will you do if that doesn't happen? What will you
obsess about then?"

She glanced up. "You're saying I need this?"

He eyed her. "Maybe part of you. Face it, Ellery. You get off
on drama."

"Not me." She snapped her laces together and stood up.
"You're the one who always wants to make things complicated."

He grabbed her arm when she tried to pass him. "Stay," he said
softly, sliding his fingers down past the scars to her narrow wrist.
"We can talk about it."

She turned her arm so their fingers touched, but did not meet
his gaze. "Go home, Sam. Julia will be wondering where you are.
I'll see you in the morning, okay?"

Mute, he released her and she pushed out into the night heat. Tree creatures chattered at her from tall pines; white gravel crunched under her feet as she made her way to her truck. The New England humidity melted her T-shirt against her sticky skin. Ellery paused, her hand on the door, and glanced around her into the thin edge of the forest. She had chosen this quiet town because it was so removed from the big cities filled with thousands of people. A few of the guys at the station would sit around during the slow times, which to be fair was most of the time, and talk about what they would do if a major crime ever hit sleepy little Woodbury. A bank robbery, maybe, as if anyone would come to their tiny downtown, with its pharmacy, post office, and handful of shops, thinking he could hit the local bank for a million bucks. The boys in blue were sure they would stop the bad guys red-handed before they ever reached the town limits. Sam, who knew better, smirked at their self-aggrandizing, sometimes tried to catch her eye across the room to share a wink at the guy's expense, but Ellery always looked away and thought, *Be careful what you wish for.*

She climbed into her truck and switched her cell phone back on, its screen casting an eerie glow over the otherwise dark interior. The missed calls and texts showed she had been unusually popular over the past hour. A missed call from her mother, no message. A text from Brady that made her smile: *6 new kittens today. Am covered in miniature but terribly fierce claw marks. Send help!* But her smile vanished when she saw the other missed call, this time with a voice message. "They're fighting again, please come quick," came the young, frightened whisper on the other end.

Ellery tossed the phone down and yanked the truck into gear, gravel spitting from beneath the tires as she tore out of the motel parking lot. She did not even stop to call it in because the time stamp on the call said that she was already twenty-three minutes late. Thanks to the late hour, there was zero traffic and she made it across town in record time. The neighborhood was quiet as she pulled off the main road, the houses dark and set in some distance from the street. The average family in Woodbury was poor in cash but rich in land. The result was large, overgrown yards separating small, run-down houses that had been built en masse after World War II and had mostly sat untouched since, with their identical striped front awnings faded and warped by the passing of time. As she slowed near her destination, Ellery's headlights caught the peeling white paint on the picket fence and an overturned child's bicycle lying in the front yard.

Yellow light spilled out from the open windows but Ellery saw no one moving around inside. She killed the engine, and in the silence, her heart beat faster as she imagined the confrontation to come. Domestic disputes were the most unpredictable part of her otherwise routine work. As much as she was fixed on her campaign to Sam about their missing persons problem, Woodbury's last official murder had been in 1983, when Tom Pickney shot his brother Terrance after Tom found out Terrance had been carrying on with his wife.

Despite the humid summer night, Ellery retrieved her Woodbury PD jacket from the floor of the passenger seat and removed her police-issue revolver from the locked glove compartment before approaching the house. She knocked sharply on the screen door, and the heavy inside door swung open almost at once, like someone had been waiting for her. Darryl Franklin filled the entire doorway with his massive frame, blocking out the light and anyone who might have been standing behind him. "Whad'you want?" He sneered down to where she stood on the stoop.

"We got a call about a disturbance at your residence, Mr. Franklin."

"What? Who called you?" He peered up and down at his neighbors, but the street was quiet and dark. "I don't see nobody out."

"Never mind who called. I want to see Rosalie and Anna."

He stank like sweat and alcohol, his face puffy and his dark eyes unfocused. He considered her request for a moment, and then broke into a toothy but malevolent grin. "There isn't no disturbance happening here," he said, and he paused to take a sip from the can of Bud he held in his beefy hand. "Go home, Ellie. It's late for a girl like you to be runnin' around all by her lonesome. Somethin' could happen to you."

Ellery squared her shoulders, her hand resting lightly on her holster. "It's an official call, Mr. Franklin. You know how this works. I can't leave until I see Rosalie and Anna."

"It's my house. I know the law. I don't have to let you into my house unless you got a warrant." He swayed a little as he said it, sloshing beer onto the pavement between them.

"Then we can all go down to the station and visit with the chief. He'll be real cranky if we have to wake him up at this hour." The truth be told, Sam probably was slinking in the back door of his house right about now, but Ellery forced that thought out of her mind.

Franklin muttered a string of curse words at her, but he stood aside just enough to allow a narrow opening for her to pass through into the house. She brushed the sweat-stained cotton covering his rotund stomach as she stepped over the threshold and into the family home. The place held a heavy, forceful quiet that Ellie recognized as the aftermath of sudden violence. She took a few more steps over the threadbare carpet. The living room TV was on but muted. The scent of cigarettes and leftover dinner, something involving grease and peppers and onions, hung in the close, thick air. Ellie let her eyes travel over the overstuffed brown microfiber sofa, its cushions lopsided from years of use, to the burned-out hole in the arm of the old La-Z-Boy recliner and the fist-size dent in the wall behind it. The dent had been there the last time Ellie showed up in the middle of the night like this.

"Rosalie? Anna? Are you in here? It's Ellie Hathaway." Her skin tingled because she still had no proof of life and now Franklin stood between her and the door. She made sure to keep her body angled so she could see him in her peripheral vision, where he was drinking his beer and feigning disinterest.

After several tense moments, Rosalie Franklin and ten-year-old Anna shuffled around the corner, Rosa's arms around her daughter's shoulders and her eyes downcast. Even from fifteen feet away, Ellie could see the welt swelling on Rosalie's left cheek. "Officer Hathaway, you didn't need to come out here so late."

"Are you okay?" Ellery asked her, closing the gap between them so that she could get a better look at the other woman's injuries.

"I'm fine." Rosalie turned her face away from Ellery, hiding behind her dark curtain of hair. "You should go."

Franklin pushed open the screen door so hard that it slapped against the outside railing, making the women jump. "Yeah, you should go now. They're fine, as you can see."

"In a minute," Ellery said, more to Rosa and Anna than to Darryl. "Why don't we step outside? You, me, and Anna."

She herded them toward the door, knowing that Rosalie would allow herself to be pushed along despite her fear because this was how she lived every day, following orders that went against her own self-interest. Ellery felt a twinge of regret at capitalizing on Rosalie's indoctrination, but there was no way she was going to convince her to press charges with Franklin just six feet away, pawing at the floor like a bull in the pasture.

When they reached the doorway, Franklin blocked them with one solid arm. "S'pose I don't feel like letting you by," he said, his voice hard.

"Then I radio downtown and explain how you're holding an officer of the law hostage, and you go to jail for a really long time."

They all stood frozen while Franklin digested this information. Finally, he dropped his arm to let them pass. Ellery exhaled in relief as they hit the night air. Rosalie and Anna were both barefoot, Anna dressed in some sort of Disney princess-themed nightgown that barely covered her bottom, and Ellery ushered them both over the half-dead grass to the edge of the lawn. Franklin remained at the front door, saying nothing but casting a long shadow. "What happened tonight, Rosa?" Ellie asked her in a low voice.

"Nothing," Rosalie insisted, hugging herself and glancing over her shoulder. "I'm okay."

"He hit her because he wanted tacos for dinner tonight but Mama didn't have the time to go shopping today."

"Anna!"

"It's true." The girl folded her thin arms and glared at her mother.

"It's not true. He was just upset because his boss reduced his hours this week," Rosalie said in an urgent whisper.

"Last time it was because his back was acting up," Ellery replied. "What excuse is he going to give you next time?"

"You don't understand," Rosalie murmured, her shoulders slumping, her gaze trained on the ground. Ellie looked away, up toward the streetlamp that hosted a frenzy of swarming gnats, because she knew she could raise her sleeves, march Rosa into the white light, and show her the scars. *I lived,* she could say, *and you can too*. Maybe then Rosa would listen to her and get that order of protection. She could kick Darryl out, get a better job, go back to school, make a peaceful home for herself and Anna, and cook whatever the hell she wanted for dinner every damn night for the rest of her life.

Ellie swallowed hard as she imagined it because she knew she wasn't going to do it. She wasn't going to blow up her whole fragile existence just for a pile of maybes. Ellery drew in a long breath and fixed Rosalie with a hard stare. "You don't have to take this from him. You don't. Say the word, and I can take you away from here, you and Anna, right now, to someplace safe. Or you can swear out a complaint against him and I'll have him arrested on the spot."

"You?" Rosa looked her up and down in skeptical fashion.

"Me," Ellery said, with more certainty than she felt. She risked a look at the door, where Franklin was watching them with a sullen expression, and she wondered if he kept a gun in the house. Ellery was five seven and athletically built, but Franklin had nearly a foot on her and outweighed her by more than a hundred pounds.

"He's not gonna go anywhere with you. Besides, what good would it do? You take him away and he'll be back here in a day or two, and then me and Anna, where're we supposed to go?"

There was a women's shelter one town over, but seeking it out meant walking away now with the clothes on their backs, and Ellery knew Rosalie wasn't wrong about the likely outcome: she could arrest Franklin, but it would be for simple assault and he would be out on a minimal bond, probably within twenty-four hours. The house was his. The bank account was his. Rosa and Anna would have to start over again from nothing. "There are people who can help you," Ellery tried again, her frustration rising as she realized she was losing yet another battle. "I will personally do everything I can to help you."

She heard the limitation of that statement even as she said it, read the truth in the way Rosa's expression shut down. "No, no. We just have to make it a few weeks, just through the summer, then his hours'll pick up this fall and everything will be okay. You'll see." Rosalie tugged her daughter back toward the house, and Anna twisted around in her grasp, stumbling over the uneven ground as she shot a pleading look back toward Ellery. Ellie took a few steps after them, but she was helpless under the weight of the law.

The screen door opened and closed again with a sharp slap, and then Rosalie and Anna disappeared from view, leaving Ellery alone again with Franklin. He was huge and back lit, his face in shadow, but she could make out the whites of his eyes as he stared her down. "Stay away from my family," he said, holding up a warning finger at her.

"Stop giving me reason to come out here, and I will."

He dropped his hand, chugged the last of the beer, and crushed the can flat between his strong, fat fingers. "You come out my way, maybe I'll do the same to you."

"What do you mean by that?"

He shrugged and tossed the can at the ground near her feet. "You drop in at my house like this in the middle of the night, seems it's only fair if I return the favor. You live out down Burning Tree Road, ain't that right? Yeah, seems I've been out there hunting once in the woods, and I seen where you live. A little old farmhouse. All alone."

"Are you threatening me, Mr. Franklin?"

He held up his palms in an exaggerated gesture. "Hell, no, Officer. I'm just bein' neighborly."

"We're not neighbors," Ellery told him flatly. "If I see you on my property, I will shoot you."

He grinned again. "Now, is that a threat? Or maybe it's an invitation. Either way, you can be sure I'll see you around, Officer Ellie. Oh, yes, I will."

Ellery gripped the wheel of the truck a little tighter as she navigated the long bumpy dirt road that led to her house. The previous owners had smoothed the road before putting the tiny farmhouse on the market four years earlier, but the intervening seasons had thawed and frozen the ground into a lavalike series of mounds and crevices. The lack of summer rain thus far meant the road was cracked and dusty, kicking up pebbles and grime as she rolled on home. It had never been a working farmhouse, not in the commercial sense, zoned at best for perhaps a pair of horses and some chickens. Ellery liked it because it was set well in from the main road and backed up against the thick woods, acres upon acres of protected land, because that was how she felt living by herself among the stars and the trees: protected.

"Don't you worry about bears and coyotes and that sort of thing?" Her mother had fretted back when Ellery first moved into the place as a twenty-four-year-old new homeowner. Ellery had used the last of her funds, the blood money, to make the down payment, marking a clean break, she thought, between her past and her future.

"No bears around here," she had reassured her city-slicker mother, not mentioning, of course, that surely her mom must realize by now that there were plenty of things out there more frightening than bears.

As she stepped out of the truck, Ellery inhaled the cool, dark scent of home in the summertime: a unique mix of wildflowers, cut grass, and the earthy smell of the forest just beyond. It was dark, the only light provided by the pinprick stars and a wedge of moon overhead, and quiet enough that she could hear the thick rustling of the distant trees. At her porch, she took the pair of worn-down wooden steps in one stretch and unlocked the dead bolt at her front door. Immediately, she heard the scratching of toenails on the wooden floor. "Hey, Bump," she called, just before her basset hound came hurtling into the room with a frantic wagging tail. "Did you miss me?"

She knelt with a grin and rubbed his long, silky ears as he pressed his solid, wriggling body as close as possible to hers. He snuffled every inch of her, cataloging her outside adventures with his generous nose, and she figured he got a good whiff of Darryl Franklin in there someplace. Franklin's attempt at intimidation did not frighten her; he was a dumb heffalump who spent most evenings drunk off his ass. If he tried anything stupid, Ellie knew she'd see him coming a mile away.

She gave Bump's ears a last scratch before rising to her feet. "Let's go out back so you can do your business, okay?" He trotted after her eagerly, through the living room, down the short hall, and into the kitchen, where she undid the dead bolt on her back door and let the dog out into the small yard. "Just stay away from skunks this time," she called as he bounded into the shadows. She flicked on the back-porch light in an effort to keep the unwanted critters at bay while Bump scampered out to the forest's edge. She couldn't see him well, but she tracked him by the jangling of the tags on his collar. While Bump went about his routine, Ellie pulled out her cell phone again and found no new messages or texts, not even from Sam, which was actually kind of a relief.

She opened her messaging program and saw the little green dot that indicated Brady was online. *It's 2 A.M.*, she wrote him. *Go to bed.*

Can't, he typed back. *Feeding time.*

He sent her a picture that showed his large hand, a small bottle of milk, and adorable ball of gray-and-white fur. Brady Archer worked at the Angelman Animal Shelter, where she had adopted Speed Bump a few years ago, soon after she moved in. They had struck up a friendship of sorts over a shared love of animals and '80s music. What cemented the relationship was that he was an insomniac, like her, so they could chat like this in the wee small hours of the morning. *Cheesiest ballad,* he would write.

Easy, she would type in return. *"I'd Do Anything for Love" by Meat Loaf. The man's name alone makes it a surefire win.*

I'm going with "Don't Stop Believing." The lyrics are just a bunch of random stuff the guy sees outside. Street light. People. What the hell does it even mean, anyway?

Blasphemy! That song is a cultural touchstone, and Journey is a legend.

Yeah. Legendarily awful.

Trading zingers with Brady reminded her of late-night talks she'd shared with her brother, Daniel, in their hot Chicago walk-up, nights when it seemed like the heat might peel the paint from the walls. They would sit by the overworked fans in the window with sweaty cans of pop and make up stories about the people down on the street. Ellie hadn't told Brady about Daniel, or much about anything personal, and he hadn't asked for any details. This was why their friendship worked. She hadn't believed she could have any friends, because friends tended to ask questions she couldn't answer, like *Where are you from?* or *How'd you get those terrible scars?* They wanted to come visit your house and talk about your family and just basically pry open the whole box of your life and rummage around inside. But Brady was different. She'd waited, cautious at first during their initial conversations about big-haired dogs and big-haired bands, but the barrage of questions never came. They kept the discussion loose and fun, and finally she had relaxed a little, just enough to allow herself one friend. The terms seemed to suit him just fine. She got the feeling that Brady had a rough upbringing too, just from the one sentence he'd ever uttered about his mother: "She lives in Texas."

Sometimes, it was hard not to share more, like when he'd typed to her, *Know anyone famous?*

Yes, she thought, *me.* Or maybe infamous was a more apt descriptor. Last year she'd switched on the TV to find some skinny blond girl playing her in the movie of the week, only she was named Annabelle in the film and had much more of a chest on her than Ellery ever had at age fourteen. The movie was called *Mind of a Madman,* but it wasn't her story; she was neither the hero nor the villain, just an inexorable link between them. *We live in Woodbury,* she'd typed back to Brady. *What kind of famous person shows up here?*

Why are you up at this hour? He wrote to her now. *Can't sleep?*

She looked down at the glowing screen as she thought of the three missing people. When Ellery was lost, a whole city had turned out to look for her. No one was searching anymore for Bea, Shannon, or Mark. In a few weeks, there would be a new name and a new search, with officers and volunteers spanning out in lines through the woods, like ants at a picnic. Ellery bit her lip and typed her question quickly, before she could think about it too hard. *Would you trade your life for someone else's?*

There was a long silence before Brady replied, *Depends on who it was.*

A stranger, she sent back.

Another long pause. *Maybe, I guess. I'd have to think about it.*

Ellery had thought of little else for almost three years.

She signed off with Brady and called Bump back inside the house, where he tanked up at his water dish and collapsed with a doggy groan on the hardwood floor. Ellie went to the second bedroom, which she had set up as an office, although she rarely had to bring any work home with her. The Bluetooth speakers connected to her phone automatically, and the music picked up right where she had left it that morning: in the middle of "West End Girls." Ellery liked to fill the silence of her house with music, because when there was noise outside her head she didn't have to pay too much attention to her own thoughts. The '80s songs, she had learned to love them when she was a kid riding around in her father's van as he made weekend deliveries. Her father was long gone now, but Bruce Springsteen would be with her forever.

Her desk had a locked file drawer at the bottom, where she kept what little information she had on the three missing persons cases. This time, she bypassed those folders in favor of a plastic Snoopy pencil case she had owned since the third grade. The Snoopy and Woodstock sticker was faded and worn away at one corner. She popped the lid and found the usual treasures: a photo of her, Daniel, and Mom taken down by the pier at Lake Michigan by her father the summer before he left them; a ribbon she'd received for winning the fifth-grade spelling bee; Daniel's Yoda watch; and a card from the FBI.

She lifted the card and read the name to herself. Reed Markham. The man playing him in the TV movie had a strong jaw and black hair that flopped in his eyes. She had no idea if Markham still worked at the FBI or if he would agree to help her. Sam was right that she had precious little evidence of any sort of crime, let alone proof of the monster she felt was out there, probably stalking a new victim even now. When summer rolled around, her fellow cops looked at her like she was the crazy one, rambling on about murder, but they didn't know how it was. They hadn't been close. They'd never sat in a killer's closet and felt the claw marks in the wood, left there by the girls who had already died. *Touched*, Ellie liked to think of it sometimes as she traced her scars in the dark. She'd been touched.

Ellie knew "touched" could mean gifted or insane. Maybe she was both.

But she wasn't wrong, and if anyone out there was ever going to believe her, it was Reed Markham. Because he'd been touched once too.

2

Reed Markham knew women. He had a genteel, warm-hearted mother and three older sisters, none of whom seemed to mind that they'd had to go outside the family to get their longed-for baby boy. He'd grown up in their pink-and-white bedrooms, ensconced on the flowery bedspreads while they confided in him about their victories and troubles, big and small, like the time Kimberly managed to convince their mother to let her put up a single poster of Kurt Cobain, even if it had to be on the inside of the closet door, or when Lynnette's best friend inexplicably stopped speaking to her through all of eighth grade. His sisters argued constantly with each other, but never with him, and so Reed just shuttled between the rooms and became the only member of the family to know all its secrets—a role he honored by keeping each and every one. "Thank the Lord and heaven above that Mama and Daddy found you," his sisters would declare with high drama, enveloping him in tight perfumed-scented hugs that squeezed his heart as hard as they squeezed his body.

Because if they were his found family, then it was possible that maybe he could lose them again. So he made sure to become everything they'd ever wanted.

All those years of practice paid off, because as he grew, Reed found himself in other girls' bedrooms, girls who were not his sisters but who liked how he listened completely to their stories without interrupting them, how he was willing to brush their hair, how he knew to compliment their shoes because they'd tried on eighty-seven pairs before buying the perfect ones. He had not appreciated at the time he was watching his sisters model endless clothes that this experience was somehow priming him for the right winsome smile, the exact special words, that made other girls want to take their clothes off. Later, after many girls, when he found he could use those same intuitive skills to ferret out criminals, his colleagues would sometimes ask, "How do you read people so well?" He would answer that it was easier than anyone believed; people would gladly tell you who they were if you only cared to listen.

So yes, indeed, Reed Markham knew a lot about women— everything except the name of the one in bed with him. His head hurt like it was in a vise and his dry tongue felt too large for his mouth. He shifted gingerly under the sheets as he assessed the situation. It was her house, he realized, blinking owlishly in the gray morning light, taking in the unfamiliar beige walls and the dresser that seemed crowded from end to end with miniature porcelain . . . he raised his head for a better look . . . whales? He fell back into the pillow with a thud that made him wince, but the woman next to him did not stir. He remembered the bar and the first couple of rum and Cokes. He tried to conjure the moment the woman approached him so that he could replay her name inside his head, but his brain recalled only the scalloped neckline of her tight yellow dress. Debbie? Donna? *It was something with a D,* he thought, rubbing his face with both hands so that the stubble scraped across his palms.

Dimly, he heard a buzzing sound, and it took him a few moments to realize it was his phone vibrating across the nightstand. His companion stretched and blinked as Reed shot out a hand just in time to keep the phone from falling. There was no name on the caller ID, but he recognized the central office number. No one had phoned him from the office in twenty-seven days now, and he was under the impression they liked it this way. He cleared his throat twice before answering. "Hello?"

"Agent Reed Markham?"

"Yes."

"I have an officer on the line from . . . Woodbury, Massachusetts. She gives her name as Ellery Hathaway and she wants to speak to you. Says it's urgent. Normally, I wouldn't bother you with this, but she says she worked with you on one of your earlier cases. Would you like me to transfer the call?"

Reed sat up against the headboard, still holding his head with one hand. The name didn't mean a damn thing to him, but he was currently hungover and naked in a bed that wasn't his. "Uh, sure, put her through." He tried to not notice that his bed partner was watching him now with obvious curiosity.

"Agent Markham?" A new female voice came on the line, this one less certain, less officious.

"Yes, how can I help you?"

There was a beat of strange silence, as though, Markham thought, she couldn't figure out an answer, despite the fact that she had been the one to call him. As the seconds passed, he grew irritated, embarrassed to be put in this awkward situation. "You said we worked a case together?" he prompted when she did not say anything.

"In a way. It was a long time ago. You knew me then as Abigail. Abby." She took a long breath. "Abby Hathaway."

Holy shit. If the woman next to him was a blank, the one on the phone was a bomb. Just the sound of her name set off a hundred tiny fuses in his head. Adrenaline surged through him, tightening his chest and quickening his breathing. "I, uh . . ." He scrambled off the bed and away from the force of the memories, momentarily forgetting his nudity as he careened around the unfamiliar room looking for a door. He found the bathroom and shut himself inside it, not bothering to turn on the lights. "Abby," he repeated in wonder, once he could talk again. "How are you?"

"It's Ellery now. My middle name."

In his book, he'd called her Patricia. Had she read his book? It spent thirty-six weeks on the bestseller list and was now in its third printing. It was a bit old for her, wasn't it? *No, wait, she isn't fourteen anymore,* he reminded himself. Maybe she was writing a book of her own and that was why she was calling. It would be a bestseller too, he knew it instantly. *Oh, God, what if the cameras come around again looking for fresh quotes? Look what had become of him now.*

"Back then," she said, penetrating his panic, "you said if I ever needed anything, I could call you."

No one asked Reed for help these days. Even his six-year-old daughter looked at him with sympathetic, doubtful eyes when he asked if she needed any assistance buckling herself into her booster seat in the car. *No thanks, Daddy, I'll do it myself.* Now he was standing naked in the bathroom of a woman he couldn't name, and Abby Hathaway was asking him to make good on a promise from fourteen years ago. "What is it?" he asked cautiously.

"I've been working in Woodbury, Massachusetts, as a police officer for the past four years. Three years ago, we had a missing persons case—a nineteen-year-old college student who was home on break for the summer disappeared one Sunday night in June. She had a volatile relationship with her boyfriend, and they fought loudly the night Bea vanished. The State Police investigated, but without a body, no one could prove she was even dead, let alone that her boyfriend had killed her."

Reed leaned his head against the door. "That is a terrible story, but I don't see—"

Ellery cut him off, her voice hard but steady. "The next summer, almost a year later, Shannon Blessing disappeared. Shannon was an on-again, off-again alcoholic, and she lived alone, so it took us awhile to realize she was gone. Her apartment was a mess but there didn't seem to be any signs of struggle. She had an ex-husband, but they weren't in touch and anyway he lives in Tennessee now. Her car was gone too, and investigating officers decided she had either just driven off to find some other life or took a wrong turn and ended up at the bottom of a lake somewhere."

"Did you search all the nearby bodies of water?"

"Shannon had no immediate family." She paused, as if gathering herself. "There was no one in particular who cared to find her. Dragging the lake and river, that costs money. We have eight officers in our unit, Agent Markham. Just three patrol cars, and the chief does the repair work on them himself."

"I see." Reed knew well the realities of small-town policing, how more than half the country's local police agencies consisted of fewer than ten officers. Cop shows invited the American public to think they were protected by bustling, large-staffed precincts filled with technologically savvy officers like on *The Shield* or *Law & Order*, when for most of them, the truth was a lot closer to *Mayberry RFD*.

"Last summer, Mark Roy went missing. He was depressed at the time over the recent death of his three year-old son due to drowning. Medical records showed Mark had been hospitalized for depression with suicidal ideation more than fifteen years ago, and he was taking antidepressants. After a brief investigation, it was concluded that Mark most likely went off somewhere and killed himself, but no body has ever been recovered."

Reed frowned. Suicide victims often did not leave neat explanations behind—only about half left some kind of note—but it was exceedingly rare for them to plan thoroughly enough that they could not be found. At most, they sought privacy just long enough to complete the act.

"These are open missing persons investigations," she continued, "but no one is actively investigating them. I think the cases are connected. I think it's the work of one individual, someone who is abducting these people during the first two weeks of July."

"It's July second now," Reed observed absently.

"Yes. That's why I need you to come right away."

"Come? You mean come up there?"

"No one here believes me," she said, her voice taking on a note of desperation. "I've tried everything to get them to listen, but the chief is unconvinced that the cases are connected. I thought with your background, your expertise, maybe he'll believe you."

Three potential victims, different ages, male and female. He wasn't sure he believed the story himself. Not to mention the hell to pay if Assistant Director Russ McGreevy found out Reed was taking on cases without the FBI's official sanction, especially not now. Not after what had happened last year. He swallowed and chose his words carefully. "Officer Hathaway, I'd like to help you, but I don't know what you've been told. I'm not actually with—"

"He sends me cards," she cut in quickly.

For a moment, there was only the sound of her heightened breathing on the other end. "Cards?" Reed finally asked.

"Birthday cards, on my birthday. Each year, after another

person goes missing, I get a card. They're all the same. There's a painted clown on the front holding some balloons and a hand-printed note inside that says, 'HAPPY BIRTHDAY ELLERY.'" She gave a significant pause. "I don't talk about my birthday around here, Agent Markham. It's not like it's common knowledge."

Who would want to talk about it? Abby Hathaway had been abducted the night of her fourteenth birthday, an ironic twist that made it into every story written about Francis Michael Coben. She was a minor at the time so the press kept her name out of it, but this juicy detail was too good not to share. "And you think . . . what?" he asked her. "These missing persons are some sort of gift for you?"

"I don't know what to think. The cards have no signature, no return address, and no usable prints. But I traced them to a man-ufacturing company that went out of business ten years ago." She hesitated, as if deciding how much to say. "They were based in Chicago."

The words dragged up a dozen different memories, all jum-bled together: the oppressive heat bearing down on the city like a boot to the throat; photos of the mutilated young women, all missing their hands; Coben, smiling, giving a cheery wave, as he walked out of the Chicago precinct as the SAC muttered, "Not our guy." Abby had been missing twenty-four hours by that point, and most of his team presumed she was already dead.

He turned on the light, leaned on the hard porcelain sink, and regarded the mirror in front of him, trying to recognize the face looking back at him in the unflattering gray light. *You saved her,* he told the face. *You.* But his haggard expression did not appear to be convinced. "Maybe . . . maybe I could come up for a day or two," he found himself saying slowly into the phone. "Just to look around—off the record." It wasn't like he had much else to do.

"Thank you," she said with relief. "Thank you, that would be great."

"You realize," he said before she could break the connection, "people are going to wonder how we know each other. There may be questions." He had loved to talk about this case at one point, but he would bet that she did not especially welcome the memories.

"I know. Tell them . . ." She sighed. "Tell them anything you want."

He wondered what she looked like now, how her story had turned out. He had left her fourteen years ago pale and bandaged and huddled in a hospital bed. All this time, he'd swelled with pride whenever someone asked him about the case. The last girl, the one who lived: Reed Markham had rescued her. Now he was going to get to see for himself whether she was truly saved.

His cell phone rang again that afternoon as he was driving his rental car toward Woodbury. He knew it was definitely not the woman from last night, whose name turned out to be Lauren, he'd discovered, much to his chagrin, by pawing through the prescription bottles in her medicine cabinet after he had hung up with Abby. When he'd finally emerged from the bathroom with a towel around his waist, Lauren had been curled on her bed wearing a robe and a suspicious expression. "You were in there a very long time. At least tell me it wasn't your wife on the phone."

No, it wasn't his wife, although he had one of those too, if only in the most technical sense since she had asked him to move out last year. So it was not surprising that this time when his phone rang it was her on the other end. "You're not here," she said flatly by way of greeting, and Reed cringed as he realized he'd forgotten his agreement to take their daughter, Tula, for dinner and a rare sleepover that night.

"I'm sorry," he said. He said that a lot these days.

"This is twice now, Reed. You're familiar with the three-strikes laws, yes?"

"Sorry," he repeated, this time with feeling. "I should have called you. Something came up—an emergency."

Sarit snorted on the other end. "What's her name this time?"

He hesitated just a second. "Abby Hathaway."

There was a stunned silence, and he felt a moment of triumph that he'd managed, this once, to surprise her. "What?" she breathed finally. "The Abby Hathaway?" Sarit Ranupam was one of a handful of people who knew the girl's real name, and that was because she was the one who convinced Reed to write the book in the first place, back when they had first met at the mayor's gala event to combat domestic violence. Sarit had been a young reporter on the rise at the *Washington Post,* and Reed was two years removed from the Coben case, but it was all over the news at the time because Coben was finally on trial. Reed had no talent for writing; he relied on Sarit's clear prose and sense of story to guide him, and together, they had crafted *Little Girl Lost,* a tale that had riveted the nation.

"Yeah," he told her with a trace of amazement, scarcely able to believe it himself. "She called me this morning about a string of missing persons cases in Massachusetts. She's a junior deputy or something now."

"How did she seem? Does she have a family? Is she thinking of coming forward with her story?"

Reed almost smiled at this connection to his old Sarit, the journalist who smelled a lede, the storyteller who always wanted to know the ending. "I don't know. I haven't seen her yet. She's pretty shaken up by these disappearances and she wants my advice."

"And this couldn't have waited another twenty-four hours?"

"She said it was urgent."

Sarit made a tsking noise, one he had heard often over the past few years. "This isn't your job anymore, Reed. You don't go hopping a plane the minute someone turns up missing or dead halfway across the country. When we go see the judge next month, he's going to ask what efforts you've made to keep in touch with Tula. What are you going to say then?"

He thought of the day his daughter was born, unusually calm and serious for a new person who had just been through the trauma of birth, how she had laid still in his arms and gazed up at him with wide, trusting eyes. Every monster he'd hunted down since then was for her. "Tell Tula I am so sorry, and I love her. I should be back tomorrow, Monday at the latest. I will call her and we'll plan a *My Little Pony* sleepover. I'll even be Princess Chrysanthemum."

"Princess Celestia," Sarit corrected absently. She made a small humming noise that Reed knew meant she was still thinking. "Reed . . . I don't understand it. Why you? Why now?"

"I told you. She wants my professional opinion." Sarit had the grace not to point out that apparently Abby Hathaway was the only one who did. What Reed didn't say was the odd, niggling feeling he'd had in the back of his brain ever since his call from Abby. The birthday cards from Chicago meant someone else had figured out her secret, someone who, even if he wasn't a murderer, was getting a sick thrill out of subtly menacing her. Whoever that was had to know the Coben history inside and out, which meant he—or she—would no doubt recognize Reed as well.

When at last he took the exit for Woodbury, it was as if the forest rose up around the road, trees thick as a bear's fur, the sun rendered as a distant, filtered light. Reed followed the rolling hills into town, where the woods had been cleared away to form a small outpost of civilization. There was a gas station, a post office, a pharmacy, a white-steepled church that was cut straight from New England lore, a handful of other storefronts, and at least one restaurant/bar. It took Reed less than five minutes to get through the whole downtown. He spotted a squat brick building with a white painted sign in front, whose fancy script lettering proclaimed WOODBURY POLICE DEPARTMENT, SINCE 1903. As advertised, there was only one patrol car parked on the street outside.

Reed performed a U-turn so he could pull up behind the vehicle, his thoughts on Abby and what it would be like to see her again. When writing the book, he had made a perfunctory check-in with her mother to see how the girl was doing two years later so they would have some good news to put in the afterword. "Oh, Abby's doing just fine," her mother had said at the time, "Top marks. She's the star shooter on her high school basketball team. You can hardly even see the scars on her now. She's applying to colleges and she can go anywhere she wants now thanks to all the money people sent after she was rescued—places we never could've afforded before—so in a way, what happened turned out to be a blessing." Reed had dutifully relayed the inspiring epilogue to the public, with Abby's name still protected, of course, but he realized now that he had never verified any of the details with Abby herself. He hadn't wanted to be the one to call up bad memories.

The heavy wooden door stuck in the humidity, forcing Reed to lean into it so that he stumbled more than walked into the Woodbury station house. No one was the in the entryway to witness his embarrassment. Instead, he found sterile white-and-gray linoleum, a short row of plastic chairs, and a narrow Formica counter with a sliding glass window behind it. There was a bell to ring for service. Reed tapped it once, and the glass slid open a moment later to reveal a bland-faced officer with a dark buzz cut. "Can I help you?" he asked.

"My name is Reed Markham. I'm here to see Ellery Hathaway." Reed congratulated himself on his use of the correct name.

The man turned and hollered over his shoulder. "Hathaway! You've got company."

She materialized almost immediately from the other side of the metal door, and Reed blinked in surprise a few times. He had been mentally casting her as a slightly larger version of the girl he had known—thin and gangly, with dirty blond hair, pale eyes that would not look directly at anyone—but the woman in front of him had dark hair, pulled back neatly at her nape, a toned, athletic frame, and a cool, assessing gaze. Only her eyes were the same, like cracked marbles the color of sagebrush. If he ever saw the eyes, Francis Coben would've been able to pick her out of any lineup, no question: *That's her. That's the one I took.*

"I didn't expect you to just show up here," she said, and Reed didn't know whether she meant the station house or Woodbury altogether.

"You said it was urgent," he replied, and a faint smile appeared on her lips.

"Yeah, well, I'm not used to people believing me. Come on back."

She led him into the inner sanctum, where six desks sat mashed up together. The three other officers in the room all turned to stare, and Reed realized with dismay that they would have exactly zero privacy here. A man who Reed presumed was the chief stepped out from the partitioned office at the far end of the room. He had a sheaf of papers in his hand and he pulled down his reading glasses for a better look at Reed.

"That's Chief Parker," Ellery muttered to him. "I don't exactly have his blessing on all this, as you're about to find out. I hope that's not a problem."

Reed didn't have the FBI's blessing either. "No problem," he said, straightening up as the chief approached.

The chief stuck out his hand toward Reed. "Chief Sam Parker," he said with a welcoming but curious tone. "Is there something I can help you with?"

"Reed Markham. I'm here to see Officer Hathaway."

"Oh?" Parker looked him over from head to toe, slowly taking in the Ralph Lauren polo shirt, the dark, designer-wash jeans, and the leather loafers. Reed wondered if he should have stopped to put on a suit.

"Can we talk in your office?" Ellery asked.

Parker stretched out a magnanimous arm. "By all means."

Parker's office was barely big enough to hold his desk and chair, a file cabinet, and two other chairs. They crowded in and sat down. Ellery was picking nervously at the blue piping on the edge of her uniform, and beneath the cuff at her wrist, Reed thought he could just make out the faint line of a white scar. Of course, he knew exactly where to look.

"So, Mr. Markham," the chief said, leaning back in his chair. "What brings you to the Woodbury Police Department today?"

"Agent Markham," Ellery corrected, and Reed felt a flicker of guilt go through him. He hoped no one called up the FBI to check his references. "He's graciously offered his help with the missing persons cases."

Parker's bushy eyebrows knit together and his mouth turned downward. "FBI," he said, eyeing Reed with new suspicion.

"I'm with the Behavioral Sciences Unit," Reed supplied. Technically, it wasn't untrue, but you could hide a whole mess of stories behind the word "technically."

"A profiler," Parker translated.

"Of sorts."

The chief turned his gaze to Ellery and narrowed his eyes a bit. "I didn't realize you were so cozy with the Feds, Ellie."

Color heightened her cheeks, but Ellery stood her ground. "You've always told us to be inventive with our limited resources, sir. I simply made a phone call. As long as he's here, what's the harm in Agent Markham taking a look at the files? Like you've said yourself a hundred times—the cases are at a dead end. Maybe he can see something we've missed."

"We're a long way from Quantico up here. You in the habit of checking into missing persons cases on the basis of one phone call from a patrol officer, Agent Markham?"

Reed felt Ellery freeze at the question; he'd wanted to let her be the one to explain their connection however she preferred to define it, but she had no words, and now the lack of response fell heavy over them. The seconds ticked by in the tense, silent room. "I'm an old family friend," Reed said at last, and he felt her unclench at his side. "I'm here as a favor, that's all."

"I see." Parker looked from one to the other, and Reed could tell he wasn't quite buying the story. "Well, I appreciate that you came all this way to offer your services, but I'm not in the habit of handing out our files to anyone just on the basis of a favor. That's not how we conduct business around here."

"You promised." Ellery sat forward, her outrage on the loose now. "You promised me that if I found a new angle that we could revisit these investigations. Well, I have. Agent Markham is one of the top behavioral experts in the country, and he's generously agreed to give us his opinion on the cases. Do you really want me to have to tell Annie and Dave Nesbit that we turned him away just because of some ridiculous adherence to office protocol?"

Anger flashed across Parker's features, but he reined it back in fast. "Don't you go bothering the Nesbits about this," he warned her. "They've had enough from you, stirring them up with your stories every summer."

"They deserve answers."

"Real answers, yes. Not some cracked-up story about a serial murderer." They glowered at each other for a long moment, and then Parker heaved a long, worn-out sigh. "Give me a day to think about it," he said. "I'll talk to Jimmy about our files, see what might be relevant."

"A day! We don't have time to wait an extra day."

"That seems more than fair," Reed interjected smoothly, cutting short Ellery's tirade, and she turned in her seat to glare at him. "I was planning to stay in town anyway. Is there a nearby motel you could direct me to?"

A strange look passed between Ellery and the chief, as though for some reason this was yet another question nobody wanted to answer. "There's a place down the road toward Pittsfield," Parker answered gruffly after a moment. "Ellie can give you directions if you need. Officer Hathaway, why don't you see our guest out, and then come back in here so we can discuss this further."

Her answer was a tight, "Yes, sir," and Reed followed her back out to the main bullpen, where the other officers were watching with naked curiosity. He noted the careful way that Ellie pretended not to see them as she crossed to her desk, pulled out a piece of scrap paper, and wrote out the address of the motel. Reed glanced at it briefly before tucking it in the pocket of his jeans. "Walk me out?" he offered.

Ellery trailed him into the warm summer afternoon, where the sun was only beginning to dip in the sky. Reed kept glancing back at her because it was a marvel just to see her walking around. He remembered the awful stench and total silence he'd found when he pried open the closet door and seen the full horror of Coben's work. He'd thought he was too late, that she was dead. Now here she was standing whole and healthy right in front of him—and furious enough to spit nails. "He swore we could reinvestigate the cases," she told him as they lingered by Reed's car. "But now it's just more of the same old bullshit. Wait and see."

"Twenty-four hours isn't too much to ask," Reed told her. "If we went through official channels, it would take much longer." He didn't add the part about how Parker could relatively easily determine that Reed had no official channels at all at the moment. *Stress leave,* they called it when it was suggested to him, but to Reed, it had sounded like: *Leave, and don't come back.*

"Yeah, well, I have some unofficial copies I can give you now," she said, leading him around back to a tiny parking lot. He was amused when she led him to a beat-up green truck and unlocked it to reveal a small stack of folders sitting on the passenger seat.

"You travel around with these? You're hardcore, Officer Hathaway."

"I figured we'd be meeting up later today," she replied defensively. "Anyway, it's not nearly everything. Only the stuff I could gain access to."

"It's a good start, thank you." He tucked the folders under his arm. "What about the birthday cards you received? Do you have those too?"

She flushed and hesitated a moment, but then reached back in to retrieve a plain brown bag from the glove compartment. "They're in here," she murmured as she handed them over.

He slid them out to see that they were exactly as she described. Envelopes filmy with fingerprint dust, the cards themselves picturing a somewhat garish clown holding balloons. Inside was even black printing: HAPPY BIRTHDAY ELLERY. "Do you mind if I keep these awhile?" he asked.

She frowned, clearly not expecting this. "What for?"

"Just to look them over in detail in the context of the other files."

"Oh. I, uh, sure . . . I guess that's fine."

"We could arrange a meeting later this evening to discuss the cases if you like—maybe at your place?"

"No," she replied too quickly, and then stammered to cover it. "I mean, my place is a wreck. You must be hungry. Why don't we get together over dinner, say in two hours? There's a decent place for burgers and beer down by the motel where you'll be staying. It's called the Dive Bar because they open a pool out back during the summer."

Reed's throat went dry at the mention of a bar. He hadn't had a drink all day, opting instead for soda on the plane. For years he had avoided anything harder than an occasional beer, unsure of what addiction legacy might be lurking in his inscrutable family tree, even as he'd watched some of his colleagues pickle themselves silly in between cases. Now he understood the attractiveness of alcohol: it coursed through your insides like a river over a rock, smoothing you out so you didn't feel so damn much.

He cleared his throat, aware Ellie was staring at him. "The Dive Bar. Sure, I can find it."

Reed took her files to his rental car as Ellery went inside to receive her tongue-lashing from Chief Parker. Maybe raking her over the coals for insubordination would get the irritation out of Parker's system and he'd be cooperative in the morning. Reed set Ellery's files next to him and dug out the name of the motel she'd suggested: the Shady Inn.

It was hot in the car, baking as it had been in the summer sun, but Reed suddenly broke out in a cold sweat. He pawed through the files to find the bag with the birthday cards. The plain black printing on the cards was eerily similar to the scrap paper he held in his hand. *No, you're imagining things,* he told himself as he looked at the cards and back again. *It's just printing. All plain printing looks alike.*

But in his head, he remembered Sarit's parting words on the phone: *That poor girl,* she'd said of Abby. *I think if it had happened to me, I'd have gone crazy.*

3

It wasn't his fault that his face appeared in her nightmares. She knew which team Reed Markham played for and remembered her rescue, but when her brain opened the closet door, only two faces waited on the other side, and one of them was his. She wondered if his brain opened the door and saw a fourteen-year-old girl. Maybe that was why she kept her uniform on when she went to meet him at the bar.

Reed was already there, also dressed in the same clothes as earlier in the afternoon, but now he sported wire-rimmed glasses that made him look like a cross between a J.Crew model and an algebra teacher. He was nursing a Sam Adams and picking at a bowl of stale popcorn when she slid into the booth across from him. Outside, through the open patio doors, she could hear the sounds of laughter and splashing from the pool. "Are you still on the clock?" he asked, taking in her dark button-down shirt.

"Came straight from work," she said, although this was a lie. She'd been home for at least a half an hour to feed and walk

Bump, but the less said about her house, the better. She had already deflected him once when he tried to invite himself over, and she wasn't looking forward to a situation where she had to explain that Bump was the only male who was allowed through her front door.

"I read your files," he said, taking a swill from the beer as he nodded to the stack of folders on the table to his left. "They're clear, detailed, and well organized. I'm impressed."

She felt her face go hot. "Yeah? Did you like my typing too?"

He set down the beer and tilted his head at her. "You think I'm bullshitting you? I've combed through a lot of case files in my day, and half of them looked like they were thrown together like a fifth-grade book report. Yours are careful and insightful—like the part where you noted that Mark Roy ordered a new work uniform three days before he disappeared."

"That's always bothered me. Why would he spend that money if he was planning on killing himself?"

"It's a good question. In fact, you've got lots of good questions in here. I'd say Woodbury is lucky to have you on the job."

Ellie ducked her head. "No one back home really figured I'd enjoy law enforcement. My mother once suggested I should be a toll-booth operator if I wanted to wear a uniform."

Reed grinned. "You're kidding."

"No. She said it must give a person plenty of time to think."

The waitress showed up, a college-age girl who smelled faintly of chlorine. "You know what you want?"

"I'll have the cheeseburger and a Sam Adams," Ellie said.

"Cheeseburger for me too," Reed added.

Ellie nodded at the bottle in his hand. "You want another one of those? It's on me—least I can do after you came all this way."

He took an oddly long time with his answer, as though he

had to run a personal inventory first. "Uh, no, thank you. I'd better stick with one." He cradled it closer, holding it almost protectively.

"Let me know if you change your mind," the waitress said, and Ellie watched Reed's gaze follow the girl's bouncy ponytail all the way back to the bar. She was still regarding him curiously when he swung his attention back around to her.

"How's your mother faring these days?" he asked as he reached for a handful of popcorn.

"She's fine. Still in Chicago, still in the same apartment. She calls on Sundays to update me on the neighborhood in excruciating detail."

"And your brother?"

Ellie looked away at the question, into the faceless crowd. No one had asked her about Daniel in many years now; he became one of the people she'd had to leave behind. "He died," she said at last, remembering his pale face and sunken eyes the last time she had seen him. "About a half a year after. After I came back."

"I'm so sorry."

She gave a half shrug and contracted in on herself. "He'd been sick for so long by then, it wasn't really a surprise." Coben had yanked her off the street in an instant, but leukemia took her brother slowly, draining the life from him over four years in a kind of torture that only Mother Nature could design. Ellie wondered sometimes, especially on the hot summer nights, whether Daniel might have lived if she had died, as if somehow the universe had said, *Pick one.*

Reed was watching her with unblinking eyes. "Your mother didn't mention his passing when I spoke to her." Off her questioning look, he explained, "I talked to her briefly a couple of years later, just to see how you were doing. She said you were thriving in school, but she didn't mention Daniel."

"I'm not surprised. Losing him was the worst thing that's ever happened to her."

Reed didn't get to reply to this because their waitress returned with the cheeseburgers. They were thick and juicy, requiring both hands, and as Reed reached for his, Ellie noted he wasn't wearing a wedding ring, but there was a slightly paler band of skin there, as if he'd taken a ring off quite recently. He wolfed down a bite or two and then paused to wipe the juice from his fingers. "So why Woodbury?" he asked her.

"I wanted to get out of the city. This is where the job was."

"The city," he repeated. "Meaning Chicago?"

"Boston," she corrected as she picked up a wedge-cut fry. "Where I got my training."

When she did not elaborate, he tried another tack. "And you've been living out here four years?"

"Four this fall, yes."

"Made a lot of friends?"

She frowned at him, burger in hand. "I thought we were here to discuss the cases, not my social life."

"Right, the cases," he said, as if reluctant to change the subject. "I see they were all investigated initially by James Tipton."

"He's our detective. Worked out of Philly until a few years ago, when his wife wanted to move somewhere closer to her family—out in Worcester, I think. Sam was looking to bring in someone with experience, so I guess the timing worked out for both of them."

Reed made a thoughtful noise. "What do you think of him?"

"Tipton? He's all right, I guess," she replied as she paused to consider. Jimmy Tipton laughed too loud at his own jokes and had a creepy sixth sense for when she was changing in the narrow locker room, but he never overtly hit on her or derided her, even as she was openly investigating his cases in her spare time. Mostly if she brought him a new theory, he would just mutter, "Yeah, I looked into that already," and go back to playing solitaire on his computer.

"All right? You've been checking the man's homework for three years now, and that's all you've got to say about him?"

She sat back in the booth, trying to decide if he was genuinely interested or just messing with her. "Fine," she said at length. "Here's what I think: Woodbury is largely a low-crime area. The cases we get, even the ones where Jimmy's called in, they don't take a Sherlock Holmes kind of intellect to figure out, if you know what I'm saying. A lady calls up and says her ex-husband broke into her place and stole her stereo system—well, you know, nine times out of ten, she's not wrong. Jimmy's a good enough cop, but he's used to being right because it's easy to be right around here. That goes on long enough and maybe a person starts mistaking his opinions for facts."

"Hmm."

"Hmm? What does that mean?"

Reed took a sip of beer. "Mind you, I haven't met the man, but I have a feeling he might say the same thing about you."

"And you? You've read the files now. What do you think?"

"I can see why you haven't made any headway with your theory. You've got three missing persons of different race and age, two of whom might have had good reason to disappear on their own, with no link among them or any concrete evidence of murder. The coincidental timing could be just that, a coincidence, and there's nothing on the birthday cards to suggest they are connected to the disappearance of these three people."

Ellie fought a rising tide of frustration at having the same conversation yet again. "So you're just like the rest of them, then. You think I'm a conspiracy theory nutcase."

"What I'm saying is, individually, each case might not add up to much. Collectively, I agree with you: they are unusual in a way that raises concern. Woodbury and its environs can't contain more than fifteen thousand people. Perhaps one person decides to run off to a new life without leaving any kind of word behind, but three people in three years . . ." He broke off and shook his head. "Something isn't right." He pushed aside his half-eaten burger and shifted the files to sit in front of him. "This first one, Bea Nesbit, has the most complete information."

Ellie leaned over her plate, her own food forgotten now. "Her parents made a lot of fuss, said there was no way Bea would just have run off. The State Police took over pretty early in, although they kept Jimmy in the loop because he worked the local angles. Everyone decided that if Bea was killed, her boyfriend, Derek Chin, must've been the one who did it. He has two priors, one for possession, one for assault—a bar fight that witnesses say Chin provoked—and, interestingly, one arrest for assault on a previous girlfriend. She claimed he choked her, and she had the bruises on her neck to prove it." Ellie fingered her throat to illustrate the pattern. "But she dropped the charges the next day and insisted the whole thing was a big misunderstanding."

"Isn't it always," Reed murmured as his eyes scanned through the file. "Bea's mother said she'd seen similar bruising on her daughter?"

"Once. About two months before Bea disappeared, she and her parents had lunch together for Mother's Day, and Annie Nesbit noticed a discoloration on her daughter's neck that she thought looked like fingerprints. Bea brushed it off when Annie mentioned it. If you've read the file, you'll know why."

"Sex games." Reed cleared his throat. "BDSM."

"Derek is into some pretty kinky stuff. When the State Police searched his apartment, they found all kinds of . . . apparatus. Also pictures of him and Bea engaged in various kinds of play."

She had seen some of the photos—Bea tied up in black ropes from head to toe in ritualistic fashion; Derek wearing a mask and holding a riding crop. His crooked smirk came back to her, the way he had looked at her almost in invitation the time she'd asked him about his unusual sex life. *Free your mind, Officer Hathaway, and your body will follow.*

"I see a reference to pictures of him with some other girl— Aimee Winthrop."

"Jimmy and the rest of them figured that's what Bea and Derek were fighting about the night she went missing, but Derek never confirmed it."

"You've talked to him. What do you think happened?"

She considered a moment. "Derek is very good at manipulating the conversation—the longer he talks, the more comfortable he feels. But he always stops just short of being actually cooperative or helpful. Back then, I thought like everyone else did, that he probably killed her. But then the next summer Shannon Blessing went missing, and there isn't any reason at all to think Derek's involved there. Or with Mark Roy."

Reed was still sifting through the pages, running his fingers over them as though reading by touch rather than sight. "Bea was adopted," he said after a moment.

Ellie remembered the framed snapshot on the Nesbits' mantel, the one taken in China two decades ago when they traveled to bring their baby daughter home. Annie and Dave's cheeks stretched to the edge, almost unable to contain their joyous smiles, while Bea in the middle looked a bit mystified by her instant family. "So?"

"So am I."

This sudden revelation felt like a test of some sort, and Ellie chose her response carefully. "So? You think it matters?"

"Oh, it always matters." He closed the file and set it aside.

"I meant to the case," she clarified.

"So did I." He cast around again for their waitress. "You know, on second thought, maybe I will have another beer."

He seemed smaller than the man from her memory, the one who had pried the nails from Coben's closet and carried her to freedom. She'd never told anyone how she had laid there and played dead for him, fetal on the floor in the pitch-black, splinters pricking her skin, surrounded by the smell of sweat and blood. She had thought it was Coben coming back with the knife to kill her, to take her hands like he promised he would, and in her delirium she'd thought maybe she could pretend it had already happened and he would just go away again. Instead it was a different voice, this one slightly Southern and as fearful as her own: *Abby . . . Abby, is that you?*

No, she'd thought, almost dreamily. *Abby's already gone.*

She held her head in her hands for a moment as Reed got started on his second beer. Maybe she'd been wrong about him. Maybe she should have paid closer attention back then after it happened, when what she mostly remembered from that time was that she'd been the one in the hospital for a change, with her mom making sure the bedsheets were smooth and comfortable. How delicious that first sweet ginger ale had tasted as it trickled down her swollen, parched throat. She'd had a color TV with remote control, right in her own private bedroom. Flowers and teddy bears. Nana came to visit. Everyone kept her far away from the news stories. Nana had called the reporters "jackals" like it was a dirty word, and Ellie had visualized them mobbed like hungry beasts downstairs outside her window, waiting for any chance to devour her, bite by bite.

Afterward, when she was grown, Ellie knew vaguely that the stories were out there—she'd heard snatches of it on television, at school, or even idle chatter on the streets of Boston, as Coben transformed from reality into legend, a spook story to be mined for public entertainment—but she'd never bothered to learn the details of her rescue. A hundred officers had looked for her, but Reed was the one who opened the closet door, and that was all she'd needed to know. Now she was starting to wonder if he was really the genius everyone had said he was.

"How did you find me?" she blurted at him.

He jerked, almost spilling his beer down his shirtfront. "I'm sorry, what?"

"Back then. How did you know it was Coben?"

He licked his lips twice, nervously, which did not give her confidence. "You . . . you don't know?"

She shook her head slowly. This was his big story, right? It had to be. He must have told it a million times by now. *Go ahead,* she thought. *Impress me.*

But Reed did not have the air of a decorated war general reliving his greatest battle. He skimmed the worn edge of their wooden table with his fingers and worried his bottom lip with his teeth. *Maybe,* she thought with sudden dread, *it was just dumb luck.* Finally, he took a deep breath and touched his fingertips to his inner wrist. "Actually, it was the tattoos," he said, punctuating the words with a small, quick smile, like he couldn't believe it even after all these years. "A couple of people in your neighborhood reported seeing a black Acura around the time that you were abducted. We had similar reports of a dark sedan from when Michelle Holcomb disappeared, and forensics matched the carpet fibers found on her body to the Acura, so we knew this was potentially an important lead. Coben owned one of nearly a thousand blue or black Acuras, and he had an arrest record— two minor arson incidents in his late teens and a complaint of assault from a young woman, but that claim was subsequently dropped."

"Aren't they always," muttered Ellie, harkening back to his earlier words. She wished she'd thought to order a second beer too.

"The arrests were enough to get Coben called in for an interview," Reed explained. "I wasn't nearly senior enough to be the one conducting it—in fact, I was mostly combing through the records of other owners of Acuras and occasionally offering advice to the local officers who were manning the tip line. But I saw Coben come in and I saw him leave. The agents who interviewed him said he had almost as many questions for them about the investigation as they had for him. 'I'm a bit of a true-crime buff,' I think is how he put it. He seemed wowed by the agents, happy to cooperate with the FBI. He said he had a solid alibi for the night you were abducted, that he'd been at a gallery showing of his latest work. A hundred people would vouch for him. So we kicked him loose," he said with a shrug. "Nothing to hold him on."

"But?"

"He had those tattoos. Right at both wrists, black bands at the exact spot the pathologists told us that the girls' hands had been cut off."

Ellie tucked her own hands deep into her lap. She could remember it now, the lines marking the ends of his arms as he'd reached for her.

"So I followed him. I'm not sure why. It was partly the tattoos and partly because he seemed to be so happy on his way out of the precinct. The others we brought in left white-faced and sweating, relieved we were turning them loose, but Coben practically bounced out of the station like we'd been throwing him a party. I followed him to his apartment and sat outside watching for a while. Then he came out with some sort of large wrapped package that looked like it might have been a framed picture, and he took that across town to the gallery. That's where I got to see his work."

Ellie could not repress a shudder. She'd seen some of it; she had no choice. Coben's huge close-up photographs of people's hands were part of pop culture now. She had heard that one piece fetched over three million dollars at auction last year. No one owned the pictures that turned out to be the dead girls, she knew that much. Those would live locked up in evidence forevermore.

"I called it in, said someone should come down to have a look. But by then they were onto Tom Moody."

Ellie looked at him with confused eyes. She had no idea who Tom Moody was.

"A supermarket butcher who had the unfortunate luck to drive a black Acura and an arrest record for statutory rape," Reed told her grimly. "They had him downtown for an interview, and he was being evasive about his whereabouts for the night of the abduction. No one wanted to give up a prime suspect to look at some photographs. So I did a little checking, and I found out Coben's stepfather had owned a working farm in Marengo, only sixty miles away. I figured I could go there and check it out, and well . . . you know the rest."

Cold. She'd been so cold with him that night when they'd hid in the woods together, her leaning heavily on the rough twill of his trousers, trying not to lose consciousness. She'd had no way to be sure he was really an FBI agent, but he'd pulled her out of Coben's closet and so she was willing to go anywhere he wanted. Her teeth had chattered as he'd said somewhere over her head, "Listen to me—Coben is the guy. Francis Coben. I've got Abby with me in the woods but Coben could show up back here at any time. Get some people out here *now*."

Her shoulders slumped as he finished the story. It should have made her feel better because, on some level, he deserved all those accolades that they'd draped over him years ago. He had spotted the clues the others failed to see. Yet she had so few clues to offer him now, it was hard to know where to begin. No killer was going to go skipping out of her precinct, conveniently inked up with meaningful body art.

"Tell me about the cards," he said, as if reading her mind. He slid them out of the paper bag but was careful not to touch them.

"There's not much to say beyond what you already know. I get them on my birthday or the day after if it falls on a Sunday. There's no return address and they're postmarked in Worcester."

"I see you've lifted some prints."

"Nothing of note—well, except for one slightly weird thing. Mark Roy's prints are on the first two envelopes, but that could be expected, because he was my mailman."

"Still," Reed said ponderously, "an interesting connection."

"It's a small town. We're all connected in some way or another."

"Who else knows about the cards?"

She flushed so hard she felt it to her toes. "No one. I thought about telling Sam. I mean the chief. But then I would have to explain why I thought they were connected."

She recalled Sam's red face in the office that afternoon as he'd lambasted her for insubordination. "I let you have copies of some of our files, and you use them to go out behind my back and bring in the FBI. I hope you're not under the impression that our relationship gives you special latitude to pull rank like this, Ellie, because if that's what you're thinking, you're sorely mistaken."

Of course it was true, whether Sam wanted it to be so or not. Why else did he think she'd gone to bed with him in the first place? He was still her commanding officer, but she outranked him in power now. Sure, her career would be tarnished too, if their affair came out, but Sam had a lot more to lose.

"Maybe the cards aren't connected to the missing persons cases," Reed suggested as he nudged one aside. "Maybe there's someone out there who just wants to mess with you."

"No one knows me here." She blurted the first response that came to mind, the truth that kept her apart from everyone else in this small town. People had asked after her history when she'd first arrived, a stranger in these parts where most folks had strong, sturdy New England family trees, taller and more deeply rooted than the oaks that rose up along Main Street. Ellie's one-word answers had shut down the questioning and created a separateness to her life in Woodbury that suited her just fine.

"Someone knows your birthday, at the very least," Reed said as he lined up the cards between them. "And if they know that much, then they could unravel the whole story."

She faltered, momentarily wordless in front of this man who had literally written the book on her. Coben's reign of terror had been told and retold so many times now that she could hardly form a protest: it wasn't a story. It was her life.

After dinner, they walked through the small parking lot together, the peals of laughter and splashing from the pool growing quieter in the distance. The delighted, playful noise was a stark contrast to Ellie's grim thoughts as she imagined a faceless killer lurking like a shark, ready to suck down one of the swimmers at any moment. Her birthday was only a week away now, so time was running short. "Just to warn you," she said to Reed, "Sam may not let us have those files tomorrow."

"Then we'll work around him," Reed replied, as though this was no obstacle at all. Ellie tried to share his confidence.

"What did you mean when you said it mattered that Bea was adopted? You think . . . you think she was abducted because of her race or her background or something?" The other victims were both Caucasian.

"I meant that everything matters when it comes to these kind of cases—any little detail that might explain how the victim was in a position to come into contact with the perpetrator. If your suspicions are correct that these three cases are the work of one individual, then that person had reasons for picking Bea, Shannon, and Mark. They might not be reasons that are obvious or make sense to us, but you can believe he had a purpose in mind when he took them. There are no random victims."

"I was." She had been out minding her own business, riding her bike, when Coben happened to spot her.

Reed halted on the asphalt and looked down at her with something close to understanding, or tenderness, with an empathy that made her squirm. She figured this was the part where he corrected her with some essential part of the Coben narrative that she had missed, that Coben had been stalking her for weeks. Instead, he took off his glasses and wiped the muggy film from the lenses with the hem of his shirt. Nearby, the cicadas in the trees hummed like a live wire.

"Bea was a college freshman," he said finally. "She was probably starting to think seriously about who she was and how she fit in with the world, to explore her identity. She'd spent her life until that point getting good grades and doing exactly what her parents expected of her. Now she had a boyfriend, someone who maybe didn't treat her very well. Their relationship was rocky. Her relationship with her parents was strained by these new choices. Emotionally, psychologically, Bea Nesbit was going through a lot of turmoil at the time she went missing. That's all I'm saying."

Ellie turned this information over in her mind and compared it with the other victims. Shannon Blessing was struggling to stay sober. Mark Roy was depressed over the death of his young son. Years ago, Abigail Ellery Hathaway had been fourteen years old and alone at midnight on her birthday, a celebration that had never occurred because Daniel was rushed to the hospital that morning. Ellie blinked back sudden tears. *Vulnerable,* she thought. *We were all vulnerable.* She drew a shaky breath, suddenly eager to change the subject. "Well, that's, ah, it's cool that you were adopted. I mean, it's interesting."

He smiled a bit, just a flash of even white teeth. "Yes, it was interesting to every single newspaper writer we encountered growing up. The captions on the family photos always read: 'Pictured, right to left, State Senator Angus Markham, his wife Maryann, their three daughters, Kimberly, Lynnette, and Suzanne, and their adopted son, Reed.'"

Oh, she thought, wincing. *Wrong topic.* "I'm sorry."

"It's fine, really," he said, waving her off. "They love me. I love them. That's never been a question." Implicit in his words was that there were other questions, but she knew better than to voice them. "It's what I was getting at before, though, about how people's stories matter. I wouldn't be standing here if I hadn't decided to look for my birth mother when I was eighteen. My parents were hesitant at first, but they gave me their blessing and what little information they had—and then the help of a first-rate private investigator. He found her pretty easily, buried in a Las Vegas cemetery."

"I'm sorry," she said again. She had wondered through the years if maybe her father was dead too. Maybe that was why he'd never called, never come back, but she'd been too chicken to try to find out.

"She was murdered," Reed continued, squinting toward the sky.

"That's awful."

He nodded. "Found strangled inside her apartment. I talked

to the detective who investigated, and he was very polite, very sympathetic, but he had no real answers for me about who she was or what had happened to her. I knew then I wasn't going to be a poli-sci major as originally planned."

She saw it then, how if he had not switched careers, she wouldn't be standing here either, and maybe there were other women out there, even now—girls who would have been Coben's next victims if Reed had never stopped him. She hugged herself, feeling a deep stab of envy at these women who didn't even know what they had missed.

"Please let me see you home," Reed said, breaking the silence, but Ellie shook her head.

"I'll be fine."

Reed placed a hand to his chest in dramatic fashion as they reached her pickup truck. "Please, I insist. I'm originally from the great state of Virginia, you see, and so I am constitutionally obligated to escort a lady to her door."

"That's not necessary, really. I've got the same measure of protection you do," she said, indicating the gun at her hip.

"Yes, but I'm not the one receiving the cards. Someone in these parts knows your secret, Ellery, and they want your attention."

Ellie paused. "Well," she said after a beat, "they can be sure they have it."

He waited a moment and then seemed to realize she wasn't going to change her mind about asking him home with her. "Good night, then. I'll phone you in the morning, shall I, and we can plot our course for the day?"

"In the morning." She squared her shoulders and climbed into her truck, determined not to be peering into every shadow. A sudden thought struck her, and she lowered the window to call out to him. "Agent Markham? Did they ever catch the person—the one who killed your mother?"

The top of his hair was flecked silver in the moonlight as he stopped and shook his head. "No," he called back. "They never did."

She was still thirsty, so she stopped off at the lone convenience store, the tiny shop that was attached to the gas station. Big, bald Joey Bartlett barely looked up from behind the counter as she stepped into the store. He had one eye on a tiny television that played the Red Sox game and the other on his cell phone, and behind his ear sat one cigarette, awaiting his next smoke break. "Evening, Joe," she said. "How are the Sox doing?"

"Losing," he replied with disgust. "Just like usual."

Ellie picked up a couple of bottles of Coke, one for now, one to grow on, and added a candy bar at the last minute. She was just about to pay when the door opened, tinkling the bell, and Detective Jimmy Tipton appeared under the garish fluorescent lighting. He didn't look surprised to see her in the store, but then again, Jimmy never did look surprised about anything. He had concocted a world-weary air of self-assured ennui: nothing transpired in his life that he did not fully expect. "Hey, there, Ellie," he said casually as he sidled up beside her. "I hear you've been digging around in my old cases again."

She lifted her chin, ready for a challenge. "It's July already," she explained again, as though they hadn't been over this a million times before. "We need to do something."

"I understand that something is the FBI," Tipton said. He made a scrunchy face at the rows of chips, as if trying to decide between regular and nacho flavor. "Reed Markham."

Ellie glanced over in mild surprise. "That's right."

"He's the guy that broke the Coben case back in Chicago."

Fear crawled up the back of her neck like vines. "Yes," she managed after a beat of silence. "I . . . I heard that."

Jimmy looked at her sideways, making eye contact for the first time, and his gaze was so intense she had to force herself not to look away. "Man, what a trip that must be, to have nailed Coben's scalp to your wall. He was like the ultimate psycho. I heard he had sex with those girls after they were dead—you know, necrophilia and shit."

Ellie's hand fluttered and she clamped it to her leg. "I . . . I didn't ask about his past cases. I want his help here now, with our missing persons investigation. I don't care what he did before." Her voice was high and thin to her own ears, and she realized how incurious and ridiculous she sounded. Any cop worth his or her stripes would want to know about Francis Coben.

"Not me," Jimmy told her. "I'd take him out for a beer and get the whole damn story. All the stuff he didn't put in the book, if you know what I'm saying." He snatched a bag of chips off the shelf. "Yeah, I'll just bet Markham has some tales to tell. Too bad because he shit the bed last year."

She was so focused on not throwing up or running out of the store that it took her a minute to parse what Jimmy had said. "What do you mean?"

He shrugged. "I looked him up when the chief told me Markham was here. Some kidnapping out in Idaho last year and your buddy fingered the wrong guy. A little boy died."

"What?"

"Seems the FBI wants nothing to do with him these days. I guess that explains why he's got time on his hands to come up here and hang around with you." He tossed the chips back on the shelf. "Shouldn't be eating this garbage, am I right? We've gotta stay in shape." He clapped a heavy hand on her shoulder.

"See you later, Hathaway. Be careful out there. I hear we've got a big, bad killer on the loose."

She stood there rooted to the floor as he sauntered away whistling, without buying anything, leaving her to wonder if he had come inside looking for her all along.

At home, she rushed Bump through his late-night routine, and then they both moved to her makeshift office, where she powered up her laptop and did what she had once sworn to herself she would never do: she searched deliberately for Reed Markham. His name returned hundreds of hits, with the book being number one. *Little Girl Lost*. The title alone made her shudder, and although she had never dared to read it, she couldn't work up any ire at Markham for writing it. She was really no better, she supposed. Markham's bestselling book. Coben's million-dollar pictures. After what she had done, Ellie was in no position to judge anyone making money from the whole sordid tale.

She steeled her stomach as she clicked on Reed Markham's Wikipedia page. She skipped over the part about his famous politician father, his personal life, the Coben case and a handful of others, down to the last link available: the Adam Kennedy kidnapping. Clicking this link produced the face of a red-haired, freckled little boy smiling out from his own Missing poster. Apparently he'd wandered away from his parents in a Boise furniture store, and by the time they figured out that he wasn't asleep in some bed somewhere, whoever took Adam was long gone. Reed had joined the case early and leaned hard on the local pedophiles, in particular one named Barnaby Tate, who was caught on security footage at the fast-food place next door to the furniture store around the time Adam disappeared. Everyone in Adam's life was also interviewed, including his family, teachers, and neighbors, but there was no trace of the boy. After forty-eight hours, Adam's parents went on television to beg for their son's safe return, and Reed apparently spoke too (there was an embedded link to that video, which Ellie did not watch). The text said Reed had promised the kidnapper that they would never stop looking for Adam.

Two days after that, little Adam was found dead in a city Dumpster. The autopsy placed the time of death only twelve hours before, meaning Adam had been alive for several days after his abduction. Hair and fibers on the body led to the arrest of Paul Cryderman, a construction worker who had been part of the team that installed the new playground at Adam's school earlier that month. Cryderman had been questioned and released earlier in the investigation. Upon his arrest, he supposedly told authorities that when Agent Markham said they would never stop looking for Adam, Cryderman felt he had no choice but the kill the boy and dump the body. Adam's parents were threatening to sue the FBI for negligence, and Reed Markham had stepped down from his position in the Behavioral Sciences Unit.

"Funny, he didn't mention that part to me," Ellie said to Bump, who raised his head and thumped his tail in agreement. Markham was supposed to be the answer man, the one who saw what everyone else missed. Turned out he could be just as wrong as the rest of them—wronger even, because the stakes were so high.

Bump froze and cocked his head, listening toward the window for something. Ellie swung the chair lazily around to look at him. "What is it, boy? Squirrel in the well again? Or maybe it's a fox."

Bump growled low in his throat and the fur at the back of his neck stood on end. He was still staring toward the window, so Ellie got up to go take a look. It was too dark to see much out in the yard, but she didn't notice anything amiss. Behind her, Bump got up on his stubby legs and repeated his warning growl. "Okay, okay. If it'll make you happy, I'll go take a look, all right?"

Her revolver in hand, she turned on the outside floodlights, and some sort of animal—a raccoon, maybe—scurried at the edge of the shadows, disappearing into the thicket of trees. Ellie walked around the perimeter of her yard but didn't see anything out of place. The night was cool and strangely quiet; she heard only her boots in the wet grass and the sound of her own breathing. Beyond that, there was silence. She looked up the empty road into the black night as she recalled Darryl Franklin and his threat to pay her a visit.

Summer moths darted back and forth in her spotlights, like tiny ballerinas on the stage. Bump had propped himself up in the window to watch, his long face sagging because he'd been left out of the action. Ellie took a few more steps toward the edge of the light, where the shadows on the ground seemed joined with the tall trees. Bump barked his encouragement—or was it a warning? She ventured farther into the dark, her short, quick breaths taking in the damp night air as gooseflesh broke out across her arms. *You've been in these woods hundreds of times,* she reminded herself as she picked her way through the low-lying branches and the soft crust of dank moss and brambly bushes. Somewhere, she hoped not close by, there was a skunk.

"This is ridiculous," she muttered after a few minutes, but as she said the words, her foot hit something, a glass bottle that rolled at the touch of her toe. She picked it up and immediately caught the scent of beer. "What the . . . ?" As she held it toward the light for better inspection, she saw her house, right there just beyond her hand. The trees parted just so to allow anyone standing in this exact spot a perfect view of her east-side windows. Her kitchen. Her bedroom.

You ever get the feeling like someone's watching you? Reed

Markham had asked her just a few hours earlier. *Following you around?*

Ellie had scoffed at the idea. *Of course not. Believe me, I would notice.*

Her blood went cold as the night creatures chattered down at her from the trees. In the distance, in the warm yellow windows of her beloved home, Bump began to howl.

4

It was the Fourth of July, a holiday for the rest of the country, but for Reed it was just another day off. He squinted out at the bright morning and took in the decorations as they drove through Woodbury: the American flags, already limp in the summer heat, and the slightly faded red, white, and blue bunting on the town streetlights. "Do you think people can ever change?" Ellery asked him from behind the wheel of her truck as they headed toward the Nesbit home.

"People change their behavior all the time," Reed answered, not turning his attention from the window. It was barely nine o'clock but already the sun had burned off any clouds from the sky. "They quit smoking. They become new parents. They find God on the road to Damascus and renounce their wicked ways."

"I'm not talking about behavior," she corrected him. "I mean can they change who they are. Become someone else."

Reed stared out the window at the waving meadows, careful not to catch his reflection in the glass. His own life had become one he did not recognize. Growing up, he'd always had a knack for finding lost things. His mother would misplace her glasses somewhere in their thirteen-room stately brick mansion and Reed invariably found them just by imagining his mother as she moved through her tasks for the day. He could close his eyes and call her up, how she would be in the kitchen, where she laid out the eggs and bacon next to the stove for cooking, and it would soon the sizzle would be perfuming the downstairs, and Mama would go wash her hands in soft soap at the sink, where the bird feeder stood just outside the window, and oh, was that a painted bunting pecking away at his own breakfast, until his vermilion belly was stuffed and fluffed to bursting? Better take off the glasses for a closer look. Sure enough, that's where they would find them, set forgotten on the windowsill next to the African violets.

Since those early days, he had crossed the country a hundred times in search of the lost. Their faces were plastered on the news, on posters and flyers and milk cartons, these missing people who were everywhere at once and yet nowhere at all. Reed would learn their lives as best he could and try to trace them back to the beginning, to the place they'd been standing when it all went wrong. Sometimes he presided over a happy reunion; more often he discovered only bones. "Each time you go, you come home a little bit less than you were," Sarit had told him once, "like you leave part of yourself behind at their graves." She didn't understand what it was like to be the one who had parted the woods and performed the miracle, the one he could never quite repeat. The awed whispers, the palpable hope at his arrival—*that's the one who found her, the Coben girl*—he felt his own history sit heavy on his shoulders each time he joined a new scene, because more often than not, the victim in question was dead before his plane even touched down. He consoled himself with the knowledge that he'd done everything he could, that there was no way he might have changed the outcome. Only the last time, in Idaho, the words turned out to be a lie.

"I don't know you anymore," Sarit had said the day she asked him to move out of their home, a solid brick colonial that had stood through the Civil War and yet it couldn't keep his family from falling apart.

Reed turned his face back to Ellery and studied her profile—the determined set of her chin, the porcelain shell of her ear, and the dark tendrils of hair that had escaped the knot at her nape. *Who would you be,* he wondered, *if Francis Coben hadn't intervened?* But out loud, he said, "I think there are many ways a person can be lost."

Ellery tightened her hands on the wheel and did not ask him any more questions.

Dave and Annie Nesbit lived in a Cape-style white house with forest-green shutters and well-tended bushes. As Reed stepped out of the truck, the overpowering scent of cut grass hit him like a silent scream. There was a large stone pot on the porch filled to overflowing with pink and white impatiens, and a cheery red mailbox out front. There was a row of houses down the block just like it, shaded by the protection of tall, leafy maples that signaled the strength of the neighborhood's history. It looked, Reed thought, like nothing bad could ever happen here. Grackles jabbered at each other in the trees and a trio of young boys went sailing past on their bikes clear on the other side of the road, as if to avoid passing too close to the Nesbit property line.

When Dave and Annie Nesbit opened the door, both of them together crowding the narrow space, Annie's hand shook slightly as she reached to greet Ellery, and Dave's blue eyes held a wild and desperate look, as though he were holding back the sea. *Hope is the thing with feathers*, Emily Dickinson wrote, and Reed felt the truth of those words every time he met the families. Hope could take you so high that you no longer saw the ground.

"Thank you," Dave said, pumping Reed's hand with forced enthusiasm. "Thank you for coming. The FBI didn't want the case three years ago—they said the State Police were doing an adequate job with the investigation, and they would reconsider if more evidence became available."

The bitterness in his voice told Reed all he needed to know about how Dave felt regarding that assessment. "I don't know what Officer Hathaway has told you," he said carefully, "but I am only here to take a look at the facts and offer any insight I might have. There have been no new developments."

"Anything . . . anyone who wants to help us find Bea, we're grateful for the help," Dave replied.

They sat on the back patio under the shade of a navy blue umbrella, and Annie Nesbit served them iced tea in tall glasses that started sweating immediately in the warm summer air. She had a pleasant oval face that sagged a bit around the edges from middle age, and huge brown eyes that rimmed with emotion when she talked about her daughter. "Bea only knew a handful of English words when we brought her home, but she was talking so much by age two that her pediatrician made a note of it in her charts." Almost shyly, she drew out some childhood photos that showed a delicate Chinese girl in various growing-up stages, in one shot wearing a pink party hat and sitting in front of a birthday cake with three candles on it, and in another playing the violin on a school stage. "She made straight A's all through school and participated in a ton of clubs—debate, French, yearbook. She also played on the volleyball team and volunteered on weekends sorting donations at the local food bank. Partly it was to look good for college applications, of course, but Bea really seemed to love doing it all—you know, pushing herself, seeing how many different activities she could cram into one day. We used to tease her that she was so good at everything, she would never be able to pick one profession—she'd be a musical cowgirl doctor who illustrated comic books in her spare time."

Reed heard the familiar bewilderment in Annie's words: How could a girl with that much potential have ended up like this? "She went to Amherst?" he asked gently, skipping the story ahead to where Bea's life started to lose some of its glow.

The warmth drained out of Annie's face as they left Bea's childhood behind and entered the place where the story went wrong. "She was so excited to get in," Annie said. "It was her first choice. We were just happy she wasn't going to Stanford, her number two, because it was so far away. Bea was just going to be down the road." She shook her head to show how foolish she'd been. "I got a cat around the time she moved out. Smokey. Bea had begged and pleaded with us for years to get her a pet, but we always said no. She was so busy with her activities, how could she look after an animal? But we adopted Smokey a few weeks before she left for school, and Bea laughed at me. I said the cat was to keep me company when she was gone, but she said it was a bribe to try to get her to come home on weekends."

Dave reached over and squeezed her hand. "Bea was right."

Annie smiled sadly. "It didn't work, though."

"Bea struggled with a few of her classes during that first semester," Dave continued, taking over the story. "For the first time, she didn't make easy A's. She didn't get along with her roommate."

"A little floozy named Nicki," Annie cut in tartly. "More interested in boys than books."

Dave patted her arm, maybe because he recalled where Bea's tale ended. "We tried to talk to her through it, but everything we suggested just made her angry. So we tried backing off and waiting for her to call us. She did, finally, at which point she accused us of not caring about her life. We couldn't do anything right."

"Still, we were so happy to have her home with us at winter break. My family came up for the holidays and Bea seemed to relax a little." Annie's voice was wistful. "Then she went into Boston with her friends for First Night. That's where she met Derek."

"Her boyfriend," Reed said, recalling the files.

"Bea didn't tell us much about him," Dave said. "She said he was in school at BU, but that turned out to be a lie."

Reed wondered whether Derek had lied to Bea, or Bea had lied to her parents. "Did you meet him?" he asked.

Annie looked at her lap, and her hair fell, covering her face. "Not until the candlelight vigil," she said softly. "We held it a week after she disappeared. The whole town turned out and the local news covered the event. We hoped . . . we hoped whoever took Bea might be watching and decide to let her go. Derek came with a few of his friends."

Dave's jaw tightened with disapproval. "He showed up wearing leather pants and stinking of cigarettes."

"Bea was staying the weekend in the city with him at the time she disappeared. She was supposed to be back here on Sunday, but she texted us to say she would be late, don't wait up. That was a little after seven P.M. and we never heard from her again."

"Records show her cell phone pinged last from the Worcester area, near the Mass Pike," Dave added.

Annie's eyes welled with tears. "She was coming home."

Reed picked up one of the photos Annie had brought out, one that appeared to be a senior portrait. Bea's dark hair gleamed with light, and her smile was confident and happy, like she knew she was going to embark on great adventure. "What do you think happened to her?" he asked the Nesbits.

They exchanged a lingering look. "We used to think Derek was the one who took her," Dave said, letting out a long breath. "But Ellie's made us reconsider, after what's happened with Shannon Blessing and Mark Roy."

"Is that why you're here?" Annie asked, leaning forward. "Do you think she's right that one person took Bea and the others?"

Reed could feel Ellie's eyes on him as he answered. "It's a possibility we're looking into," he said. "Did Bea have any relationship with Shannon or Mark?"

"We didn't know Shannon at all," answered Annie. "Mark was our mailman. The kids around here used to set up a lemonade stand in the summers, and Mark would always buy three cups and drink them all in a row. They loved him for it. We felt just awful when he lost his boy, Dylan. People used to say he wasn't the same after that, but how can you be?" She picked fretfully at the edge of a damp paper napkin.

Before they left, Reed asked if he could take a look at Bea's room, and Annie led him upstairs to a tidy bedroom that had clearly belonged to girl in transition to adulthood. Smokey the cat lay curled up asleep atop the pink-and-gray bedspread. Reed stood in the doorway and took in the white lace curtains, the blue ribbons pinned on the wall, the drawings of dragons and kittens and snapshots of Bea with her high school friends. "They'll all be graduating college this year," Annie said tightly, following his gaze. Her voice was a hoarse whisper, raw and filled with pain. "You know what I keep thinking about?" She said it as if she were confessing a secret. "I think about her other mother, the one in China. We never knew much about her except the province she was in at the time Bea was born, but I wondered about her all the time. We wanted so much to have a child. I lost six babies to miscarriage before we finally gave up and decided to go for adoption." She bit her lip, hard enough to turn it white. "I know it's not the same thing, losing a baby that wasn't born yet versus giving up your actual child, but sometimes I think I know how she must have felt, letting Bea go. I prayed all the time that God would tell her that Bea is happy, that we love her, that we would keep her safe."

Reed wondered briefly about his own mother, and whether she'd had the same wish. The woman who had birthed him died just a few months later, so if there had been any kind of prayer during Reed's youth, maybe she was in heaven to receive it.

At the door, the Nesbits shook his hand one more time, hanging on even as he edged out onto the porch. "We're realistic at this stage," Dave said, drawing himself up as they finally parted. "After three years, you don't think it's likely you're going to get a happy ending. We just want to know what happened to her. We want to bring Bea home."

"We will keep you informed of any news," Ellery assured them. "You have my word."

As they walked down the path from the Nesbits' home, Ellery glanced back over her shoulder to where the couple was still watching them from the doorway. "They say they're realistic," she murmured to him, "but Annie sends me every news story of a missing person who reappears after a long absence, like maybe it was some cult leader who snatched Bea off the streets and he's holding her in his compound somewhere."

"The thing with feathers," Reed muttered.

"What?"

"Never mind." He was eyeing the cruiser just turning the corner down the street. "Isn't that your boss headed this way?"

Ellery stifled a curse as the car rolled to a stop behind her truck and Chief Parker got out, his boots heavy on the hot sidewalk.

He did not look pleased. Sweat beaded up the back of Reed's neck, and his cotton shirt clung like a second skin. "Ellie," Parker said as he approached. "I thought I told you to leave these poor people well enough alone." He spoke through gritted teeth, a half smile plastered on his face because presumably the Nesbits were still watching.

"They wanted to meet Agent Markham," she replied. "They deserve to know what's going on."

"Nothing's going on!" The mask of pleasantness slipped and he turned his back to the Nesbits' front door. "We don't have anything new to offer them, and all you're doing is stirring them up with crazy theories and terrible memories. They don't need your kind of help."

"But—"

"Don't 'but' me. You call in outside investigators without consulting me, and then you deliberately disobey a direct order. I've half a mind to pull your shield right now."

"Go ahead, then. Do it."

Reed watched with interest as Parker worked his jaw back and forth, his nostrils flared with barely suppressed fury, but for some reason, the chief didn't call her bluff. "I came out this way also to tell you that I won't be giving you the rest of those files," he said, enunciating every word slowly. "Tipton and I looked through them, and there's nothing there that hasn't been thoroughly investigated already."

"So then what's the harm in letting Agent Markham look them over?"

"The harm is you going around scaring people in the town with unsubstantiated rumors."

"They should be scared," Ellery shot back. "Someone else is going to go missing soon, and we've done nothing to protect them."

"Yeah?" Parker spread his arms in angry defiance. "Tell me who. Who's going missing? Tell me where and when to send my units, Ellie, and I'll get right on it." He waited a beat through her silence. "That's right. You can't tell me anything but the same old horseshit about the bogeyman hiding in the bushes. Well, until you have something—I mean a solid piece of evidence that these people are dead, or that the cases are definitely connected—I want you to drop it. You understand me? Drop it."

"And if I don't?"

Parker's eyes darkened to the color of steel. "Then so help me, I will take your shield. I don't care what the consequences are." They stood there, glaring at each other, until Parker's radio went off from inside his cruiser. He narrowed his gaze at Ellery. "I've got to get ready for the parade today," he said. "I suggest you go get a lawn chair and take in the music. You seem like you could use the rest." He turned to Reed, as if seeing him there for the first time. "You might want to bring your friend here too. I called down to Quantico, and they tell me he's been under a lot of stress."

He bit out the last word and then turned on his heel to leave. Reed and Ellie stood on the sidewalk and watched the cruiser's taillights disappear back around the corner. Reed cleared his throat. "Look, about what they said in Quantico—"

"Don't worry about it," she cut in swiftly, not looking at him. "I don't need to know. You're here to help, and that's all that matters."

Reed looked down at the cracked sidewalk and shook his head. He wished like hell he had a drink, something cold and hard to fill the space where his certainty used to be. He was nobody's hero, not really, and he feared what her reaction would be when she finally figured that out.

"What do you want to do next?" she asked him as they climbed back into her truck. The dark leather seats practically singed his skin, and the color of Ellie's face had turned to a bright, glowing pink. "You want to see Shannon's apartment? I know the woman renting there. Or we could drive Mark's mail route."

"I have a different idea," Reed said carefully, watching her closely for a reaction. "I have a friend at the Massachusetts State Police Crime Laboratory. I called her this morning to see if she might be willing to run DNA analyses on the birthday cards you received, and she's agreed to take a look."

Ellery raised her eyebrows at him as she turned on the engine. The roar of the air-conditioning sprang to life, but for the moment it blew only more hot air. "DNA analysis? On a holiday weekend? She must be some friend."

Back in college, Danielle Wertz had once been a friend with benefits, nothing serious on either of their parts, but with enough remaining affection that she didn't immediately hang up on him when he requested she do him an enormous favor on her day off. "What do you think?" he asked Ellery. "Fancy a trip to Maynard?"

She seemed to hesitate for a fraction of a second. Maybe, as he feared, she had her own reasons for not wanting the cards analyzed by an outside party. "I'd have to drop off my dog with a friend first," she said at length, "if we're going to be away that long."

"By all means," he agreed, settling back in as the cool air began to flow at last. She put on the radio, some '80s pop tune he dimly recognized, and barreled down the road like she was driving into battle, body pitched forward, both hands on the wheel. *The other guys in my unit think I'm crazy,* she'd confessed to him last night, and it seemed possible that they were right. But Reed had been the lone voice in the wilderness once, following an evidence trail that no one else seemed to see, and now here she was

alive as a result. For the moment, until he had proof it was foolish to do otherwise, he would continue to follow her lead.

Ellery's dog turned out to be one of those long-eared, slobbery
creatures that always looked to Reed like evolution had played
some sort of practical joke, in which a long, sturdy animal was
equipped with laughably small legs. The dog's addition to the
front seat of the truck made a close ride that much hotter, as the
animal wiggled and dangled its enormous pink tongue all over
the left side of Reed's face. "Couldn't he ride outside in the back?"
Reed asked in desperation as the tongue came swinging at his ear
for the third time.

"Bump would love that, but the road grit is bad for his eyes."
She glanced over and gave him what was the first honest-to-
goodness smile he had ever seen on her. "Besides, I think he likes
you."

"I've had entire romantic relationships that did not involve
this much tongue," Reed replied as he wiped the slobber off his
arm with a tissue.

This made her laugh, a sound that somehow turned his ears
hot. "Guess you're going steady, then," she said as she turned off
the road into a parking lot marked Angelman Animal Shelter.
"Come on, Bump. Let's go find Brady."

The dog leapt from the vehicle with all the grace of a hippo
performing a belly flop, and Reed trailed him and his mistress
into the shelter. It smelled like antiseptic and fur, making his nose
tingle. Ellie waved at some woman in the office and then wandered into the back like she owned the place, so Reed followed,
down the hall, into a room with sad-looking animals in various sizes of metal cages. They all stirred at the arrival of new

visitors, barking and yowling and sticking wet noses out as far as they would go. Reed hardly knew where to stand without getting a snout in his face.

At the commotion, a young man in a gray lab coat turned from mopping the floor. "Hey, Ellie," he said, pulling out his earbuds and silencing his music player. "What brings you by?"

"Sorry for just dropping in like this. I was hoping Bump could hang out here with you today," she said, reaching down to scratch the dog's comically large ears. "I have to head across the state for work this afternoon, and I'm not sure exactly when I'll be back."

"You know I love the Bumpmeister and he's welcome anytime." Bump was running around sniffing at the various cages, wagging his enthusiastic tail behind him. "What's the fire today?"

"Oh, the usual. You know."

The young man nodded. "Yeah, it's July again."

Reed wondered if there was anyone in the town who had not heard Ellery's theory of the missing persons cases. "Sam's stonewalling me," she was saying to the other guy. "He won't give me full access to the case files."

"What more could you need at this point? You've been collecting stuff for years."

"The State Police have records on the Bea Nesbit investigation that I haven't seen. For one thing, there's surveillance video from the gas station she stopped at the night she disappeared. Jimmy Tipton said it's useless, but I'd like to see for myself."

The guy looked surprised. "I'm pretty sure you can—if you've got a computer and a credit card."

"What are you talking about?" Ellery asked. Reed sidestepped Bump, who had become interested in running his nose all over Reed's shoes.

"Come on, I'll show you." He put aside the mop and wiped his hand on his jeans before extending it to Reed. "I'm Brady Archer."

"Oh, sorry," Ellery said. "Brady, this is—"

"Reed Markham," Reed supplied. "I'm a friend of Ellery's."

"He's FBI," Ellery said flatly as they followed Brady deeper into the bowels of the shelter.

"FBI." Brady let out a low whistle that carried back down the dark hallway. "It's good to have friends in high places." They reached a lighted nook at the end of the hall. "Welcome to my abode. I'd offer you a chair, but there aren't any."

The three of them squeezed into the small, windowless room that appeared to act as Brady's office. It featured concrete walls covered with various animal pictures, some of them pen-and-ink sketches done by an individual with actual artistic talent. Brady had captured the impish gleam in the kitten's eye and the baleful, lonely gaze of the mongrel mutt. There was also a battered old metal desk and a stool whose stuffing was coming out on one side. The desk was piled high with empty cans of Mountain Dew, and stacks of different-colored forms littered the rest. Brady opened his laptop and bent over it. "There's a group of people online who follow unsolved cases, collecting information and exchanging theories. I guess they all think they're Sherlock Holmes or something. Anyway, a few of them are interested in Bea Nesbit."

"How did you find out about this?" Ellery asked, plainly surprised. Reed wondered how the magic of the Internet seemed to have passed her by.

"I looked her up one day out of curiosity, after she disappeared," Brady said with a shrug. He looked a little embarrassed. "She came in here with her mom once when they adopted a cat. Seemed like a nice enough girl."

So this guy knew Bea Nesbit too, Reed observed. He imagined trying to map the connections of everyone in Woodbury, and envisioned the result looking like a spider's web.

"Here." Brady pointed at the screen. "This guy posted a link and a PayPal account for someone calling himself 'Oil Can Boy.' Oil Can will supposedly sell you the video from the gas station the night Bea disappeared for twenty bucks. But if you read through the thread, it seems like the posters agree with the cops on this one—the video isn't helpful."

Ellery was frowning. "Why didn't you tell me this before?"

"I assumed you knew. Googling your victim and your suspects—isn't that, like, Police one oh one?"

Ellery's face turned pink, and Reed realized then that she might have good reason to avoid any sort of true crime message boards or chat rooms—any space loaded with curious, prying people who had a lot of time on their hands and imagined themselves to be professional investigators. Reed ended the awkward silence by pulling out his wallet. "Well, I have a credit card," he said. "May I?"

"Be my guest," Brady said, backing out of the way so Reed could request a copy of the video. As he entered the information, Reed heard Brady and Ellery talking quietly behind him.

"How are the kittens?"

"Armed and dangerous. Check out my palms."

"I don't even see a Band-Aid. I think somehow you'll live."

Reed straightened up as his request went through. "There," he said, "I guess now we shall await a return missive from Mr. Can."

"We've got to go," Ellery said, touching Brady's arm. "Thanks again for looking after Bump today."

"My pleasure, Officer," he replied, giving her a grin and a mock salute. Then he grew serious. "And, listen, I'm sorry if I messed up by not telling you . . ."

"No, no," Ellery assured him quickly. "You didn't mess up." She turned with Reed to exit, but at the door, she hesitated, so

Reed stopped too. "What do they say about who killed Bea?" she asked Brady. "The people on the Internet?"

Brady's dark eyes were wide and guileless. "I haven't looked in a long time. Last I saw, they still believed her boyfriend did it."

The Massachusetts State Police Forensic and Technology Center was located in the sleepy suburb of Maynard, right in the midst of a residential area, although it looked more like a prison than a modern science laboratory. The foreboding concrete face had long narrow windows and a few shrubs around its base. Reed phoned Danielle Wertz, who met them at the lobby. He noted that her long, flowing blond hair had been replaced by a tousled bob that bore flecks of gray, but she still had the same intelligent blue eyes and warm hug that he remembered from years ago. "It's been too long," she said as she pulled away. "How are you? How are Sarit and Tula doing?"

Reed coughed and rubbed the back of his neck. "Good. They're, uh, good. How's . . ." He tried to call up the name of her long-term boyfriend. "Scott?"

She made a face. "We broke up last year."

"Oh, I'm so sorry to hear that."

"Not half as sorry as my mother. She was always so sure we were getting married. Now she's trying to set me up long-distance with her cable guy."

"Hold out for a satellite provider," Reed advised, and Danielle tilted her head back with a laugh. "Danielle, let me introduce Officer Ellery Hathaway of the Woodbury Police Department."

"My mother once tried to set me up with my cousin," Ellery told her as they shook hands.

"Holy crap, really? I think you win—or lose, as the case may be."

"He was a second cousin, but my objection still stands on the record."

"Thank you for coming in to help us today," Reed said. "I owe you one."

"You owe me about three by now," Danielle said, eyeing him up and down. "But you get a discount this time because my A/C is out and there's no way I was going to sit around frying my eggs off at home. You said you wanted some letters analyzed?"

Reed nodded and pulled out the cards Ellery had given him. "We're hoping you can pull saliva samples from these envelopes. Maybe we'll get lucky and there'll be a hit in the system."

"Should be easy enough to check," Danielle replied as she accepted the bag with the cards in it. "Why don't you guys help yourselves to a soda and I'll let you know if we even have anything here worth testing?"

"Actually," Ellie said, "I was wondering if you could test something else too."

Reed regarded her with mild surprise, and he noted for the first time that she was holding a small paper bag.

"There's a beer bottle in here," Ellie said. "I was hoping you could check it for prints or DNA."

"Where is that from?" Reed asked, because there was nothing in the files about a beer bottle. Ellie took a long time with her answer.

"The woods behind my house," she said finally. "I found it last night."

Danielle looked from one to the other. "Just what funny business do you two have going on here?"

"That's what we're trying to find out," Reed said, but he was still looking at Ellery.

"Well, like I said, take it easy for the next twenty minutes or so and I'll let you know what I can do."

Reed and Ellery found the soda machine and bought a couple of Cokes. Reed drank his sitting on the hard bench, but Ellie paced the length of the floor in front of him. "You didn't tell me about the beer bottle," he said as she walked past.

She halted with a shrug but did not meet his eyes. "It may not mean anything. Tad and Erin Bashir next door have a couple of teenage boys. Could be they were drinking in the woods."

"You ever see anyone out there?"

"No, never."

He took a long swill of cold soda. "Have you given any more thought to who might have sent you those cards? Even if we get DNA, we may need a sample to compare it to."

"Of course I've given thought to it," she replied impatiently. "And I've told you—there's no one. I have been very careful not to talk about my background with anyone."

"What about going back farther—to the training academy, to college. Maybe you told a friend or a roommate."

She shook her head. "I'd changed my name by then. I've been Ellery Hathaway for ten years now."

He thought back to the hundreds of people involved in the case at the time. Everyone from the patrol officers to the EMTs who showed up in the woods behind Coben's farm would have known a piece of the story, and there was a time when those pieces might have fetched a pretty penny. The public's appetite for the story seemed insatiable. A few years ago, Reed had dental surgery, and just as the anesthesia hit him, making his head float free from his body, the nurse's voice had materialized out of nowhere: "Mr. Markham? Tell me . . . what is Francis Coben really like?" His fat tongue had laid numb in his mouth, too paralyzed to answer. If these strangers haunted him with their questions, what would they do to Ellery when they found her out?

"You really haven't talked to anyone about it?" he asked her.

"Even people who might swear to keep your identity confidential—no reporters, no doctors, no lawyers."

"No," she insisted, almost stamping her foot, looking more like the fourteen-year-old girl he remembered. "There's no one." The instant she said the words, her cheeks developed two bright spots on them. "Well, okay, there's just one person. But it was a long time ago, and she's dead now."

"Tell me."

Ellery cast a long look down the empty hall before sighing and walking over to join him on the bench. "After it happened," she said in a low voice, looking straight ahead and not at him, "some people sent us money. Not a lot, usually—twenty bucks here or there. But this one woman, Jacqueline MacKenzie, she wanted to give us thousands, as in almost one hundred thousand dollars. My mom worked as a paralegal in a small firm. Daniel had medical bills. One hundred thousand dollars was a lot of money back then."

"It still is."

She took a deep breath. "Anyway, for that kind of money, she wanted to meet me. See how I was doing. I didn't want to do it, but we really needed the money so I said okay. She sent a driver to come get me in this enormous burgundy-colored Cadillac. I remember he opened the door for me and gave me a bottle of cold water for the drive. The backseat was the size of my twin bed at home, and the driver kept checking me out in the rearview mirror, like he couldn't believe he was chauffeuring around this poor kid from Albany Park. My mother wasn't allowed to come with me; that was part of the deal. Mom didn't like it, but she didn't feel like she could question Jackie if we wanted the money."

Reed remembered holding the slight weight of the girl in his arms as he had run from Coben's farm, not knowing for sure whether she was even breathing. How desperate must her mother have been to send that same girl out the door to relive the whole ordeal alone with a total stranger. Surely there must have been another way to pay the bills.

"So we drove to her huge house in Old Town," Ellery continued. "It must have had three or four stories—practically as big as my whole apartment building back home. We sat and had tea in her front room. The tea tasted like dirt to me, but I felt like I had to force it down anyway, what with all the money she was going to be giving us. She said, 'Call me Jackie-Mac, everyone does.' Then she started with the questions."

"What kind of questions?"

Ellie bowed her head. "What was it like when Coben took me? What did his farm look like? What did he do to me? That sort of thing. She wanted to know all the details."

"Why?"

Her head jerked up and she gave him a pointed look. "What do you mean *why*? Why did you write your book? Why did so many people read it? Because of course everyone had to know the gory details. Jackie-Mac just happened to be rich enough to go straight to the source."

Reed stiffened from the bitter sting of her barbs. He remembered the shining light in Sarit's eyes as he'd told her the story. *You've got an amazing tale here, Reed*, she'd told him. *Bestseller material! People would eat this right up.* He knew she wasn't wrong, because he'd felt it from the start, the unending public hunger for more of Coben's story. He'd thought he was informing them, edifying them about the psychology of violent offenders. Sitting now with one of the victims, seeing how she curled protectively in on herself just at the mention of Coben's crimes, he felt dirty, no better than the old bat who'd dragged a vulnerable teenager from her home and justified the sin with money.

"I just answered her questions as quickly as I could and prayed like hell the whole thing would be over," Ellery said wistfully. She leaned back against the wall and looked at the ceiling. "I figured if I could tell the cops about what happened for free, I could tell this lady for a hundred thousand bucks."

Reed rubbed his face with one hand as he absorbed the story. "I'm sorry," he told her finally. "I'm sorry she did that to you."

"Yeah, well. It wasn't the worst thing that's ever happened to me, you know?"

The night of the rescue, Reed had been surrounded by reporters before he'd even had a chance to change or to think about what he would say. It all happened so fast. Later, he had watched himself on the news stammering, "No comment, no comment," looking like a hunted fox under the bright TV lights. It was only then he noticed that Abby's blood had spilled all down the front of his shirt.

"She summoned me back a few times over the next few years," Ellie continued. "I went each time and answered more of her questions. By then, Coben was on trial, and she used to videotape the news reports on the proceedings and then want to watch them with me. I pretended to watch but mostly I went inside my head and counted backward from one thousand. I told myself I was counting all the money we would get from her, the crazy old bag."

"Jackie-Mac," Reed repeated, musing on the name for the first time. "You know, her name actually sounds familiar."

"Her husband was some real estate mogul in Chicago. In any case, she died while I was still in high school. Left me another fifty grand in the will, so I guess it was all worth it. Her money was my ticket out of there."

"Reed?" Danielle poked her head into the hall. "I've got good news for you."

Reed and Ellie tossed their empty soda cans into the trash

and walked back to the entrance to the laboratory area. Danielle had donned a white coat and gloves. "What did you find?" Reed asked her.

"Two envelopes and the beer bottle all have usable samples, but I only have time to do one today—which one do you want first?"

"The envelopes," Ellie said, at the same time Reed said, "The bottle."

Danielle spread out her arms. "Pick one."

"The envelopes," Reed said, reluctantly revising his answer. If Ellery was unbalanced enough to be sending herself anonymous birthday cards, he needed to know sooner rather than later. But he'd also seen her house, when he'd been sitting in the truck while she went in to fetch the blasted dog, so he knew how isolated she was out there. The idea of someone camped out in the woods watching her filled him with a creeping sense of dread. It was becoming apparent to him that Ellery had not mapped the Coben history at all—she had no idea there were kooks on the Internet who believed in Coben's innocence. Women who wanted to marry him. Men who wanted to be like him.

Reed himself had seen Coben in person only once, when he interviewed him for twenty minutes as fodder for his book. Coben had shaved his head and tattooed eyeliner around his deep-set eyes. His smile had been predatory, and he had just one question: "Where is Abigail?"

"Okay, the envelopes it is," Danielle said, breaking into Reed's thoughts. "I'll be in touch with the results as soon as I have them. Maybe as soon as tomorrow. The beer bottle is going to have to wait."

"Great, thank you."

"Yes, thank you," Ellie echoed.

They exited the building into the summer heat, which to Reed felt like walking into a wall. Waves shimmered off the parking lot pavement, making him momentarily dizzy. "I forgot my sunglasses," he said. "Go on and I'll catch up."

He jogged back into the building, where he went to the trash and carefully picked up Ellie's soda can. Danielle was already back in safety goggles inside the lab, and he knocked to get her attention. "What is it?" she asked when she emerged.

"The envelope samples," he said. "Could you please test them against this can?"

Danielle did not look thrilled to be given another task. "That'll delay your results," she said.

"I understand. Can you test it anyway?" He glanced back to make sure Ellery wasn't watching.

Danielle looked concerned for the first time. "Reed, whatever you've got going on here, I hope you're being careful."

He wasn't sure which answer would be worse: that Ellery was sending herself menacing birthday cards, or that someone else was. "Test the can," he said softly. "As soon as you are able—and thanks."

On the journey back to Woodbury, the air-conditioning in Ellery's old truck could hardly keep up with the shimmery heat outside. Reed rolled up his shirtsleeves and let himself be lulled by the hum of the road noise and the banality of the passing scenery. Thick, bushy trees, grasses browned from the summer sun. A blue sky whipped with clouds that looked like cotton candy. "If you want, we could stop and get a drink," Ellery offered, breaking the silence.

A drink. The word called up a vision of a tall beer in a frosty glass, cold foam at his lips. But this time, it felt like a reward for a hard day's work and not the first step toward sweet oblivion.

He had to stay straight and sober to figure out what the heck was going on with her, this woman he'd pulled back from the brink. His idle mind had a new beguiling puzzle. So yes, he was thirsty again—but not for booze—and the realization filled him with some relief. The alcohol felt like something he'd been auditioning in the wake of all his losses, something to fill the void. Maybe also it had been a kind of secret test. Reed had no specific knowledge of his genetic background, no idea what he might have been flirting with when he cracked open that first bottle of Jack Daniel's. *Maybe,* he'd told himself, bleary-eyed when looking in the mirror, *maybe this is who you really are.* Now he was far from home, rolling down the Mass Pike with a woman who might be certifiably nuts, but he felt the sanest he'd been in almost a year. "Is there a bookstore around here?" he demanded suddenly.

"Uh, sure, as part of the mall up here. I think so. Why?"

"Please, can we stop there? I have something I'd like to check out."

Ten minutes later, they were standing together in the True Crime section as he pulled the latest edition of *Little Girl Lost* off the shelves. Ellie looked on with apparent interest as he started thumbing through the pages. "What, you don't have it committed to memory by now?" she asked.

She might even have been teasing him, but Reed felt acutely self-conscious holding the paperback in his hands with the actual lost girl standing two feet away. "I just want to check something," he said.

Ellery stretched out her hand. "Can I see it?"

He drew up short, blinking, and then slowly passed it to her. She took it carefully, as though it were an ancient artifact. She fanned the pages so quickly he knew she couldn't have caught any of the content; rather, she seemed to be weighing it, feeling the shape in her hands. "My part is really small, when you think of it," she said finally. "Hardly worth centering the title around. I didn't come in until the very end."

"Neither did I. But you have to admit we made an impact." He smiled at her gently but she didn't return the weak humor.

"You, maybe," she acknowledged, ducking her head. "I didn't do anything."

"Yes. Ellery . . ." He waited until she looked up again. "You lived." The doctors hadn't been so sure, the night he took her from the house, whether she would pull through, given everything that had been done to her body. *At least she's still got her hands,* one of the physicians had remarked. Reed let his gaze drift to the scars at Ellery's wrists. Coben had liked to cut them slowly, with a small knife.

Ellery kept her eyes on the book. "The person who's sending me the cards—why do you think he's doing it?"

Reed shifted uncomfortably, glancing around at the other customers. No one seemed to be listening. "Coben is infamous— probably half of America knows who he is. You notice how we call serial murderers and presidents by all three of their names? There's a fascination there, a kind of awe. Some people want to feel connected to the story so they learn everything they can about the killer. They write to him in prison. Collect souvenirs. They retell the story with themselves at the center somehow, inexorably linked to the killer."

"Hmm," Ellery mused, tilting her head. "Kind of like you."

His face burned as she held his book out toward him. "No, I . . ." he stammered as he took it back. "Not like that. I'm referring to mentally disturbed people."

"Keep talking," she advised darkly. "You're just digging yourself in deeper."

There was a glint of amusement in her eyes, and he realized

with a start that she was very definitely poking fun at him now. He shook his head, embarrassed at being slow on the uptake. "Funny," he said lightly. He was running secret DNA tests on her, and yet somehow he still really wanted her to like him.

"Come on," she said, walking away. "Let's go pay for your book. Or maybe if you agree to autograph some copies, they'll let you have it for free."

"Cute," he called after her. "You're better than my publicist."

"And after you pay for the book, you can buy me dinner," she said as he caught up to her. "Think of it as my share of the royalties."

He had no recourse to object to this. Really, it was the least he could do.

They found a hole-in-the-wall Mexican joint, and the ribbing continued over tacos as Ellery decided to read the opening to his book. He sat on the other side of the booth and tried not to care. "You had horses growing up?" she demanded, arching an eyebrow at him as she peered across the table. "Competed in fencing? Here, open wide so I can check your mouth for a silver spoon."

"My parents have money," he said with an agreeable smile. "I was born with nothing."

"Hey, I know from nothing, and believe me, this ain't it. My mother used to send us to school with mashed potato sandwiches because meat was too expensive." She paged through to another spot in the book. "Princeton, very nice. I'm sure you were top of the class."

"Why don't I just take that."

She held it away from his grabby hands. "No way, it's mine now."

What could he say to that? Of course it had always been hers.

He sat back in the booth, tugging the tortilla chips toward him with a sigh. He chomped them as she read.

"Huh," she said after a moment.

"What?"

"You were twenty-eight at the time. That's how old I am now."

Somehow, she seemed younger. "Yes, it was my first big case."

"So I am finding out," she replied. "I just can't believe you were only twenty-eight back then. You seemed much older."

He felt older. "You were fourteen," he said, spreading his hands in a magnanimous gesture. "I suspect to a fourteen-year-old, anyone over the age of twenty seems positively calcified."

"So that makes you forty-two now," she said as she worked out the math.

He dipped a chip in the salsa. "Practically a mummy." The word "mummy" triggered a flash of memory as he recalled why he had bought the damn book in the first place. "May I see that a moment? I promise I'll give it back."

She handed him the book, and he flipped around until he found the page he was seeking. "Yes," he said, "I thought I had recalled the name. Coben's surname came from his stepfather, who adopted him when Francis was eight. As a young boy, he lived with his biological father, Frank Galluzzi. Frank himself had a half brother named Mark MacKenzie, a self-made millionaire in the real estate industry."

Ellery's face went pale. "Wait, you're saying Jacqueline MacKenzie was somehow related to Francis Coben?"

"If I've worked out the family tree correctly, she would have been his aunt." Reed had explored the Coben family history at the time he wrote the book, fascinated as he was by genealogy. "But listen to this: Mark MacKenzie had a child, a boy, who would have been Francis Coben's cousin. I don't recall his name, but I could certainly find out."

"This cousin, he would have known about me, right? After all, his crazy mother was pumping me for every bit of information."

"Maybe. We'll have to locate him and see what we can learn about his recent whereabouts."

At that moment, Reed's cell phone buzzed twice in his pocket, alerting him to a new e-mail message. Ellery seemed troubled and distracted as he withdrew the phone to check it. "Don't worry," he told her. "If he's the guy who's harassing you, we'll find him and shut him down."

Reed had expected perhaps to hear from Danielle, but instead, it was Oil Can Boy thanking him for his purchase and directing him to a link where he could enter a code to download the video. "Mr. Can has accepted my legal tender and provided me with a link to the supposed surveillance video," he told Ellery, who perked up a bit at this news.

"Really? Let me see."

"It's still downloading," he said as she joined him on his side of the booth. This was as close as he had been to her since he'd scooped her off the floor of the closet fourteen years earlier. She smelled like salt and soap and cotton as she leaned into him to get a better look at the phone. "Ah, here we go," he said as the movie began to play.

The video, as it was, could not be authenticated and could never be used in court. Still, he found he was as eager as Ellery to see the grainy footage. A dark-colored Honda Civic pulled into view and a girl who appeared to be Bea Nesbit got out of the driver's side door. Bea used her credit card to pay for a tank of gas, then she got back in her car and drove away. No one appeared to bother her. She did not interact with anyone as far as Reed could see. "Seems the Greek chorus of the Internet might be right about this one," Reed said with dismay. "If this was indeed taken the night she disappeared, it doesn't show anything about what might have happened to her."

"Wait a second." Ellery placed a hand on his arm. "Go back and start it again."

"Sure." He replayed the footage and it looked just the same to him: a girl filling her car with gas.

"There," Ellery said abruptly. "Stop it there."

Reed tapped the screen to freeze it. "What?" He peered down at Bea for a closer look.

"The woman at the pump behind Bea—that's Shannon Blessing."

Reed and Ellery puzzled over the new discovery all the way back to Woodbury, but neither could make heads or tails of it. That Shannon Blessing should show up on screen with Bea Nesbit the night she disappeared, at a gas station thirty-five miles away from anyplace either of them called home, seemed like it ought to be of significance somehow, but of course, Shannon was no longer around to ask.

It was dusk when they reached town, and Ellie texted Brady to say she could pick up Bump. Brady answered that he and the dog were down on the town square, preparing to watch the evening fireworks with the rest of the locals, so Ellery and Reed swung by to retrieve the animal. Reed waited in the truck, watching from a distance as Ellery accepted Bump's leash and patted Brady on the arm in thanks. Moments later, the dog bounded back into the vehicle, greeting Reed with an enthusiastic kiss. "Yes, yes," he said, shoving Bump toward the middle. "I'm ever so delighted to see you too."

They were heading back to Ellery's place to tackle the task Reed had been mulling since he'd arrived: a map of any connections they could find among the victims, or between the victims and Ellery herself. Unfortunately, Ellery didn't drive fast enough to outrun the fireworks. Bump yelped as the first boom hit and climbed solidly into Reed's lap, quivering and huddling against him.

Ellery shot him a chagrined look. "Sorry. Bump doesn't like fireworks."

"Yes." Reed spat out a mouthful of fur. "I had rather picked up on that detail."

The trio turned off the quiet road onto Ellery's even more deserted driveway. The truck ambled over the peaks and troughs, jiggling them along until civilization had completely disappeared from view. Except, Reed noted, for one police cruiser sitting in front of Ellie's house. "Looks like you have some company," he observed, and Ellery answered with a deepening frown.

She stopped the truck, and they all got out. Bump let out a warning growl as a figure in the shadows shone a bright flashlight beam directly in their eyes. "Sam," Ellery said, shielding her face from the glare. "What are you doing here?"

"I came to apologize," he said, not sounding at all apologetic. "Didn't expect you'd be out so late."

"You should go," she said as she walked toward the house.

"Aw, don't be like that."

Reed heard a slight slur in Sam's words, suggesting the chief had been drinking.

"I brought you those files you wanted," the chief said, his voice turning hard. "I thought you'd be pleased."

"That's nice of you, thank you, but I think you should go now. Julia will be looking for you soon, if she isn't already."

"Seems you're popular tonight, Ellie," he continued as though she hadn't spoken. "Look what was sitting here waiting for you when I got here."

Reed squinted in the darkness to try to make out what the chief was holding. It looked like a package with a bow. Downtown, the fireworks picked up the pace, exploding in a frenzy for the big finale, and air was redolent with sulfur smoke.

"Let me see that," Ellie demanded as she grabbed the package from Sam's hands. "What did you do?"

"It wasn't me," the chief grumbled. "I told you—it was sitting on your porch when I drove up. Is it your birthday or something?"

All of a sudden, Reed knew. He knew what would be waiting inside the box. He saw it the same way he could always find his mother's missing eyeglasses. "No, Ellie, wait—"

Too late. She ripped open the package and then dropped it with a small cry. She stumbled backward away from it, stuttering and gasping for air. "No. No."

"What? Whazzat?" The chief staggered to his feet and shone the flashlight down on the small square box. Reed forced himself closer so he could look too, and yes, there it was, nestled in the tissue paper: a human hand.

5

The first young woman to go missing courtesy of Francis Coben was twenty-two year-old Michelle Holcomb. Ellie had heard her name in the news, and later, once it was over, she had looked her up on the computer at the school library, just to see the place where it had all started. Michelle had long, wavy dark hair and charcoal eyelashes and perfect caramel-colored skin, although she rarely smiled in photographs because she was self-conscious about her crooked front teeth. She was just pretty enough that when the high school boys whispered to her in backseats that she was so gorgeous she could be a model, she believed them. She never paid attention on her odds-and-ends jobs because they didn't matter; she was going to be moving to New York soon, where she would get her teeth fixed and become famous, if only she could get the money together to make it happen. Her lack of focus caused her to be fired from one job after another, so she couldn't manage even to make rent, let alone a new smile, and thus she drifted from one tentative roommate situation to the next—people desperate like her, so her promises of an extra fifty bucks a week were enough to earn her a spot on the dilapidated living room couch. When she disappeared, everyone thought she'd finally done it, finally scraped together enough cash to make her dreams come true. It was five months before her aunt, concerned that she hadn't been able to reach Michelle through any means or find anyone else who had seen or talked to the girl in weeks, reported Michelle missing to the Chicago Police Department. They dutifully took down the details and that was that, until Michelle Holcomb was discovered murdered in Busse Woods, with both of her hands removed.

"How awful, that poor girl," Ellie's mother had said when the evening news played its grim report, but her voice had held no real horror back then, because why should it have? Daniel wasn't sick yet and the police themselves hadn't understood that Michelle was only the beginning. Ellie had been eleven years old at the time and cared about the news only when the Cubs score came on.

The hand in the box lay on the ground right where she'd dropped it. Sam was over at his car, radioing back to dispatch. "I don't care that the fireworks display is just letting out," he snapped. "The crowd can control itself this year. I need Herrera and Taylor over here at Ellie Hathaway's place, and I need them now. Get Tipton too. All units, you understand me?"

Reed, who had somehow had the presence of mind to scoop up Bump's leash amid the chaos, ambled over to stand next to her. She felt rooted to the earth, like the tall trees surrounding them. "I think . . ." she said, her voice hollow as Sam continued to bark orders at the dispatch controller, "I think he believes me now."

"Here," Reed said, thrusting the leash into her hands. "Take this."

She accepted control of Bump as Reed pulled his cell phone from his pants pocket. "What are you doing?"

"I'm calling Terre Haute," he replied. "I want someone to put eyes on Francis Coben."

"What? You think he did this?" Her pulse skittered as she glanced again at the package with its cheery polka-dot wrapping paper and pink ribbon. Coben had been tried in federal court and sentenced to death twelve years ago, at which point he'd been housed with other male inmates awaiting the same fate in Terre Haute, Indiana. Maximum security. Ellie bit her lip as Reed stalked off into the shadows with the phone pressed to his ear. It seemed impossible that Coben could have escaped from death row and found her again, but she had defied statistics twice already, first when he took her and then again when she lived. If you're the sucker who gets hit by lightning once, a one-in-a-million chance starts to feel downright ordinary.

"Ellie!"

She jumped as Sam started charging in her direction, and Bump responded by weaving his way back and forth between her legs, effectively tying her up with his lead. When Sam got up close, she could see his watery eyes and the gun in his hand.

"Come on, we need to secure the scene," he said. His breath still bore the sweet, fetid scent of alcohol, and he nodded in the direction of her house. "Let's go."

"Inside? No one's been inside," she said, but she realized she couldn't really be sure of that. The front doors and windows appeared unmolested, but the interior sat cloaked in dark silence.

"Dammit, Hathaway, someone left you a friggin' human hand wrapped up like Christmas in July. Let's be damn sure whoever it was isn't still with us on the premises." Her heart went full tilt as Sam turned toward her front porch and began walking.

"Markham," Sam yelled back over his shoulder. "You stay here with the evidence. When the boys roll in, don't let 'em touch anything. Ellie, get rid of that damn dog and come with me."

Reed, still on the phone, turned and offered a distracted wave. Ellery hesitated a moment before tying Bump's leash to the wooden railing and following Sam up to her front door. Sam stood over her, training the flashlight on her hands as she opened both locks. The door creaked as she pushed it open. The air smelled familiar but faintly stale, the odor of an old house that had been shut up tight and baked in the summer sun all day. Sam stepped inside, weapon drawn, flashlight splitting the dark of her previously sacrosanct home. Ellie watched the invasion for half a second and then forced herself to follow.

She hit the wall switch and held her breath as the lights came on. Green sofa, black-and-white pillows. Bookcase crammed to overflowing. She wilted, relieved that nothing seemed out of place. Sam was already across the room, heading for the kitchen. The sound of his boots on her wood floor made her skin tighten. "All clear," he called back to her.

She checked the hall. "Clear."

Sam was walking toward the back, nearing her bedroom. *Wait,* she tried to say, but the word got stuck in her throat.

She heard the jiggle of the closet door. "What the hell? Hathaway!"

Ellie closed her eyes briefly in regret. It was a small life she had made for herself here, but it had belonged to her alone. "Chief?" she asked as she moved to join him in her bedroom.

"What the hell is this?" he asked, pointing at her closet and the nails that held it shut.

"It's a closet," she said, matter-of-fact, like it was just any other part of her home. There were two others exactly like it that she hoped he would never see.

"It's full of nails."

"There's nothing in there," she said. "The house is clear."

"Ellie. Why's your closet nailed shut like this?"

She felt the balance of their relationship shifting in his favor again as they stood there in front of the evidence of her insanity. Coben had given her an early, brutal lesson—sex is power—and for years afterward, she'd kept her body sequestered from the male gaze, hidden beneath baggy sweatshirts and loose jeans, lest anyone try to take it from her a second time. Only later had she realized that she could trade on men's hunger, that she could give up her body and nothing else, and so they always wanted her more than she wanted them. Now here was Sam standing too close, precisely where she never wanted him, waiting for her to do the one thing she would never do: explain herself.

"I, uh . . ."

She was saved when Reed appeared in the room. "Chief, the cavalry's arrived outside, and they're awaiting your orders." It was then that Ellie noticed the red-and-blue lights dancing against her bedroom windows from the squad cars in the yard.

"It's the holiday weekend," Sam muttered, almost to himself. "We're going to have no choice but to send the damn thing up to Boston." He tromped out of the room and Ellie nearly went weak with relief.

Reed crossed the floor until he came to stand where Sam had been, and he reached out to touch the row of nailheads poking out along the wooden closet door. He stroked them gently for a minute and then turned to her with solemn eyes. "Coben's confirmed to be inside his cell at Terre Haute," he told her.

They stood and looked at each other for a long moment as the words sank in, deep down inside Ellie, to a pit of dread she couldn't close off even if she had a thousand nails.

It wasn't Coben who did this. That meant there was another one.

Ellie felt naked as a peeled grape as she watched her colleagues trample the grass around her home. She tried to detach, to think of it as just another crime scene, but her heart lurched every time she heard their footsteps go up and down the wooden steps on her front porch. Jimmy Tipton came roaring up the driveway in his Nissan Coupe. She knew the color was black cherry, but in the dark it simply looked black, shaped like an arched cat and low to the ground, so that Tipton himself might have been Batman arriving at the scene of some outrageous caper, a purposeful conceit that probably explained why Tipton had shelled out close to a year's salary for the thing in the first place. All boys wanted to grow up to be Batman.

"Holy shit," he said, drawing out every syllable as he walked across her lawn. "Is it true?"

Ellery turned to look at him but could not see his face clearly thanks to the squad car's high beams trained at her house. Her quiet cottage shone like a carnival funhouse, and everyone wanted to step right up and see the attraction. She swallowed down the bile at the back of her throat and answered Tipton with a short nod. "There," she said, indicating the package on the ground with a haphazard wave of her flashlight. She and Reed had been elected to stand guard while Parker led the others on a search of the property to make sure there were no other body parts lying about the place.

Tipton switched on his own flashlight and squatted down for a better look. "Jesus," he murmured. "That's the real deal, all right. You can smell it." He straightened up and came to stand beside Reed. "What are the odds, huh? You show up in our little town here and all of a sudden someone's chopping off people's hands."

"You're not insinuating he did it," Ellery said testily. "Because first of all, that's crazy, and second of all, he was with me all day."

"Cozy," Tipton remarked, and then he scowled. "Of course I'm not suggesting he did it, but it sure looks like someone rolled out a very specific welcome mat for him, don't you think?"

Ellery held back her instinctive retort, which was that the hand had been left on her doorstep, not Reed's. She rubbed the scar at her wrist with her thumb, a nervous habit she'd never been able to shake. Coben had tattooed himself at the same place on both wrists, an obsession that had apparently been his undoing as the ink roused Reed Markham's suspicions all those years ago. In hindsight, it seemed blindingly obvious, almost like Coben hung a neon sign on himself that said, *It's me, I'm the one*. Only no one could see it until it was too late. Ellie watched the men combing the tall grasses at the outskirts of her yard and wondered what she wasn't seeing.

She risked a quick glance at the hand in the box, noting the gray-green skin and curled fingers. Certainly, this new guy was into conspicuous messaging. The hand looked on the small side to her, and Bea was the most petite of the missing victims, but the flesh seemed relatively plump and free of obvious decay. *Maybe*, she thought with a sudden chill, *this gift means he's already got a new one*.

"Are you cold?" Reed asked at her shiver, ever solicitous with his slightly Southern accent. "I can stay here if you'd like to fetch a jacket."

"She's not cold. She's scared." Tipton eyed her with a devilish gleam. "What's the matter, Hathaway? I thought this was everything you always wanted."

"Nobody goes looking for this," Reed said quietly, but with

the certitude born from experience, and it was enough to shut Tipton up.

Sam rejoined the group, now somewhat winded from traipsing back and forth across her property, shouting orders. Sweat slicked his brow, making his hair stick to his forehead like he was a little boy fresh from the bath. "Jimmy, good, you're here. I've called the hospital for transport to Boston, but I want you to go with the bus—make sure they understand this is special circumstances. We're not waiting around six weeks for answers on this one."

"How long could it possibly take 'em for the autopsy?" Tipton said gruffly. "It fits in a goddamn jewelry box."

They all peered down at the box with the hand in it. Ellery knew the massive backlog of cases at the medical examiner's office often meant weeks to months of waiting for a complete report, especially for more routine cases. The State had been conducting only external exams on many bodies to try to ease the backlog, a practice that did not meet national standards but was about all the understaffed office could manage these days. Massachusetts was supposed to have at least seventeen full-time examiners but currently employed only nine.

"Somehow I think they'll clear the decks for this one," Sam said, "particularly when the press gets hold of the story—as we know they'll do."

"Can't we keep it quiet?" Ellery asked, trying to tamp down the note of desperation from her voice. "At least for now?"

Sam gave her a strange look. "You're the one who wanted all the noise. I'd think you'd be leading the parade."

"The press gets the story and we'll be crawling with news vans and lookie-loos," she said. She remembered them lined up three rows deep outside the hospital years ago, and how the administrator had led Ellery and her mother out a private entrance on the day she was released so she wouldn't have to face them all at once.

"I can't argue that," Sam said, "but I don't see how we can keep a lid on this one for long." He looked Reed up and down, as if seeing him for the first time. "I guess it's lucky for us that the FBI is already on the scene. Downright prescient of you, Agent Markham."

Reed blinked his usual owl-like stare. "Ellie's the one who called me, Chief."

"Hmm," Sam said thoughtfully, turning his attention to her. "That she did. What do you say, Ellie? Any ideas on who would want to send you a severed human hand?"

She felt everyone's eyes on her as she struggled to answer. "No, I have no idea who might have done this." She hadn't told Sam about the birthday cards because explaining their significance would mean revealing her whole personal history. However, there was one new development she could share. "But there may have been someone in the woods here the other night." She pointed with her flashlight toward the trees. "Bump started barking and growling like he heard someone on the property, and when I went to check it out, I found a beer bottle on the ground. It had remnants of beer still in it, so it hadn't been there very long." She glanced at Reed before continuing. "Agent Markham has a friend at the State Lab who is analyzing the bottle for us. Maybe she'll get a hit."

Even as she said the words, Ellery tended to doubt their veracity. While it was true that careless mistakes brought many a criminal career to a swift end, they were talking about someone who had abducted three people and left no trace of evidence behind, to the point where no one could be sure a crime had even occurred. This did not strike Ellery as someone who was likely to go skulking in her woods and leave a beer bottle with fingerprints on it for them to find.

"You what?" Sam's sharp question made her flinch. "You not only ignored my direct order to drop your investigation, but you went and logged evidence at the State Lab without my permission or knowledge?"

"It's not evidence of anything," Ellery protested. Then she added, "Yet."

"Do you mind if I have a word with you over here?" Sam snapped.

"Can it wait?" Jittery and tired, she didn't much feel like another heated exchange over her apparent insubordination. As far as she was concerned, the festooned body part lying on the ground at their feet completely validated every move she had made on this case since day one.

"No, it can't wait," Sam replied slowly and evenly, as if she were a dim-witted child.

Reluctantly, Ellie followed him away from the idling cars and the bright headlights, until they stood in her side yard, well clear of the others. "You should have told me," Sam was saying. "You should have at least had the courtesy to pick up the damn phone, Ellie."

She was done apologizing. "Someone was out here spying on me, Sam. Someone who may be into dismembering people, if you haven't noticed. What did you want me to do? Just wait around and—"

"It was me," he broke in, hissing at her under his breath.

Shock made her close her mouth for a moment. "What?"

"The beer in the woods. It was me." His jaw worked back and forth in frustration. "You have that bottle printed, and it's going to come back to me, you understand?"

"What were you doing out there?" He said nothing, and she took a step backward. "How many times have you been out there, watching me?"

"You don't answer your phone half the time," he said petulantly. "You don't ever let me come over. I worry about you out here all alone, Ellie."

"Bullshit," she said, running both hands through her hair. "What the hell were you thinking? You have no right. You have no right to spy on me like that!"

"It's not like that," he said. "You and me have a relationship."

"Not anymore we don't," she replied hotly. "God, Sam. What the hell?"

"Listen," he said, reaching for her. She jerked her arm away, but he closed in on her in a hurry. His voice was low and urgent. "Listen, we don't have the luxury of time here for you to lecture me about my behavior. You have to stop that analysis on the beer bottle, okay? You have to stop it now or the whole thing is going to come out."

"You mean the whole town will find out what a creeper you are?" She felt angry, violated, and ashamed of herself by how deeply she had misjudged him.

"Tell yourself whatever you want," he said. "But you fix this. You fix it fast, Ellie, because it's not just my ass hanging in the wind on this one. This comes out and everyone will find out about you too."

Prickles of fear broke out across the back of her neck. Her ears started to ring and her tongue swelled inside her mouth. "What . . . what do you mean by that?"

His eyes were flinty in the low light. "Test me," he said, "and you'll find out." He rotated his neck, cracking it with a terrible pop. "Make that can go away and we'll pretend none of this ever happened."

She turned her head away and focused on keeping her breathing even so he could not see her fear. Sam let out a short, irritated chuff. "You should be glad it was me," he told her, "and not the sicko who's leaving you body parts. Fact of the matter is, I should probably move in with you until we catch this guy."

"No." Ellery snapped her attention back to him. "That's not happening."

"Someone should stay out here with you in case this sicko comes back."

"I have all the protection I need," she said, indicating her sidearm.

"I can assign Watkins if you prefer." His tone actually softened a bit. "I'm serious, Ellie. This guy means business, and you're out here all by your lonesome."

"Reed will stay." The words slipped out before she thought about them, but she knew immediately it was true.

Sam snorted, and the hard tone was back in his voice. "Reed," he repeated. "He'll keep you company, will he? Play house? Tell me, Ellie, are you sleeping with him too?"

Her face went hot. "None of your damn business."

Sam grinned without any humor and nodded to himself. "It would explain a few things, like why he trotted on up here just because you made a phone call."

"Unlike some people, Agent Markham believed I had a case."

Sam squinted at the pine trees, which were lined up like sentries in the dark. "Well," he said finally, "I'd say you've made true believers out of all of us now."

Much later, after the fireworks had died down completely and the hand was ensconced in a biohazard box and speeding its way toward Boston, Ellery served iced tea for herself and Reed in tall, mismatched glasses. She carried them carefully into the living room, feeling alien in her own home, where she had lived for four years without entertaining a single guest. Bump, too, clearly sensed a disturbance in the force, because instead of passing out on the nearest patch of floor, paws up and snoring, he lay quiet but watchful at Reed's feet. Reed himself had the file on Bea Nesbit's disappearance spread out on the coffee table. Maybe Sam had forgotten the files in the furor of the evening, but he had left them behind and so now they had, as far as she knew, a complete picture of everything the police had on the case.

"I've at least glanced through all of it now," Reed said as he accepted the glass. "And I don't see any reference to Shannon Blessing. I don't think she was ever questioned about Bea Nesbit or determined to be a witness."

Ellie sat as far away as she could from him on the other end of the sofa. "I think once everyone saw the videotape and realized there was no one lurking in the shadows to grab Bea, they didn't bother to examine it further. Shannon wasn't missing at the time, obviously. Why should it mean anything to anyone back then?"

"It's not entirely clear it means anything now," Reed said with a tired sigh. "But it's a strange enough coincidence that it bears looking into—I think we should go to the gas station tomorrow to check it out. At a minimum, it's the last location we can confirm for Bea, so it might be helpful to retrace her steps from that night."

"I've tried that several times," she told him. "It got me nowhere. I did the same for Shannon too—the last place we could confirm she was at was the local craft store, where she was buying pink and white yarn. She told the checkout girl that she was knitting a hat and booties for her soon-to-be niece. We found the hat and the socks already completed inside her apartment, so either Shannon was the world's fastest knitter, or someone else must have seen her before she went missing."

"What about Mark Roy?" Reed asked, reaching for the folder.

"Mark completed his mail rounds on July eleventh last year and didn't show up for work the next day. I've traced his route a dozen times since then, but it's not like that helps any—he went over the whole damn town." She sat forward and placed her glass on the table next to Reed's, where she was struck anew by how odd the two looked together. Usually, her glass sat alone, and that was how she liked it. She felt itchy and strange. He wasn't an overly large man, but he seemed to be everywhere now. When he shifted his weight, the couch moved under her own body.

"Well, maybe we can do that tomorrow too," Reed said. "Trace Mark's mail route."

"Want to know where it ends?" she said, because the delicious irony had always intrigued her.

"Where?"

"Sam's house. Chief Parker."

Reed blinked at her for a moment. Honestly, the man probably had a genius IQ but he had a knack for looking totally befuddled by the most ordinary pieces of information. "Ah," he said finally. "The chief. He seemed to have more heated words for you again this evening."

Suddenly, she remembered the beer bottle and regretted even mentioning Sam's name. "He was just spooked by the hand," she said. "We don't get that sort of thing happening around here."

"Did you tell him yet?" When she did not answer, he persisted. "About Coben."

Ellie ducked her head, and the silence stretched between them. "No," she admitted at length. "And I won't, not unless I absolutely have to."

"Someone gift-wrapped a severed hand for you and left it on your doorstep. I think that time may have come, don't you?"

"It's not Coben who did it. You said so yourself."

"No, but it's someone who knows his history—and yours."

She curled deeper into the couch cushions, away from him, and shook her head. Here he was in her living room, voicing the fear she'd carried alone for years now, but it gave her no comfort to know he saw the danger too. "Even if it's someone who is imitating Coben, we can mention that without having to get into my connection with the case."

"Ellery." Reed's tone was gentle, but exasperated.

"Look," she said, more sharply than she'd intended. "I get that this is academic for you. You solved the case and wrote a really lovely book, I'm sure. So you can go on TV and give lectures and make movies or whatever else you did to celebrate the victory the last time. You earned it, and I won't deny that. But here? This life? It's mine. If I tell the department who I am, then it gets out to everyone, you understand me? That's it, it's over. Everyone would know, and they would never look at me the same again. They'd know these scars aren't from some bike accident when I was a kid. They'd know how he took me and locked me up, how he cut me, how he . . . he . . ." Reed had to know everything that had happened on Coben's farm, but she hadn't talked about it in years. She barely had the words. "They'll know what he did with the farm tools," she finished in a whisper, unable to look at him.

After Ellie was rescued, the doctor at the hospital had directed the news of Coben's brutality to her mother, even though Ellie was sitting right there. *It's possible she'll never be able to have children. We just can't say for sure.*

To her utter horror, tears had started to leak down her cheeks. She swiped them away angrily, and she felt more than saw Reed moving around the room. A moment later, he pressed a tissue into her hand. "I'm sorry," he said softly.

"I don't want you to be sorry," she said, crumpling the tissue in her fist. "Everyone will be sorry. That's the whole damn point."

Her cell phone buzzed, indicating a text. Grateful for the interruption, she sniffed hard and whipped it out, figuring it had to be Brady. It was.

At bar with friends—keeping the party going! I'd say come join us but there's this story going around about a murder at your place tonight?

She typed back: *Can't talk about it.*

So it's true?

Can't talk about it.

There was a short silence and then his reply came through: *Are you ok? I can come over . . .*

The last thing she wanted was more male company. *I'm ok,* she wrote quickly. *Reed's here.*

Ok. Call me if you need anything.

She put the phone aside and resumed her huddle at the end of the sofa. "Rumors are starting to circulate," she said. "Brady heard there was a murder out here tonight." The press would not be far behind.

Reed appeared to digest this bit of news. "Brady—is he your boyfriend?"

She closed her eyes wearily. "Why is everyone so damn interested in my love life tonight?"

"Because like it or not, you're at the center of this, Ellery. The details of your life are going to matter." He paused significantly. "All of them."

"You don't know that," she protested weakly. "I didn't know Bea at all, and Shannon, only a little bit. Mark, I only talked to him when I had to sign for a package or something. These people had no particular bearing on my life, so I don't know why we have to start categorizing every last bit of information about me."

"The birthday cards," he reminded her.

"They may not mean anything." She'd spent years believing otherwise, but now that he was saying it, she didn't want it to be true. "You don't know for sure."

"I know," he said. "Because you told me."

"What are you talking about?"

"Back at the beginning, when Bea was just a single missing persons case and Shannon and Mark were still walking around town just like they always did, back then, Ellie, you knew something was up, because you saved that first card."

She looked down at her hands and thought back to the day she had slid the initial card from the envelope. Just the stamp on the front had been a shock. You don't get first-class mail when you're living a third-rate life. She had seen the message and felt the wind go out of her, the past rising up like an icy wave to steal her very breath. Someone knew. Knew enough to find her birthday, and the rest would come tumbling after. She'd escaped from the paper-thin edge, run off the page of her own story only to discover she'd failed to shut the book. She had slammed the card in a drawer, locked all her doors and drawn the curtains, and waited for the phone or bell to ring. But they had stayed silent. Days passed and nothing more came of it.

When the attack first happened, there was no way she could escape it—Coben had forced himself inside her very being, and her body burned from what he had done to her. So she went somewhere else inside her head until it almost seemed like the whole ordeal happened to some other girl, some unfortunate soul named Abby who lived far away and long ago. So when that first card came, the one that said HAPPY BIRTHDAY but really meant *I know who you are,* she was afraid but also wondering, like a child who puts her hand to the candle flame. She made herself keep it. She held on to it because it made her remember everything she had to leave behind. "I don't get much mail here," she told Reed as she pushed off the couch. "It was nothing more than that."

Ellie desperately wanted a shower, but she wasn't taking off her clothes with Reed awake and prowling about the house. She felt like he could see the scars right through the walls and doors, and she was eager to put as much space as she could between them. He appeared tired when she brought him a pillow and blanket for the couch, with lines around his eyes and stubble dotting his chin. She remembered he probably had a life in Virginia that he had abandoned to come up here and help her. "Thanks, uh, for staying tonight," she muttered, careful not to touch him as she handed him the bed linens. "I didn't want Sam posting some sort of guard at my door."

"Might not be the worst idea," he replied with genuine worry, and her own concern ticked up a notch. He was an FBI agent, sure, but he was standing there in his T-shirt and shorts, sporting bare feet and wire-rimmed nerd glasses. He hardly looked menacing, so what kind of backup would he really be?

"You really think the guy would come back here tonight, while we're here?" she asked.

Reed ran a hand over his face and glanced at the door. "He left you a gift-wrapped body part today. I don't think any of us can rightly predict the next move right now. That's why it might pay to be extra cautious."

She noticed then that his gun was lying on the coffee table. "I wanted to ask you something: I know you've profiled these guys, right? You must have some sort of read by now, looking at all these files. Tell me what you think we're dealing with here."

Reed seemed to hesitate with his reply. He scrubbed at his head with both hands so that his hair stood on end like a porcupine's. "There's a boilerplate list of traits that is liable to hold true in cases such as these," he said finally. "White male, age twenty-five to forty-five. We're looking at multiple victims—adults with no real physical vulnerabilities—which suggests he is practiced, careful, and above average in intelligence. We don't know why the perpetrator in this case picked Bea, Shannon, and Mark, but you can be sure there was a reason, and that their abductor stalked them for some time before approaching them. The killer probably admires Coben, knows the history of the case inside and out, maybe even has corresponded with him. We will certainly look into that first thing tomorrow. But also he would not really be considered a copycat."

"But the hand."

"Yes, it's a nod to Coben, obviously, and to us as well. But Coben had a very specific type—young women with long hair and pretty hands—and this subject has targeted both males and females, of different races and ages. Plus, well . . ." He broke off, as if he didn't want to say this next thought in front of her.

"What?" she demanded.

"The hands were Coben's trophies. He would never willingly give one up. Not for you, not for anyone."

Ellie took her own gun to bed with her, taking care to draw the shades against anything or anyone wishing to peer inside. She locked her door, but light still shafted in beneath it because Reed was down the hall washing up in the single bathroom. Bump gave a dramatic yawn and flopped over on the small oval braided rug. Ellie envied the dog his obvious relaxation as she climbed under the sheet. Her mind was awhirl with images of the severed hand, of Bea and Shannon together at the gas station all those years ago, and of the hard set of Sam's mouth as he'd laid out her marching orders about the bottle in the woods: *Fix this*. She really didn't see how she could.

She screwed her eyes shut against the noise in her head, but already, she knew sleep would be futile. Outside, she heard Reed's footsteps moving around her house, and she started counting backward from one thousand to block out the sound. In the closet, back when it happened, she had lain on the floor and felt the boards vibrate with Coben's approach. Footsteps always meant more pain. *He's coming, he's coming.* She clutched the cotton blanket closer to her body and counted louder. "Nine hundred seventy-eight. Nine hundred seventy-seven."

Her phone buzzed loudly on her nightstand, making her sit up with a gasp.

She fumbled for it in the dark and hit the button to light up the screen and retrieve the text. She frowned in puzzlement when she saw it wasn't Brady's number, but then her heart stopped as the words came up. "Oh, God," she gulped, and threw the phone aside on the blanket like it had bitten her.

But the text was still there, glowing up at the ceiling.

I know it's you.

6

In his dream, Reed had been buried alive, not in a coffin but with the dirt piled directly over his face, right up in his nostrils and mouth so he could taste and smell it. He heard the crunch of a shovel overhead—someone was coming for him—but he couldn't move or scream for help. Finally, his rescuers broke through and Reed could feel the daylight behind his closed lids. But instead of helping him out of the hole, they turned a hose on him, with the water splashing down in a manner just as suffocating as the dirt had been. He gasped, desperate to capture a mouthful of air, and as he did so, his eyes opened and the dream vanished into the ether, leaving him prone on Ellery's couch, eye level with her dog. The fur monster wagged happily when he saw that Reed was awake and his giant tongue came hurtling toward Reed's face once more. "Ah, no," Reed said, scrambling off the sofa and away from him. "Definitely not!"

"Bump, stop it."

Reed turned to find Ellie standing in the doorway, dressed already in jeans and a faded T-shirt with a purple cow on it. Her hair was down for the first time since he'd met her, falling in dark waves around her shoulders, and he saw the ends were still damp from her shower. Her bare feet and the filtered early morning sunlight combined to make her look much younger, effectively transporting them back in time to their first meeting. She'd been pale and withdrawn then, much as now, with the same dark smudges under her watchful, steel-gray eyes. Reed became acutely aware of the fact that he was standing in front of her wearing only his boxers, having shed his T-shirt sometime during the stifling overnight. They had shut the house up like Fort Knox before bed, every door and window locked, and the result was rooms full of hot, dead air. Reed cleared his throat and glanced down at the dog, who was thumping his tail against the hard floor and staring up expectantly at Reed. "I hope you didn't acquire this cur as any sort of watchdog," Reed said to Ellie. "Because I have to warn you, he doesn't seem up to the task."

"Bump's a people person," Ellie replied with a sigh, sounding almost disappointed. "I've tried to explain that we're really just a bunch of selfish, rotten, hateful creatures, but he goes on loving all of us just the same."

Reed frowned downward at the floppy-eared animal and mentally told him the truth. *I'm a world-class fuckup at the moment, you understand? Telephone my ex-wife and ex-boss, and they'll explain my numerous failings in great detail. Sarit, in particular, has the delightfully textured vocabulary of an Oxford professor and a retired longshoreman.* But the dog continued to gaze up at him with adoring eyes. "He, ah, he has an unusual moniker. Is it a metaphor for taking it easy on the roads of life, or something like that?"

Ellie snorted as Reed reached around the dog to grab his T-shirt. "No," she said. "It's no metaphor. Stick around awhile and you'll see what I mean."

"Speaking of sticky . . ." He could still feel the remnants of the night sweats dried on his skin. "Do you mind if I use your shower?"

Ellery looked momentarily taken aback by his request, but she recovered quickly. "Sure, go ahead. There are clean towels on the shelves in the bathroom. Bump and I will just head out for our morning constitutional."

Reed halted from tidying up the couch and looked over at her. "Outside?"

"He hasn't been trained to use the john," she replied, deadpan.

"Yes, I realize as much. I just . . . just be careful out there."

Ellery dropped her chin to her chest, as if acknowledging the possible danger. "We can't hide in here forever. Come on, boy. Let me just get my shoes on and we can go, okay?"

Bump trotted after her, dog tags jangling, and Reed headed for the bathroom. It was bright white and sparkly clean, free from the lotions, makeup, and other usual trappings of female bathrooms. Ellery's shower caddy held only unisex drugstore-brand shampoo and conditioner, and some sort of ginger-lily cleanser gel. Still, Reed felt his blood warm as he stepped naked into the tub that was still wet from her shower. It wasn't a sexual reaction but a realization of how intimate it was to be sharing her space like this. His heart squeezed in sudden longing for his family. Tula, as a chubby happy baby, had showered with him on Sunday mornings while Sarit caught a few extra minutes of sleep. Tula's tiny giggles bounced and magnified off the tiles as they'd played together under the tickling spray.

Reed scrubbed away at the grit and memories, until he felt ready to face Ellery and her nailed-up house again. He dressed and left the steamy little bathroom, only to stumble at the threshold because the damn dog was lying in his path. "Speed Bump," Reed muttered as he righted himself. "Got it."

He found Ellery sitting at the kitchen table with a mug of tea. "I feel more human now, thank you," he said.

"There's water for tea, if you want it. If you prefer coffee, I'm afraid you'll have to go out. I don't drink the stuff."

"I'll do you one better. I'll make us breakfast." His stomach was so empty he felt like he had a gap at his middle.

"Um, yeah. Good luck with that," she said into her cup as he opened the refrigerator door.

He peered in at the thin collection of condiments, a quart of skim milk, and a half dozen fast-food containers. There was one lonely, wizened orange. He rotated a glass bottle of fermenting sludge-like apple juice. "What do you eat?" he asked, unable to keep the vague note of horror from his voice.

"I just take a granola bar with me for breakfast," she said with a shrug. "There are a few different kinds in the pantry if you'd like."

A granola bar wouldn't sustain him past nine o'clock. "I'll just run to the market for a few things, then, shall I? It won't take long." He would welcome the distance from her, actually; it would give him time to clear his head.

"Suit yourself."

He got the directions from her and set out in his rental car. Summer was up and on the job early, a strong sun already muscling its way over the trees into the high blue sky. The air smelled sweet and he left the windows down as he drove, the breeze ruffling his hair. He found the grocery with no trouble and parked amid the scattered other cars in the lot. However, he did not immediately go inside. He pulled out his cell phone and dialed the number he still considered home. "Sarit here," she said when it rang through.

"It's me," he replied, grateful for her familiar voice. "How is Tula doing?"

"She's fine. She's dressed in three layers of pajamas plus a princess dress that's trailing glitter all over the household. I'm sweltering just looking at her, but she swears the costume is necessary for the royal tea party." There was a pause. "Never mind us. How are you faring? Did you meet Abigail?"

It was strange now to hear Ellery's old name, as she had become someone completely new to him in the space of a few short days. "Yes, I met her."

"And? What is she like?"

He pictured her, nose to nose with Chief Parker, arguing her case despite its lack of merit, or the hint of humor in her eyes as she'd skewered his privileged upbringing. He thought of her quiet, lonely house with its closets nailed shut. *She's like a soldier back from the war,* he wanted to say. *She's strong. She's shattered. Surprisingly funny, if she wants to be. You would like her, presuming she's not certifiably crazy.* He was still waiting on the DNA analysis from the birthday cards. The appearance of the severed hand increased the urgency of the answer. Reed didn't think that Ellie was that unstable, couldn't believe she would be damaged enough to reenact some version of Coben's crimes and then call attention to that fact, but he was aware also that he did not want to believe it—which made it crucial that he keep his attention trained to the facts of the case. Facts stated that Ellery had the opportunity to leave that hand on her porch before he and she departed for their adventures yesterday, so she would remain a suspect until there was proof otherwise.

"She's, ah, she's interesting," Reed managed to reply at last. "A natural investigator. She's got something here with these missing persons cases."

"I see," Sarit said, her tone indicating that she had parsed the tea leaves of his message. "So you're staying on, then."

"I have to. We've had some . . . developments."

"And we have a mediation appointment this Thursday," she reminded him.

"I know, I know." He wanted to be there. It was part of his vow to himself when they split. Sarit had accused him of checking out of their marriage long before she'd left it, that he'd cared about everyone in the world but her and Tula. He was going to prove her wrong by showing up faithfully to whatever appointment she demanded of him. "Look," he said, taking a deep breath. "It turns out that whoever is responsible for the missing persons cases almost certainly knows Ellery's identity and the history of the Coben case."

Sarit made her usual humming noise. "That means he knows you too."

"Yes. You can see then why I need to stay."

"I don't like the feel of this, Reed. It sounds like someone with questionable motives is eager to get the band back together again. Why do you need to go along with it?"

"If this is something that was set in motion back years ago, then I don't really have a choice, do I? As you say, the players are already determined."

"Something from years ago," she repeated. "You mean there was a second killer? Maybe Coben had an accomplice? Or are you thinking there is a copycat?"

"I can't speculate at this point." He had to remember that, technically, he was speaking to the press.

"Can't? Or won't?"

"You know the rules, Sarit. This is an active investigation and I can't compromise it. I promise that when it's okay to talk, you'll be the first person I call."

"Anything new related to Coben would be front-page material, even after all these years." He could hear her turning over the juicy possibilities in her mind, but at least she wasn't angry with him anymore.

"Can I talk to Tula?" he asked.

"Let me see if I can catch her."

A few moments later, his daughter's breathless voice came on the line. "Daddy! There was a rock that was moving in the little stream at the park, only it wasn't a rock, it was a turtle! I named him Stanley, and he was going to come live with us and sleep in my bed but then Mom said I had to leave him there because he needs the water. But next time we go, I am going to bring some lettuce for him."

"Clever girl," Reed said. "I'm sure he'll love that."

"Daddy," she said, her voice wistful. "When are you coming home?"

He held the phone tight to his ear and closed his eyes against the rush of emotion. "Soon, baby. Soon." Someday, when she was old enough to hear it, maybe he could tell Tula the truth: that there was another girl whose small hand turned up wrapped in pretty paper, a girl they had yet to identify and they did not know what had happened to her, but this girl was never coming home, and so for the moment, neither could he.

Back at Ellery's, the opened windows let the cross breeze flow through, and so the rooms of the house could momentarily breathe again. Ellery loitered in the kitchen, her back to the sink, watching Reed assemble French toast and fry thick cuts of bacon. Bump was living up to his namesake in the doorway, licking his chops every so often as the bacon sizzled. "Where did you learn to cook?" Ellery asked.

"My mother taught me," he replied as he expertly flipped the slices of bread to brown them on the other side. "She loves to cook—oh, the peach pies she made in the summer were the stuff of county legend—and I am but a pale imitation of her skills. But I was at least more interested than my sisters, one of whom actually burned boiling water."

"Is that even possible?" Ellery wrinkled her nose.

"It is if you let the pot sit over the flame for three hours until it melts. Technically, I suppose, Suzy burned the pot and not the water. We're just glad she didn't burn the house with it."

"My mother's specialty was Jell-O with canned fruit in it." She sniffed in the direction of the stove. "This looks a lot better."

"Yes, well, it's about finished. Do you own any plates?"

"Of course I own plates. I'm not a complete savage."

"What percentage savage are you, then?" he asked, teasing a bit as she retrieved a couple of plates from the cupboard. "Half? One quarter? Tell me, were you raised in a barn?"

At his words, she dropped the plates, which clattered loudly and rolled in different directions, and Reed remembered with horror what had happened to her in a barn.

"I'm sorry," he said, kneeling with her as she bent to retrieve the plates.

"Forget it," she replied, not looking at him.

"I'm an insensitive lout."

"I said forget it," she repeated, and met his eyes briefly to show she meant it. "Let's just eat, okay?" She'd fixed her hair into its usual severe style, pulled back at her nape, but he was close enough to see the smattering of freckles that dusted the bridge of her nose. He could see the girl she used to be, the one she'd left behind, and he wondered what it was like to have to live every day with a huge secret. A million little lies she must have told over the years, and convincing ones at that. Just because he knew the truth about some of them didn't mean he knew them all.

He spread his hands apart and forced a smile. "It's forgotten."

He served them breakfast in silence and then watched, appreciation warming him again, as she wolfed it down. "This is really good," she said as she shoveled forkfuls of the flaky, buttery toast into her mouth. Reed admitted to himself that the dish had turned out rather nicely. A delightful aspect to New England was that one could find real maple syrup, even at the corner store.

"Mother would probably give me a B-plus for my efforts," he answered. "But it beats the hell out of a granola bar."

For a moment, there was only the sound of forks scraping against the plates, punctuated every so often by Bump's impatient whine. He seemed fairly certain the leftovers would surpass granola crumbs too. "Did you hear back from Danielle yet about the test results?" Ellie asked him eventually. She was trying to sound casual, but her eyes were trained on her plate.

"Not a word. Why?"

She squirmed. "I was thinking maybe she shouldn't bother with the beer bottle."

Reed put down his fork and regarded her. "Why would you say that? It seems more relevant than ever, given that someone snooping around your property left you a human body part yesterday. Stands to reason that he or she could have made a practice run."

"I know, it's just that Sam told me . . . he told me he was pretty sure it was just the Bashir boys from next door. He's busted them for drinking beer in the woods a couple of times in the past, so it seems likely it's just them screwing around again. I wouldn't want Danielle to waste her time."

She was selling the story better this time, making eye contact with him and keeping her voice neutral, but something unnatural gleamed in her gaze, as though her irises held too much liquid or light. He reminded himself that circumstances had made her a liar, and a good one. "Ellery," he said carefully, "is there some reason you don't want to have that bottle tested?"

She held his gaze, her eyes guileless. "No. I just think it'd be a waste of time and resources, and as you point out, we have new, more pressing evidence that needs to be examined."

They sat there looking at each other, the tension rising as he tried to figure out whether to call bullshit now or let the lie play out a little longer. Before he could decide, there was a frantic knocking on her front door, and Bump scrambled toward it, pell-mell and barking at the top of his lungs. Reed trailed behind Ellie as she went to answer the door, and he was surprised along with her to find Annie and Dave Nesbit standing on the porch, drawn tight like a pair of strings ready to snap. "Ellie, thank God you're home," Annie said, grabbing for Ellery's hand. "We're sorry to just show up like this, but Chief Parker wasn't giving us any information down at the station."

"We heard . . . there's a body," Dave added, his thin lips having trouble with the shape of the word. "Parker will only tell us that the department is investigating the possible discovery of human remains."

To Reed, the severed hand had looked like the real deal, but he supposed there was still the outside possibility that it was a brilliant fake. Ellery looked shocked and out of her depth as she stood there in the grips of the anguished parents. "I . . . I'm sorry," she said at length. "I really can't say anything more right now."

"But you promised!" Tears brimmed around Annie's eyes. "You promised us you would always keep us updated on any new developments in the case."

"And I will. We just don't have anything certain to report right now. I'm sorry. I know this is hard for you."

"No," Annie replied, shrinking back. "You haven't got the first idea how hard this is. Three years! We've been waiting three years for any kind of news at all. Now there's a body and you won't even tell us who it is."

"There's no body." Reed stepped in, hoping they would get the hint. This wasn't going to play out like one of those TV shows where the family gets to ID a beautiful corpse draped tastefully in a white sheet.

Dave went pale, making the beads of sweat stand out on his bald head and thick upper lip. "No body, or no body you can identify?"

"Please," Ellie said. "I will tell you everything the moment we have a concrete development. Right now, we have more questions than answers, and I wouldn't want to say anything that misled you or raised false hope."

"Hope? You think news of a body gives us hope?" Dave's face had twisted into a mask of anger. "What kind of sick reasoning is that?"

"Let's go," Annie cut in, tugging on his arm. "She's not going to tell us anything."

"I'm sorry," Ellie called after them as they retreated, leaving an emotional black hole in their wake. Their car engine roared to life, and Dave gunned it hard a few times, tires spinning in the dirt, before they shot down the driveway and disappeared into the trees. Uneasy quiet settled over the house again. Reed could hear Ellie's unsteady breaths, saw the twinge in her shoulder.

"That was intense," he observed.

"Yeah." She was still watching the distant spot where the Nesbits had disappeared. "I've figured for a while now that Bea was dead," she said, not looking at him. "I thought they had figured that too—you know, that when we talked about bringing Bea home, it was with the understanding that they'd be visiting a gravesite from now on." She shook her head slightly. "They don't know yet that it doesn't matter who the hand belongs to. Bea's already gone."

They left Bump happily slurping the leftover French toast and bacon from the breakfast plates and took Reed's car back toward Worcester to the gas station where Bea had made her final purchase alongside Shannon Blessing. Ellery asked Reed to drive so she could look at the files Sam had left them the night before. She started with Mark Roy because he was the most recent victim, but she was disappointed in what she found. "There isn't anything here I didn't already know. They interviewed a few more people in an effort to figure out where Mark might have gone off to kill himself—his ex-wife, his coworkers, and the bartender down at the Black Cat where Mark liked to drink sometimes—but no one had a clue to offer, and so Jimmy Tipton just stopped asking, I guess."

"What about Shannon Blessing? Have you discovered anything in there that might link her to Bea?"

She juggled the folders on her lap so that Shannon's came out on top. "It's hard to imagine they had any sort of connection," she said as she started going through the witness statements. "Bea was a nineteen-year-old college student and Shannon was a thirty-four-year-old unemployed alcoholic." Reed navigated his way onto the Mass Pike while Ellie scanned one page after another. "Huh," she said after a moment.

"What, you've got something?"

"No connection to Bea," she replied. "I can't believe I didn't figure this bit out earlier, but I guess I never saw the original incident report." She held it up for him, but he couldn't exactly slow down from 65 mph to study it. "Mark Roy was the one who first reported Shannon was missing. Or rather, he called up the station to say he was worried about her because her mail was piling up. He says the last time he saw her was July sixth, when she happened to be coming out of her apartment building just as he was putting the mail into all the slots. He gave her the mail personally, and she took it back to her apartment. Six days later, he phoned the station to say she hadn't retrieved her mail since."

The odd interconnections seemed to Reed like a deranged logic puzzle from a standardized test: *Bea knows Shannon and Shannon knows Mark. Ellie knows Shannon and Mark but not Bea. If someone abducts Bea but not Shannon from a gas station one night, why is Ellie the only one left standing?*

"Do you think it's important?" Ellie asked him.

"Yes," he replied, although he couldn't say why at this point. "What else have you got in there?"

"Nothing much," she said as she sifted through the contents. "A record of her arrest for operating under the influence back in 2012. There are a few witness statements from people in her apartment building who said they hadn't noticed anyone suspicious hanging around. No one in particular going in or out of Shannon's place. There was nothing, Jimmy notes, to convince them that Shannon met with foul play. They did serve a warrant to her bank to get her account information—the latest check on that was just three months ago—but Shannon has made no deposits or withdrawals in the past two years."

"From what you've told me, Shannon does not sound like someone with either the motivation or the acumen to suddenly go off the grid."

"No," Ellery replied flatly, and turned her face toward the window. "She's dead. They all are. The only thing that's different now is that folks are starting to pay attention."

He wondered if she had any idea of the kind of attention that would be coming their way, the kind of powder keg they were sitting on now. The fuse had been lit last night when the hand was shipped to Boston, and now they were all just waiting for the boom. The Boston area hadn't seen a serial killer of any consequence since Albert DeSalvo strangled thirteen women in the early 1960s, long before the advent of the twenty-four-hour news cycle and various social media. Everyone had a camera now. Everyone wanted to be part of the story.

His tenuous involvement was its own kind of time bomb. McGreevy would pull him out of Woodbury in a heartbeat if he knew what Reed was up to, and it was only a matter of time before he caught on. Reed had heard the skepticism in Mike Driscoll's voice this morning when he called the warden in Terre Haute to ask for visitor logs and correspondence records pertaining to Francis Coben. "You have to requisition that information through the proper channels," Mike had told him. "You know that better than anyone."

"I don't have time to go through the proper channels," Reed had replied. "Don't send me copies if it's too much—just a list of names would be fine."

Mike had gone silent for so long that Reed thought the phone connection might have cut off. "First the bed check on Coben and now you want a look at his visitor log," he'd said at last. "Just what do you think he's up to?"

"I don't think Coben himself is up to anything. I'm concerned he has a friend—an admirer—who is keen to take up where Coben left off."

Mike Driscoll knew the details of Coben's crimes better than most; he was the one who had to babysit the animal until the Feds decided to pull Coben's plug once and for all. "That," he replied in a massive understatement, "would be real bad news."

They had agreed on a compromise: Mike would look over the logs himself and flag anything that looked odd or suspicious, and then he would send the details of those interactions to Reed. Reed hated to rely on anyone else's judgment of what was "odd" in this instance, even someone as savvy as Mike, but he had no standing to object. This wasn't technically his investigation.

"Turn up here," Ellie said as they reached the fateful exit Bea had taken years ago. Reed drove them into the bustling rest stop, which was packed with holiday travelers. They waited in line at the gas pumps so that they could have number six, the one Bea had used. Reed swiped his card and put the nozzle in the tank, although the car couldn't possibly need more than two gallons at this point. Mostly, he wanted an excuse to look around.

"Shannon was at pump number seven over there," he said, pointing, and Ellie's gaze followed. "The two women definitely would have been able to see each other."

"But the video doesn't show them talking or having any sort of interaction," Ellie reminded him. She squinted at a clean-cut man with his silver Beemer, who now stood where Shannon had been the night of Bea's disappearance. "Maybe . . . maybe Shannon saw the killer that night as he was stalking Bea, and that's why he killed her too."

"Maybe. Why would he wait a full year before targeting her, though?" Reed turned in a circle as he took in the fast-food restaurant, the mini-mart, a Dunkin' Donuts, and the expansive parking lot. They were right off the highway—the Pike traffic rushed by at roaring speed—with any sideline trees set well back from the asphalt wonderland. At a peak time like this, the rest stop boasted more than one hundred cars, but it was central enough that it probably did a reasonably brisk business even at ten o'clock on a Sunday night. The short-term parking spaces close to the mini-mart would provide an excellent vantage point from which to watch the patrons at the gas pumps. "The video suggests that Bea got into her car and drove off unmolested, and yet we know she did not reach her parents' home in Woodbury. Somewhere in between her abductor intervened." He looked out at the passing traffic and tried to envision what might have occurred. "It would be hard to run her off the road without attracting any attention. Perhaps he flagged her down somehow, or maybe even sabotaged her car while it was here at the station."

"The video doesn't show anyone approaching her car," Ellery pointed out.

"Maybe then she made it all the way back to Woodbury. That would make sense, in a way, given that our other missing persons are connected to the same area. A young woman, traveling alone after dark—she might be willing to stop for a familiar face."

Ellery scuffed at the cement with her toe. "I don't know. I think maybe sometimes that's true, but I also think that people make assumptions. If there's no sign of forced entry, then the victim must have let him in—right? She must have known him. But I think people forget that folks are basically trusting, or maybe you can call it naïve. Whatever. If a stranger knocks on your door or flags you down because he says he has car trouble, you're inclined to believe him. You don't think anything bad is going to happen to you, right up until you're being stuffed into his trunk. Everyone expects the bogeyman to look like some sort of freak, but these guys, half of them could pass for Mr. Rogers."

Reed had to concede her point. The Green River Killer, Gary Ridgway, had managed to murder as many as ninety women, perhaps more than any other serial offender in U.S. history, in part because he was so ordinary in every other respect. The Bible taught that the Devil would be marked with a special brand upon his forehead, but in Reed's experience, too often the Devil was a middle-aged, soft-bellied wage worker with a receding hairline, two ex-wives, and a pair of bloody shackles in his basement.

"It would be useful to see the rest of the video from the night

Bea disappeared," he said to Ellery. "Just in case Shannon Bless-ing appears elsewhere or there is anything else of note—someone loitering before Bea arrived, for example. But I don't suppose Oil Can Boy has any more recordings on offer."

Ellery shrugged. "We could ask."

Reed scrunched his face at her. "I haven't traced the correspon-dence. We would probably need to get a warrant for the Internet provider in any case to disclose his real identity."

"Yeah, I don't think that's going to be necessary. Follow me."

She went into the mini-mart and waited in line until she could talk to the full-bodied woman with frizzy hair who was minding the register. "Hi," Ellery said brightly, but she did not introduce herself or show any form identification. "I'm looking for some-one who works here—someone with access to the video surveil-lance and a big-time thing for the 1986 Red Sox."

The frizzy-haired woman wrinkled her whole face. "You mean Alfred?"

"Alfred, yes," Ellie replied with satisfaction, as if she had known it all along. "Now where can I find him?"

"He's loading inventory in the back." Ellery turned without another word, but the woman hefted herself half over the counter to call out, "Hey, you're not allowed back there. Employees only!"

Reed smoothly withdrew his official credentials. "FBI business, ma'am. We appreciate your confidentiality and cooperation." Then he half walked, half hopped after the striding Ellie, who was already pushing her way through the swinging doors.

They found a skinny African American man who was lifting pallets of soda and dropping them onto the shelves in what ap-peared to be in rhythm to some beat inside his head. He was nod-ding along as if to music, and as they got closer, Reed could see the man had earbuds connected to a cell phone in his pocket. As might have been expected, he also wore a Red Sox baseball cap that was faded on top from the sun. Ellie walked right up behind him and announced loudly, "Oil Can Boy, I presume."

The man dropped the pallet he was holding and grabbed the buds from his ears. "Jesus, you scared me, creeping up like that."

"You're Alfred?" Ellie asked, and the man nodded.

"Yeah, I'm Alfred. What's it to you?"

"And do you also go by the online handle Oil Can Boy?" she asked.

The whites of Alfred's eyes got bigger and he took a step back. "Who wants to know?"

"Officer Ellery Hathaway," Ellie replied, showing her ID at last. Reed followed suit with his own credentials.

"I believe I'm one of your satisfied customers," Reed told him solemnly.

"FBI—what do you want with me? I ain't done nothing illegal, I swear." Reed could tell by the sudden sweat on the man's brow that he wasn't too sure of this.

"Relax, we're not here to bust you," Ellie said. "We want your help."

"The FBI wants my help?" Reed could see he wasn't convinced of this either.

"You're the one who's been selling the surveillance video of the night Bea Nesbit disappeared, aren't you?"

Alfred folded his arms across his chest. "I ain't saying anything one way or another."

"We know it's you," Ellie told him. "We can get the IP trace to prove it—get a warrant, search your home . . . or you could just agree to help us out."

"Help you out how?" Alfred was still plenty suspicious.

"We want to know if you have any other video from that night—other cameras, other times. Anything that isn't covered in your usual product."

He gave an expansive shrug. "The cops took everything the first time around. You guys already got everything we had from when that girl went missing."

Reed exchanged a look with Ellery. There was nothing in the files about additional video. "But you have copies," he said to Alfred. "Right?"

"Dunno. Maybe. It was years ago and that girl was only on the one camera, I know that much. She didn't come inside the store."

"We're interested in another woman. The woman next to Bea Nesbit at the gas pump that night."

For the first time, Alfred looked interested rather than cagey. "Yeah? You think she had something to do with that girl going missing?"

"She's missing now too," Ellie said. "We're trying to determine if there was any connection between the two women, something that might have happened here that night."

Alfred's eyebrows knitted together in doubt. "I don't recall nothin' on the video that night that was interesting, other than Bea getting gas, so I don't even know I saved the other stuff. It was plain-ass boring. I'd have to go check my files to be sure."

"Please do that as soon as possible," Reed told him. "And send the information to me at this e-mail address, okay?" Reed handed a business card to Alfred.

"I got no promises," he told them as he looked it over.

Ellery sighed with the resignation of a woman who had been chasing ghosts for three years now. "Just look," she said. "That's all we ask."

As they bid Alfred good-bye and returned to Reed's car, he gave her a sideways glance. "That was astutely deduced," he said. "I confess I didn't have you pegged as a sports fan."

"The Red Sox are a local dialect around here. You have to speak it to fit in."

"So Oil Can was not some local mechanic or fire starter," he said.

Her mouth twitched in a smile. "No, Oil Can Boyd was a star pitcher for the 1986 Red Sox."

"Hmm. Seems I heard something about them—their season didn't work out so well, as I recall. A rather disgraceful ending in the World Series in which they managed to snatch defeat from the jaws of victory?"

"Yeah, that would be them. Turns out, though, if you wait long enough, the story has a happy ending."

Back in Woodbury, they traced Mark Roy's mail route, and the only benefit Reed could see was that he now had a complete visual picture of the town. "This is it," Ellery said as they rolled to a stop outside a pretty colonial house with a wildflower garden in the front and great, green trees hanging over it on either side. The cheery painted mailbox featured a pair of cardinals, and there was a late-model Lexus SUV parked in the driveway. "This is the last house on his route. Chief Parker lives here with his wife—no kids."

"Did anyone talk to them about the day that Mark Roy disappeared?"

"Yes." Ellie's eyes went to the folder on her lap, but she didn't open it. She knew the answer by heart. "Julia says she signed for a package at around two thirty that afternoon, and that Mark seemed fine to her, but they didn't linger to chat."

Reed stretched over into her personal space so he could get a closer look at the house. The front door seemed to be open, leaving only a screen in its place, so he presumed Julia was at home. "We could go talk to her now, since we're here," he said as he drew back to his own seat.

Ellery made a choking sound that she covered with a cough. "I don't think so. I mean, why should we? She didn't see anything."

"Didn't she? The investigators who interviewed her asked questions to determine if Mark Roy might have committed suicide, not whether he might have been abducted. We've agreed that he probably went missing soon after he finished his rounds, so that makes her among the last to have seen him. If the perpetrator was stalking Mark that day, Julia might have seen something unusual, something no one thought to ask her about before."

"I doubt it," Ellery muttered. "She's not really the observant sort."

"Well, we won't know unless we ask." He removed his seat belt and got out of the car, but Ellery remained seated, staring straight ahead. He tapped on the window, startling her. "Aren't you coming?"

She rolled down the window. "Sam isn't going to like this. He won't like us questioning her without his say-so."

"Since when have you been bothered by what Chief Parker likes and doesn't like?"

She still didn't get out of the car.

"Suit yourself," he said, stalking off toward the front door, and he heard her scramble out behind him.

"Don't say I didn't warn you," she said under her breath as they reached the steps.

"I've been sufficiently warned," he replied, hitting the doorbell. It chimed from inside, and a few moments later, a dark-haired woman appeared.

Reed admitted to a certain curiosity about the woman who was married to Woodbury's bellicose sheriff. Julia Parker was slender and well put together, the kind of woman who was born on the right side of beautiful and blessed with the means to keep it up, at least for now. He didn't know if she worked for a living, but she clearly brought her own money to the marriage. Her summer outfit consisted of tailored khaki shorts and a navy button-down blouse with tiny pink polka dots. She wore a large diamond ring on her left hand and a dismayed expression on her pale face at the sight of Reed and Ellie standing on her front porch. She halted behind the screen door and looked them over, back and forth a few times, but did not open it when she asked, "Yes? What is it?"

"Hello, Mrs. Parker," Ellie said. "I hope we're not intruding. Please let me introduce Reed Markham from the FBI. We were hoping to ask you a few questions about Mark Roy."

"Mark," she repeated, plainly surprised. "Yes, it's a shame what happened to him. He was a lovely man. However, I'm afraid don't know anything other than what I've already told my husband." Reed noticed she still had not opened the door for them.

"We are exploring a new angle in the case, ma'am," Reed said with his best Southern charm smile. "We'd be deeply obliged if you could indulge us just for a few moments. I promise it won't take up more than a few minutes of your time."

The woman looked long and hard at Ellery as she made up her mind. "Sam said your fussing had somehow convinced the FBI to come up here. He didn't seem too pleased by it."

"Did he also tell you he was out at my place last night?" Ellery said boldly. "Did he tell you why?"

Irritation practically sparked off her skin. "No—suppose you enlighten me."

"I'll let the chief fill you in," Ellie said. "Best you hear it from him."

Reed figured they had at most a couple of hours left before Julia and the rest of the world could hear about it on the news.

"May we come in?" He almost batted his eyelashes as he said it. "Please?"

Julia's posture softened as she relented. "All right, just for a minute. I have a pie in the oven."

He could smell it as they stepped into the foyer—berries and sugar and browning crust. Julia didn't let them past the tiled entryway. "Go ahead, then: What is it you wanted to ask me?"

"The afternoon last year when you took the package from Mark Roy," Reed said, "did you notice anyone else in the area at the time? Anyone who wouldn't usually be here?"

She did actually appear to think about the question, at least for ten seconds or so. "No, no one."

"Maybe earlier or later in the day," Reed pressed. "It could be a delivery person, a jogger, a strange car in the neighborhood?"

"I'm telling you, no. We get bicyclists down the path all the time, so I don't pay attention to them much anymore. Maybe there was someone there. Otherwise, it was the usual assortment of characters: the Grossmans' loudmouthed dog, Maureen Mayer doing her power walking with the weights, and the Ryder boys playing hoops in their driveway. I didn't notice anyone skulking about."

"Okay," Reed relented, feeling another slim lead slipping away. "Thank you for your time."

They turned to leave and were almost out the door when Julia Parker spoke again. "You people have asked me three times about Mark, but funnily enough, no one's ever come to ask me what I know about Shannon."

Reed and Ellie turned almost in unison to face her again. "I beg your pardon?" he said.

"What about Shannon?" Ellie asked her.

Julia gave a high, brittle laugh. "You should know, Ellie. You should know better than anyone."

"I'm afraid I don't follow you."

"You mean you don't want to follow me. There's a difference."

Reed could see from Ellie's expression that she was genuinely befuddled. Julia made a huffing noise and turned her attention solely to Reed. "Shannon Blessing was the town drunk," she said bluntly. "But she has only one OUI."

"Ma'am," Reed said, "excuse me, but I don't understand your point. Are you saying that you know what happened to Shannon? That you have information that could help us find her?"

"I don't know what happened to her or where she went," Julia replied. "But as far as I'm concerned, she need not ever be found."

She shut the door on them this time—the heavy one. Reed looked at Ellie. "What the hell was that about?"

"I don't know. She's right that Shannon has only one citation for OUI on her record, and I guess that would be unusual with Shannon's history." Her cell phone rang as they were walking down the path toward car, and she dug it out to answer. "Hathaway," she said, and then came to a sudden stop as the voice replied from the other end. "We'll be right there," she said tersely. Then she hung up and looked at Reed, her eyes dazed. "They have a fingerprint ID on the severed hand from last night," she told him. "It's Bea Nesbit. Sam wants us to come to the station for an all-hands meeting. That's what he said, 'all-hands.' "

They got into the car, but before Reed could put it into gear, his cell phone trilled from his pocket. He fished it free, but his greeting was distracted, given the circumstances. "Yeah?"

"Reed? It's Danielle."

"Oh," he said mildly, glancing at Ellery to see if she was listening in, but she seemed preoccupied by the latest bit of news. "How's it going?"

"I'm not sure what to say here, but you might have given

me a heads-up—this wasn't just some little favor you asked, now was it?"

"What do you mean?"

"You show up here with an officer from Woodbury and eight hours later, the ME's office is calling, saying they've got a severed hand found in Woodbury, and could we please help them with the identification process? A severed hand, Reed!"

He winced as he navigated around a corner. "We didn't know about that part when we talked to you. I'm sorry if I've caused you any trouble."

She blew out a frustrated breath. "Just so we're clear. I can't do any more favors for you on this one. Everything has to be by the book or not at all."

"Understood. Were you, uh, were you able to get anything?"

"I didn't process the beer bottle. Officer Hathaway wrote this morning with instructions not to bother, that it was no longer germane to your case."

"What?"

"She e-mailed," Danielle said with a trace of impatience. "And frankly, it's just as well. About thirty minutes later, my boss called with the news about the hand, and I realized why you'd been in here asking for these tests."

Reed squeezed his eyes shut briefly. "Okay, okay. Anything else?"

"I sampled the birthday cards as you asked, just looking for anything under the envelope flaps and nothing else. I retrieved usable samples from two of the envelopes, and there is a high degree of statistical probability that they originated from the same donor."

"How high?"

"Think one in five billion."

"All right, that's helpful, thank you."

"There's one other thing. You asked me to run the samples against the DNA from the soda can you gave me."

He looked over at Ellery again. Her face was pale and drawn. "Yes," he told Danielle. "Go on."

"It's a match."

7

I am sorry to have to stand here and give you this news," Sam said to the unit as they all crammed together in the undersized squad room. "The hand we discovered last night has been positively identified as belonging to Bea Nesbit."

For Ellery, the truth had been three years coming, but it did not make the words easier to bear. Her brother, Daniel, had taken four years to die but the end was agony just the same. He died in the winter, the mourners huddled against each other again the biting wind, their teeth chattering as they waited for the grave to finish being dug. It was as if the earth did not want to take him. Daniel had known only some of what had happened to her at Coben's hands, and at first when she'd returned to the apartment, he had tried to talk to her about it. *Tell me,* he'd say gently when she crawled into bed with him. His body was winnowing away, disappearing inside his bones, so that he'd shivered even though summer blazed away outside behind the perpetually drawn shades. She had shivered for other reasons she could not say. She refused to add to his troubles by heaping on her own. Besides, how could she explain that the real reason she put on the same ugly purple sweatpants and T-shirt every day, the ones borrowed from the hospital? The truth was that she didn't know how to wear her own clothes anymore. Before, she had enjoyed searching out fun and funky attire at the little secondhand shops. After, she'd just looked in the closet and stared. The skirts and pants and bright pretty blouses belonged to some carefree bird of a girl, and that girl had flown away.

"Bea Nesbit's parents had her fingerprints taken when Bea was in fourth grade as part of a statewide Safe Child campaign," Sam was explaining, his head tilted downward, curly hair matted with sweat in the hot, airless room. "The medical examiner's office was able to use those prints to make a positive identification on the remains we found yesterday. Most of you were here three years ago when Bea went missing, and so you'll remember that State investigators took control of the case. With this new development, the case has been reactivated, and they'll continue to run point on the investigation, with our office providing support in any way they decide is useful. They are now officially treating this as a homicide."

About time, Ellery thought, but she kept those words to herself. Aloud, she said, "What about Shannon Blessing and Mark Roy?"

That she was still the only woman in the room was a fact she didn't think much about until situations like these, when eight pairs of male eyes turned their attention straight at her. Sam shifted his weight from one foot to the other, looking uncomfortable and a bit deflated as he considered her question. He was in full dress uniform, highly unusual for a Sunday afternoon, and the humidity made his thick hair curl around his ears. "Shannon Blessing and Mark Roy remain open missing persons investigations," he said at length. "It would be appropriate to take another look at both cases, but we don't have any new information to go on right now. There is nothing concrete to connect Bea Nesbit to either of the other two investigations."

"That's not entirely true," Ellery said, conscious that everyone was still watching. "Shannon Blessing was at the gas station with Bea the night Bea disappeared. She was filling up her car right at the same time Bea was."

Sam narrowed his eyes at her. "How do you know this?"

"It's on the surveillance video. No one ever noticed before."

At least a dozen officers must have looked at that tape over the years, but Sam clearly heard Ellie's words to mean *you* never noticed before because two red spots appeared on his cheeks and his eyes darkened to almost black. "I see," he said curtly. "Thank you for that bit of information. It's a peculiar coincidence, but for right now, that's all it is."

"But, Chief—"

"I said we'll look into the other cases, Ellie. Right now we have actual new evidence in the Bea Nesbit investigation, not to mention someone has to go notify Dave and Annie of what we've found. On top of that, you might have noticed the news vans are circling like vultures out there. If you've got some definitive proof that Shannon Blessing and Mark Roy are connected to Bea Nesbit, then by all means, please enlighten us." He paused meaningfully, knowing full well she wouldn't reply, and the room was so quiet she could hear the force of his angry breathing. The men around her were no longer staring; no, they were studying their feet in sympathy for her embarrassment. "That's what I thought," Sam concluded when Ellie had no proof to offer. "Now, as I was saying—"

"Chief, before we move on, maybe Ellie has a point." This

unexpected voice of support came from Officer Charles Taylor—
Call me Chuck, like the shoes, he liked to say—a barrel-chested,
soft-spoken guy with arms like cannons. Ellie didn't hang out
or go to lunch with him or anything like that, but she did feel a
certain kinship with Chuck since he was the only minority in
their tiny unit. *Black like the coffee,* is how he put it, and coinci-
dentally, it was how he drank it too. Ellie had tried out her theory
of the missing persons cases on Chuck before, and he'd listened,
heavy lidded, but he had never thrown any of his considerable
weight her way until now. So everyone pretty much had to listen
as Chuck Taylor, a man who modeled his usual conversational
style after Trappist monks, made something of a speech. "Chief,
the way I see it, we do have a pattern here—people gone missing
from this town during the first part of July. If Bea Nesbit is
dead, then it seems to me the others probably are too. I s'pose we
could wait until the guy starts wrapping up pieces of their bodies
and leaving them on our doorstep to declare an official connection
between the cases, but maybe instead we could try to get out in
front of this thing. 'Cause if Ellie's right, the most important
thing is that it's July fifth—and we could be looking at another
victim any time now."

All the heads turned to look at Sam for the rebuttal, and he
responded by sucking hard on his upper lip—maybe to keep from
screaming or cursing, maybe just to cover up the fact that he'd
been called out by yet another of his junior officers. "I'll take that
under advisement, Taylor, thank you."

Chuck shrugged a hulking shoulder. "Just saying—if the State
investigators are running the Nesbit case, we could concentrate
on the others."

Sam opened his mouth as if to protest but then closed it.
He took a deep breath and clutched his hat a bit tighter. "Right

now, today, we just have to get a statement together for the press and to make sure the Nesbits hear about Bea from us, not from them. State investigators are on their way here now, and Jimmy, I want you to take them out to Ellie's house to show them where the remains were discovered."

Jimmy Tipton answered the chief with a quick nod, but he glanced over at Ellie, and she thought she detected a gleam in his eye. It was her house, but somehow it was still his case.

"Uh, shouldn't I be there too?" Ellery asked.

Sam shot her a dark look. "I expect they are going to want to talk to you eventually, but in the meantime, I figured you'd want to accompany me to the Nesbits' place. After all, you're the one who's been promising them a thorough investigation for years— well, now you've got it."

The way he phrased this made it sound like she was somehow responsible for Bea's murder, as if she'd wished this to happen. She remembered how anguished and angry Dave and Annie had been when they had showed up at her place, and she swallowed hard. He was right. She had to go. "Yes, sir."

The meeting broke up, and she tried to catch Reed's eye to see what he made of this latest development, but he ducked away from her and pulled out his cell phone, heading for the exit. She wondered briefly if she should chase after him but figured Sam would pop a gasket if she set foot off the property before they had performed notification at the Nesbit place. So she let Reed go and instead chased after Chuck Taylor, who was heading for the back where the locker room was located. "Hey," she said as she caught up to him, "I just wanted to say thanks for backing me up in there. I appreciate it."

He opened the locker with a quick punch and cast a dubious eye down at her. "You're welcome, but you aren't the one I'm supporting. I'm worried about who's next." He took a pressed and clean uniform shirt off its hook and slid it on over his gray T-shirt. "I got three kids and a wife out there, you know?"

"Yeah," she said. "I understand. I just wanted to say thank you. The chief is tired of hearing the story from me."

"He's gonna be hearing it from everyone in about two shakes," Chuck said as he buttoned the shirt. "There're vans from all four networks parked outside. People are going to freak when they find out about that hand."

Good, Ellie thought. *The town should have freaked a long time ago.* "Listen, while we're here, there is one thing I wanted to ask you about, that may or may not be related at all: Did you ever book Shannon Blessing for an OUI?"

He rolled his neck around while he considered it. "One time, I answered a neighborhood disturbance call and found her wandering down over by the hardware store, carrying on about how she lost one of her shoes. Her left leg had a pretty bad cut on it and she smelled like a gin factory. I took her to the clinic and waited while they patched her up, and then I brought her back here and let her sleep it off downstairs in holding until morning. Another time, yeah, she was weaving over the double yellow line on Route 2, so I pulled her over and booked her on suspicion of OUI. Turned out she blew a one point eight on the meter."

Ellie glanced over her shoulder to check that they were alone. "I booked her once too, on Valentine's Day the year she disappeared. The thing is, if you look at her official file, the only OUI on the books is one from 2012."

He raised his eyebrows. "For real? That lady got tagged almost anytime she was behind a wheel. Soon as she'd get her license back, boom, there she'd be again, driving down to the liquor store."

"I know. That's why it's weird. Can you think of any reason

those other OUIs would be expunged from her record?" Chuck had eight years more experience on the job than she did.

He scratched the back of his head. "Can't think of one. Prosecutor could throw it out if they didn't want to pursue the case. Or a judge could do it, I suppose. Should still be on the record, though."

Ellie thought the same thing, and she wondered when Shannon's records had been altered, before or after her disappearance, and whether there was any way to find this out. She was still standing there next to Chuck, trying to think if there was a way to force the system to regurgitate its history, when he cleared his throat at her. "Shouldn't you be going with the chief to talk to the family?"

Ellery had never had to do this kind of notification before, to tell a pair of loving parents that their daughter was almost certainly dead, and that her body had been mutilated in the process. Her thoughts drifted to the other names she carried in her memory, the girls who had been taken before her but did not get out alive. *Michelle Holcomb. Gabby Walker. Rebecca O'Hara. Christine Strunk.* Someone had had to tell their families, too, that they'd been found in pieces, that they would never be whole again. Ellery wondered if her mother had considered those girls during the days that Ellie was missing, or if she had clung to the stubborn hope that Ellie would be different. "Oh, thank you, God," she had said when they were reunited at the hospital, holding Ellie, rocking her tight in a way she hadn't since Ellie was a small girl. "Thank you, God, for this answered prayer." Ellie had smelled the sweat and fear on her mother's skin, had let herself be crushed against her hair and breasts, but she could not accept her mother's sentiment. If God was the one who had saved her, that meant he'd let the others die.

"You ever have to do a notification?" she asked Chuck.

He shuddered, his shoulders rising and falling like mountains in an earthquake. "Not like this one." A pause as he shook his head. " 'Bout six years ago, we had a bad accident over on Church Street. Little tyke playing in his parents' yard chased some toy out into the road, just as a car came flying along. Robbie Coussens, the boy's name was. Three years old. He lived long enough to be airlifted to the hospital, but the doctors couldn't save him. I had the job of finding Robbie's dad at work and giving him the news. I remember driving over there to his office, thinking the whole time how I was going to be the one to ruin this poor SOB's life." He took a deep, heavy breath. "The family moved away less than a year later, but I've never forgotten them. Can't say I blame them for leaving—imagine having to look out at the street every day and see the place your child died."

Ellie had lived the remainder of her childhood in the same walk-up apartment, two blocks from the spot where Coben had abducted her, and she never made a fuss, not even when the bus stop for her junior year turned out to be within sight of the park where it had happened. Her mother still lived in the same apartment and probably always would. Daniel's bedroom was there, with the faded great white shark poster from *National Geographic* and his seventh-grade soccer trophy and the goofy pictures of Daniel with his friends or his classmates—all the evidence left in the world that Daniel Hathaway had once existed. Her mother had made a choice to stay in this place where Daniel last was, where he would always be, and Ellie had accepted this, even if it meant she could never really come home.

Back in the squad room, Reed had returned and was pacing the narrow aisle next to her desk, apparently waiting for her. "Are you coming with us to the Nesbits'?" she asked him.

He halted and looked at her funny, as though laying eyes on her for the first time. He looked, she thought, the same way he had when he took those tentative steps inside her hospital room fourteen years ago. Like she was a ghost that only he could see. "What?" he said, sounding distracted.

"Dave and Annie Nesbit. We have to go give them the news." The man had just sat through the same painful briefing that she had. Surely the task at hand was apparent to him. "Are you coming?"

"No." He looked behind her at Sam's office. "I don't think that would be wise at this stage. Ellery . . . why did you ask Danielle to stop any analysis on the beer bottle from your yard?"

Heat crept up over her ears, and she started shifting some paper around so she didn't have to look at him. "Oh, I thought we agreed—there was no point in processing the bottle when we had other more important evidence."

"No, we very much did not agree on that."

"Hmm, I thought we had," she said, hoping her flush didn't give her away. She looked up and forced herself to meet his gaze. "If you really think it's that important, by all means, go ahead and have her run it now."

"She can't now," he snapped. "This whole thing blew up with the discovery of the hand, and now she can't be seen running any favors for an investigator out of Woodbury."

"Oh," Ellie replied, relieved. "I'm sorry, then. I guess we got our wires crossed."

"Guess so," he said with his hands on his hips, fixing her with a hard glare. He obviously didn't believe a word of it.

"What are you going to do, then?" she asked him, trying to change the subject. "If you're not coming with us."

"I've got some records on Francis Coben's recent correspondence to go over, and I am trying to track down his cousin—the son of your strange patron."

"Right." She had repressed the very idea of the cousin's existence, but Reed had been clear from the start: someone knew her secret. In her pocket, her cell phone seemed to burn through to her skin. *I know it's you.* She had not deleted the text from the unknown number. She'd checked enough to learn it was from a burner phone and therefore hard to trace. "Let me know what you find out."

Reed was still watching her face closely, his posture oddly adversarial. "You're the one who invited me up here," he said after a beat. "You wanted me on this case."

"Yes, and here you are. Thank you." She couldn't guess what he was driving at.

"You asked me last night what kind of person might be behind these abductions—now presumed murders. I neglected to mention a very significant part of the perpetrator's autobiography: essentially all serial offenders experience trauma in childhood that leaves them unable to form normal emotional and psychological connections with other humans."

Her mouth went dry and her heart thrummed inside her chest. The way he was looking down at her so intently, she felt as though he were talking about her, right there with her colleagues listening in, everyone with their ears out on stems as Special Agent Reed Markham insinuated she was psychologically warped to the point she could be a serial murderer. "Lots of people have troubled childhoods," she said. "That detail hardly narrows the suspect list, and it certainly won't help us catch him."

"Or her." He seemed to want her to say it too, but she would not grant him the satisfaction. He carried on anyway. "Violent female serial offenders are rare, but they have been documented."

"We'll keep that in mind," she said. Christ, now she sounded like Sam.

At that moment, the chief himself came charging out of his office. "Hathaway, you're with me. Let's go." She was actually grateful for the escape and left Reed standing there as she fell into step beside Sam. He didn't even look sideways at her. "Keep your head down and say 'no comment,' you got that?"

He gave the order just before pushing open the door, so she had no real time to think or reply. Suddenly, there they were, a crowd of perhaps a dozen reporters from various news organizations. Cameras were rolling and the eager bodies clambered in around them as microphones poked near her face. "Chief! Chief Parker, is it true that you have found a severed human hand? Is there any connection to Bea Nesbit, who disappeared almost three years ago to the day?"

Ellie froze. Dimly, she recognized the woman with the expensive manicure and poofy brown hair as Monica Jenkins, the nightly anchor for Fox News. The media smelled blood in the water so they had sent their biggest sharks. Cameras flashed and clicked. People hollered questions, all of them speaking over one another. *Have you positively identified the hand? Where was it found? Have you found any other body parts?* In her head, the shouts echoed back to fourteen years ago, to the first time she'd tried to leave her apartment after the attack. *Abby, did he cut your wrists? Is it true he held you in the same closet where he put the others? Abby, how does it feel to be saved?* She froze at the memory, sweat breaking out across the back of her neck as her heart hammered inside her throat. She could not move and the reporters swarmed in, surrounding her as they sensed an opening. "We heard a rumor that the FBI is already involved with the case. Can you confirm?"

She heard Sam calling her name, but she couldn't see him or free herself from the lights and cameras. "I . . . I . . ."

"No comment!" Sam bulldozed his way back through the throng and grabbed her arm. "You'll have a statement from our office by the end of the day."

She gasped as he yanked her from the crowd, spiriting her away toward the fenced-off parking lot. The reporters continued to follow them, cawing and flapping about like birds all the way to Sam's car, where he finally relinquished her with a little shove in the direction of the passenger's seat. Ellie got in and slammed the door shut against the noise outside. She put her hands under her legs to keep them from shaking. "Can't let 'em get to you like that," Sam muttered as he turned over the engine. "This is only the beginning."

Ellie leaned her head back against the seat and gulped in several breaths of air. Tears blurred her vision, and she turned her face so Sam couldn't see. *You're okay, you're okay,* she coached herself the same way she had in the closet all those years ago. She pinched her leg hard enough to hurt. The pain grounded her in the moment. It told her she was alive.

"This story might go national," Sam said, sounding energized by the prospect. "Then they'll all be here before you can blink an eye: CNN, *Dateline,* Court TV. You wait and see, Ellie. We're all going to be famous."

There were reporters waiting outside the Nesbit home when Sam and Ellie arrived, those who had either beaten them to the scene or already guessed the ending to the sordid discovery. The neighbors all emerged from their homes as the squad car rolled up, as though they, too, had been anticipating this development.

No one said anything, however, as Sam and Ellie exited the vehicle. The air was thick with anticipatory dread. No breeze. The full sun slipped behind the trees as though it, too, wanted no part of this story. Ellie's nose burned with the scent of hot pavement and scorched grass. There was only the sound of their boots as they trooped up the walkway to the Nesbits' front door. It flung open suddenly before they could reach it, Dave and Annie appearing together on the threshold.

Ellie could see they had guessed the reason for the visit. Their rigid body language screamed, *No, no, go away,* but they soldiered on and opened the screen door to face the news anyway. "Evening, Chief," Dave said, his voice unusually loud. "Ellie." Annie hung back, twisting her hands in the hem of her blouse. "You, ah, you have some news for us?"

"Evening, Dave. Can we come inside and talk for a bit?" Sam said, not unkindly. He removed his hat, and Annie's face crumpled at the gesture. "We have some developments to share with you."

"Sure, sure. Come in." Dave still seemed overly jocular. Annie had fled the entryway and vanished into the house. Ellie thought again to all the times she'd talked to them before, walking them through the day Bea vanished, mining her personal history for any sort of clues. Dave and Annie were hungry to talk about their daughter and Ellie had used that to her advantage. Now she felt ashamed, even guilty, because they had been so nice and she hadn't realized they had never seen this coming, this moment, when, like Chuck had predicted, she would be the one to ruin their lives.

"Don't make us wait," Dave said, although his wife was nowhere to be seen. He gripped the back of a dining room chair so tightly his hand turned white—almost the shade of his daughter's as it lay inside the box. "What is it you've come to say?"

Sam took a deep breath. "It's about Bea," he said, and the father began to weep.

In the end, they stayed almost two hours at the house. Ellie forced down a coffee she didn't want simply because Annie needed to make it. Dave had a million questions that she and Sam could not answer, mostly because there were no answers to give. *But you can't be one hundred percent sure,* was the point Dave kept returning to, *you can't be sure she's dead. People can live just fine without a hand.*

Ellery thought of Coben and how he'd kept the hands and dumped the rest. Initially the cops thought he was trying to obscure identification of the bodies. Only later did they discover what he was really doing with them—a detail that Ellie wasn't sure made it into most books. It surely wasn't covered in any of the TV movies. There were simply some depravities no one wanted to contemplate. She had overheard a conversation between a couple of cadets at the Boston Training Center. "I heard Coben had sex with the girls after they were dead," said one guy. "Naw, it was worse," said the other. "I read the books about him. He didn't rape the girls. He jacked himself off with their severed hands." This last bit was accompanied by a rude gesture to illustrate, and Ellie had bolted the break room before she could hear any more.

As horrible as this moment was for Dave and Annie, they could have uglier ones waiting for them when the full story broke.

Sam drove them back toward the precinct in silence. Ellery figured he, too, was wrung out from the emotional ordeal at the Nesbit place, but it turned out his thoughts were elsewhere. "Julia called to tell me you came by the house," he said after a stretch. "You and Markham."

"We're continuing to follow leads on the case. Julia's a witness."

"Bullshit." He yanked the wheel so the car turned abruptly off the road. "Julia collected the mail from Mark and that's it. She's a witness to nothing."

"Jimmy asked her only about Mark. He didn't ask her about anything else she might have seen that day. Reed and I were just following up."

"Listen up, because I am going to explain this one time: you are stay away from my wife, and stay away from my house."

"Oh, but you can go creeping around in my backyard and that's okay?"

"Dammit, Ellie!" He pounded the wheel with such force that she jumped. His breathing was ragged as he leaned over toward her. "You don't get it. We're all going to start getting attention now, some of it the kind we don't want—are you following me?"

"No. Are you following me? Like, literally following me? Because that's going to get you all kinds of attention, Sam. I made the bottle go away, and now Reed thinks I'm sandbagging him on the case. I protected you once, but I'm not going to do it again."

"Believe me, you won't have to. I get it. We're done. I'm reading you loud and clear. The part where you moved a man into your house last night kind of made that obvious."

Ellery resisted pointing out that he'd had a woman living in his house the whole damn time—a suspicious, angry woman, if their earlier conversation could be believed. "I'm not sleeping with him." After the incident with the bottle, she'd be lucky if Reed was even speaking to her.

Sam gave a derisive snort. "Yeah, well, I'd keep my distance if I were you. The man who solved the Coben case shows up here, and all of a sudden you've got a severed hand on your doorstep. Seems like maybe he's got some sort of sick fan club going on."

"Bea was taken three years ago," Ellie pointed out. "Long before Reed Markham was involved in the investigation."

Sam shook his head like she just didn't get it. "I didn't tell everyone the full report on Bea's hand. It was remarkably well preserved, considering the years. The ME can't say when the hand was removed, but her best guess is that it's been frozen all this time. So you see what I'm saying? Some sicko has been keeping Bea Nesbit on ice, just waiting for this opportunity to come along. Maybe tomorrow, he'll mail us her liver. Or, God forbid, her head."

Ellie's own hand fluttered to her throat. With her thumb, she could just feel the scar by her clavicle. Coben always left his victim's hands uninjured, but he had no compunction about slicing up the rest of the body, just for fun. By the time he got to her, he'd had lots of practice, so he knew where he could cut, how much and how deep, to keep her alive as long as he wanted. A thousand times she had prayed for death to release her, but she'd kept opening her eyes and finding herself awake again. It was a pattern she'd been repeating for fourteen years now, each morning when she blinked herself free from the past and found only her shadowed bedroom. Still breathing. Still here. It was one part miracle, one part waking nightmare. Ellie wasn't suicidal; she'd fought hard for her life and won. But sometimes, especially during the longest nights, she did wonder if maybe the other girls had been luckier after all.

Back at the station, Sam holed up in his office to draft a statement for the press while Ellery met with State Investigators Matthew Tovar and Tracy Grigsby. She had spoken to them before during their earlier exploration of Bea's disappearance, but they were quite a bit more interested in her theories this time.

Tovar had a head of silver hair and a gut that hung over his belt and made her think of Santa Claus. Grigsby was younger, maybe midforties somewhere, with wide blue eyes that seemed to give her a perpetually surprised look. Or maybe it was just that she was having a hard time buying Ellery's story.

"Why do you think the perpetrator left the hand on your porch?" she pressed for the third time. "Wrapped up like a present?"

Ellie kept her cool. "Well, I do have a birthday coming up."

Tovar and Grigsby exchanged an annoyed glance. They didn't understand how much truth she had just told them. "He or she picked you for a reason," Tovar said. "It would help to know what it was."

Ellie flicked away a bit of lint from her knee. If she'd stayed inside that night when she was a kid, maybe watched the late-late show or just sat out on the fire escape and watched the people go by, she would not have been on her bike near the park when Francis Coben stopped her to ask directions. *Sometimes,* she wanted to tell them, *there isn't a reason.*

"Obviously, I don't know what would motivate someone to leave a human body part on my porch," she said. "But I am the one who has been asking questions about the case over the past few years. Maybe he figured I'd be a good person to deliver the message."

"What message?" Tovar asked sharply.

"I'm here. I'm for real. Take me seriously." All the things she'd been saying to Sam for the last three years.

Grigsby nodded at Ellie's wrist. "Out of curiosity, where did you get those scars?"

"Bike accident," Ellie replied smoothly, because when you got right down to it, that's all it was, really—an accident.

Grigsby's wide eyes narrowed ever so slightly. "Must have been one hell of an accident."

Eventually, Tovar and Grigsby tired of her, and Ellie was able to sneak down to the basement, where the holding cells were, and dial Reed from her cell phone. It rang through to his voice mail, so she left him a brief message and asked him to call her back. If he'd been in touch with Danielle about the bottle, maybe he had received the news about the birthday cards too. She also wanted to know what he'd found out about Coben's cousin.

She tapped the phone in her hand a few times as she tried to figure out her next move. It was late, way past dinner. She felt emotionally exhausted but also jittery, like she'd had too much caffeine. In truth, she hadn't eaten a thing in hours, and neither had Bump. She hit the button for Brady's number, and a few moments later, his familiar voice came on the line. "Hey," she said. "It's been a day."

"I saw the news," he said. "You kind of couldn't miss it."

"Do you want to meet me and Bump at Armstead Park for sandwiches?"

"Yeah, okay. That sounds good." He gave a sigh. "It's been a day here too. See you in half an hour?"

"We'll be there." A better friend would have asked Brady what happened to him that day to make him sound worn down and spent, but she had no energy to take on someone else's problems at that moment. Outside, she had little trouble dodging the press; the pack had thinned because they were all working on their nightly stories. It was dark but still very warm, with sticky air that bore the faint scent of salt in it, as though it had traveled all the way from the sea. Ellie went home to retrieve Bump, who greeted her with an enthusiastic slobber. She tried Reed's cell number one last time before leaving, but he still wasn't picking up. Maybe he'd said the hell with her and flown back to Virginia.

Brady beat her to the park because she'd stopped at Branson's Deli to pick up two ice-cold Cokes and classic submarine sandwiches. He stood up from their usual bench by the streetlamp when he saw her juggling the bag, the Coke bottles, and Bump's leash. "Here, let me give you a hand." He froze the instant the words left his mouth, horror plain on his face.

Ellie gasped in shock but then in laughter as her internal pressure gauge finally snapped. It wasn't funny so much as ridiculous, but she was helpless in the thrall of giggles. "Too late," she said as her eyes teared up. "Someone beat you to it."

"Tell me," he offered as he took the bag and one of the Cokes.

She let Bump free so he could sniff about the premises, and he scampered into the dark as soon as he was loose. "I can't really talk about it," Ellie told Brady with a sigh as they took their usual positions on the bench. "But the news reports are probably pretty accurate at this stage."

"They said it was Bea Nesbit."

She nodded as she unwrapped her sandwich. The smell of salami and mustard rose up from her lap, and she realized suddenly that she was ravenous. "We had to tell her parents. It was awful."

"God. That had to be rough. I'm so sorry."

They ate without speaking for a few moments, the only sounds coming from Bump's distant jingling collar, the occasional rustle of the deli paper, and the ever-present electric hum of the bugs in the trees. Eventually, she remembered he'd indicated that his day had been less than stellar as well. "What about you?" she asked. "What happened to you today?"

He waved her off. "Forget it," he said as he uncapped the soda and took a long drink. "It's nothing compared to what you've been through."

She saw then he had a bandage on his forearm. "No, what? You got hurt?"

He touched the bandage almost self-consciously. "You remember Tristan, the Rottie we got a couple of weeks ago?"

She did. The dog had been found wandering by the highway, half starved and with a deep cut on his hind leg. He had other lacerations that indicated he'd been in recent fights with other animals. The staff at the animal shelter named him Tristan and found him to be very friendly around people, but he displayed dangerous levels of aggression toward other animals. They were trying to determine if Tristan could be retrained. "What about him?" Ellie asked.

"He got out today. I'm not sure how. I think maybe his cage didn't latch properly the last time he was put back inside it. Anyway, I was in the other room, exercising the kittens, when Tristan came charging in with his eighty-seven thousand teeth."

"Oh, no," Ellie said, wincing as she pictured the scene.

"Yeah." Brady's voice was grim. "He killed three of them before we could stop him. Sheila said that was it for Tristan—we had to put him down too."

"That's terrible. I'm sorry."

Brady raised his Coke bottle in the lamplight and flashed her a humorless grin. "Some fun couple we are tonight, huh?"

"We would kill at parties," she agreed.

"Let's talk about something else. Something stupid. Oh, I know—I hear that Journey is thinking of going on tour again. Maybe they'll play downtown here on Schearer Stage."

The stage was a rickety collection of plank wood that was used to show off local music acts and drama groups during the summer. Families would picnic on the green and listen to a bunch of middle-aged guys who had real jobs at medical offices and auto dealerships fake their way through a cover of "Satisfaction." "Ha ha, I see what you did there," she groused. "You think 'stupid,' and Journey immediately comes to mind. They're one of the bestselling bands of all time, you know. Five billion people can't be wrong."

"Oh, yeah? Well, the Snuggie moved more than four million units of inventory last year. I think I rest my case."

"Let's talk about your favorite, then: The Cars. Or shall we discuss their ill-advised reinvention as The New Cars? I think that sold as well as New Coke." She waggled her bottle at him for emphasis.

"Mock me if you like. Ric Ocasek was a visionary. He's helped develop a dozen different bands since then."

"Yeah, and one of them is Weezer," she retorted, and he smacked her playfully on the arm. At that moment, her cell phone rang, and the mood broke apart. She stuffed the uneaten sandwich back in the bag and pulled out her phone. The caller ID glowed with Reed Markham's number. At least he wasn't going to leave without saying good-bye.

"This is Ellie," she said.

"It's Reed. How did the notification go?"

Ellie scanned the horizon for Bump, relaxing as she spotted him forty yards away, snuffling in some bushes. "About like you'd expect. What did you find in Coben's mail?"

She heard some paper shuffling on the other end. "The usual brand of misguided, lonely folks looking for a connection to a famous person, and religious fanatics who want to save Coben's soul. Plenty of women who think he was wrongly convicted and would like to be his pen-pal girlfriend."

Ellie shuddered. "Really?"

"Oh, yeah, a bunch of these guys wind up marrying women while on death row. They claim they've found God, but they're really out for more earthy pursuits, if you catch my meaning."

"Is that even possible?" She couldn't imagine a system that granted death row prisoners the rights to conjugal visits.

"Legally? No. But it's not without precedent. Ted Bundy conceived a child while awaiting his death sentence—a girl, I believe."

Ellie wondered what it would be like to have your father be Ted Bundy and your mother be someone who had sex with Ted Bundy while he was on death row for murdering dozens of other women. "What about Coben?" she asked. "Is he, uh, seeing anyone?"

"No one special that I can discern." There was a long pause. "You've never written to him, have you?"

Ellie fumbled the phone, such was her surprise. "What?" she said when she'd recovered. "God, no. Why the hell would I do that?"

"I don't know," Reed said, sounding speculative. "But it happens."

"Not to me," Ellie said firmly. She couldn't imagine what she would have to say to him. A page full of expletives probably wouldn't make it past the warden's inspection.

Reed sighed. "Coben's cousin looks to me like a dead end. His name is Andrew MacKenzie, age thirty-eight, and he's currently locked up on an attempted homicide charge in Pennsylvania. He's been in since 2011 and won't be eligible for parole for another six months. He's not our guy. Maybe your friend Jackie-Mac told someone else about your background."

"Maybe. But we can't ask her—she's dead." There was another strange silence on the other end. She would have thought Reed had hung up except for the fact that she could still hear him breathing. "Reed?"

"Where are you right now?"

"I'm with Brady at the park, getting Bump some exercise. Why?"

"Okay, that's fine. I guess we'll talk tomorrow."

"If you want to get together, I can meet you—"

"No," he cut her off quickly. "Tomorrow. We'll talk then."

He hung up, and she looked down at her phone, perplexed. He'd been acting strangely ever since he'd discovered she asked Danielle Wertz to can the analysis on the bottle. Maybe she shouldn't have gone around him like that, since Danielle was his friend and doing him the favor, but it wasn't Reed's case, not officially. His aggrieved tone seemed a bit over the top to her. The Feds, she thought as she stuffed the phone back into her jeans, they can be such divas.

"More trouble?" Brady asked her.

"No, just more of the same."

"You mentioned Coben. His name came up in the news reports too."

Ellie kicked her leg at the dirt and tried to sound cool. "Yeah, when you've got a severed human hand, pretty much everyone's mind goes to the same place. It was his signature move."

"You thinking he might have a copycat?"

She shook her head. "It's not that simple. Plus, like I said, I can't really talk about it."

He held up his palms in surrender. "Say no more. I was just interested when I heard you saying you were looking into his mail."

She gave him a sideways glance. "Yeah? You ever drop him a line?"

He got a strange look on his face, and for a second, she thought he might say yes. "No, no. Nothing like that. My aunt Ginny had a prison pen pal, though. A guy in Texas who was locked up for murdering his wife. She wrote him every Sunday like clockwork for years, urging him to repent and find God. He said he would pray real hard, but could she also send along a few dollars for the commissary because he needed new slippers. Always slippers or soap—not cigarettes or candy or whatever else he was really using it for. Anyway, she wrote him right up until the time he was released. I think maybe she even offered to have him come visit."

"Did he?"

Brady squinted at the trees and gave a quick shake of his head. "Naw. He got out and immediately beat some hooker within an inch of her life." He turned to look at her again, his eyes gone black in the low light. "Guess you probably know by now—there's just no saving some people."

Ellery collected Bump from his adventures, dusting bits of grass from his ears before she let him back into her truck. The night was mild, so she left the windows down as they drove through the deserted streets of Woodbury. Bump rode with his head out the window, ears to the wind, a giant doggy grin on his long face. Ellie made the turn into her driveway at half speed, lumbering the truck toward the trees. She drove like she felt: exhausted and spent.

As the woods parted to reveal her house in the distance, she hit the brakes with a sudden jolt. Light glowed in one of the upstairs windows—her bedroom. Her heart started pounding and she was wide awake now. She cut the engine and watched the window for a few moments. Maybe she had left the light on that morning. Or perhaps the State Police had been inside her home when they searched the premises earlier. Then a shadow crossed in the window and Ellie had to admit it: someone was inside.

"You stay here," she ordered Bump as she retrieved her weapon and slid out of the truck.

She walked up to the house on the grass, careful to avoid the gravel so her footsteps wouldn't give her away. Her heartbeat pulsed in her ears, creating an ache that made her feel dizzy, and the gun felt slippery in her hands. She licked her dry lips and slowly, carefully opened the locks at her front door. As she eased open the door, she could hear the sounds in the house definitively now; someone was moving around upstairs in her bedroom. *Creak. Thunk.* Then she heard the tinkle of metal rolling on the floor. Ellie couldn't move, couldn't breathe, because she knew this sound too well.

Someone was taking the nails from her closet.

8

He had quick, nimble hands from years of piano lessons but no experience whatsoever with the tools of manual labor, and the hammer felt clumsy in his sweaty fingers. Reed gouged at the wood trim on the closet door as he yanked the nails free, one by one. He was huffing from the effort and the knowledge that he was way out over the ledge here, breaking into Ellery's home and searching her things. If he was on the job with a badge behind, him he never would have dared to do something this reckless, but he wasn't on the case, not technically, and he had to know for sure: Did he rescue her all those years ago only to have her grow up to repeat Coben's crimes? The answer had been in the closet back then, and so that's where he went for answers now.

He had given a cursory search to the rest of the room, so half her dresser drawers sat open, their contents rifled, and he'd pulled a couple of boxes of old shoes and belts out from under her bed. Nothing there. The hot room smelled like dust now; he could practically feel the dirt beading up on the back of his neck. *She lied. She lied. She sent those cards herself.* The words were the driving chant inside his head, forcing him onward even as the splinters pricked his hand and the nails fell like rain around him. He'd broken about six laws already, each one easier than the next. The last time he'd done this, when he'd followed his gut and trespassed onto private property, he'd found a half-dead girl in the closet and ended the day a hero. No one back then gave two shits about Francis Coben's constitutional rights. No one would care about Ellery's either.

He gave another angry yank, and a nail came shooting out, pinging off his chest like a metal hornet. He was so involved in his effort, blood roaring in his ears, hammer clawing at the nails, that he almost didn't hear the creak of the floorboard in the hall. When reality of the noise and what it meant reached his muzzy brain, Reed froze with the hammer in midair. His body went completely still even as his heart thundered on against his ribs. There was nowhere to run or hide. He closed his eyes briefly in anticipation of what was coming around the corner.

When he opened them again, he found Ellery herself standing in the doorway, the barrel of her gun pointed straight at his chest. "What the hell are you doing?" Her gaze flicked around the room at the disarray, but the weapon did not shift from him even a fraction. Reed didn't have an immediate reply. He stood there, chest heaving, sweat streaking down the sides of his face, the nails scattered at his feet. He saw the scene suddenly as she did. He was a trespasser, a felon. A voice inside his head whispered to him: *If she's crazy, then what are you?*

"Answer me!" She took a step forward and he saw her arm tremble. One fumble with the trigger and he'd be dead. "What the hell is this?"

His shoulders sank. What the hell, indeed. "The analysis came back on the birthday cards," he told her, his voice soft but his gaze intent as he watched for her reaction. Their eyes were locked together now, and the gun was reduced to a blur somewhere between them. "The DNA on the envelopes," he continued, "the samples collected from the place they were sealed—two of them were a match. To you."

Confusion spread across her face. She was searching herself for answers, maybe because she did not think he would ever find out. Reed allowed himself to glance at the gun. His own weapon was on the bed, four feet away, where he had left it when he'd exchanged it for the hammer he still clutched in his right hand. He eyed the distance, measuring his chances, and Ellery caught him looking. "That's not possible," she said, moving to position herself between Reed and his gun.

"Danielle Wertz is the best in the business," he told her. "She doesn't make mistakes."

"It doesn't have to be a technical mistake. My DNA would have been all over those envelopes. They were delivered to me and I opened them."

"I instructed Danielle to collect samples only from beneath the seals. That's what she did. The results point to you as the person who sealed those envelopes."

"Bullshit! I didn't touch them until they showed up in my mailbox."

"The DNA says otherwise."

"Well, then it lies," she said coldly.

In Reed's experience, it was the opposite: people lied, science told the truth. But if Ellery was truly off the rails, it was possible she wouldn't remember or be able to acknowledge, even to herself, that she had sent the cards. "Do you ever have blackouts?" he asked her. "Periods of time you can't remember?"

Her brow crinkled. "What? No."

"Maybe you find things in your home you don't remember

buying. Or friends who reference a conversation you had together that you don't recollect ever happening."

"Everyone forgets stuff sometimes," she said. "I am not crazy."

He tried to keep his voice calm and soothing, but she was still pointing a gun at him. "You're hurt. You're scared. Anyone would be after what happened to you. You brought me up here to help you, Ellery. That's what I aim to do."

"By breaking into my house and searching my stuff?"

His cheeks flamed at the question. "I had to check . . . I had to be sure . . ." Adam Kennedy's killer had sat right in front of him, and Reed had just let the guy go—let him walk right out of the station to go back and suffocate a precious six-year-old boy.

"Go on, then." Ellery's voice was hard as she waved the gun at him. "Look."

He felt the presence of the closet at his back like it was a living, breathing thing. "Why don't we just talk for a few minutes?" he suggested, loosening his grip on the hammer as a gesture of conciliation.

"No!" she shouted at him, furious now. "You wanted to look so bad, so do it!"

Reed's ears tingled and he felt light-headed as he turned slowly, hesitant to put his back to her. Crazy or not, she was in her rights to shoot him. He'd invaded her home. He bent low so he could tug the last of the nails free from the door. There was only the sound of his breathing and hers, and the bits of metal clattering to the floor. At last, the nails were all gone, and Reed stood up. He cast a look behind him to gauge her expression. Ellery looked grim but determined.

"Open it," she said, enunciating each word.

The door was stuck in the frame, swollen by the summer humidity and frozen by years of nonuse. Reed gritted his teeth and pulled with all his strength, groaning along with the wood as it finally came free. The smell of dead air wafted out of the dark hole. Reed carefully set the door aside and peered into the closet. It was empty.

"Well, there you go," Ellery said from behind him. "Now you have my big, terrible secret. Are you satisfied?"

Reed stuck his head in first and then finally stood fully inside the musty wooden closet. He touched the walls and the bar where clothes should have hung, but the only thing he found was years' worth of built-up grime. He wiped his hands on his jeans as he exited the closet. "I, uh . . ." He was beginning to doubt his own theory.

"Maybe you want to check the others," she said steadily. "Just in case I'm hiding dead people in them somewhere. Maybe Coben was contagious—is that what you're thinking? He touched me and now I like to cut up people too?"

"The birthday cards," he began, but she cut him off.

"I didn't send them! I kept the first one because it was creepy, because I don't celebrate my birthday at all, for obvious reasons, and no one around here even knows when it is. My mom calls—sometimes, when she thinks of it—but otherwise, July thirteenth is just like any other day in my life. Except for three years ago, when the first card arrived. Then another one came the year after. And another. I can't explain why my DNA was under the seal, but it wasn't because I had any part in creating them. I wish I had thrown them out. I wish I'd moved to outer Siberia or something! I wish the whole thing would just stop."

Reed studied her for a long moment, taking in the anguish in her gray eyes and the dirt smudge on her cheek. If this was an act, it was a convincing one. "I'm sorry," he said quietly.

Ellery gave a bitter laugh, but at least she lowered her gun. "For which part? The part where you broke in and ransacked my home? The part where you think I'm capable of murder? Or the part where Francis Coben kidnapped me, raped me, cut me up, and shoved me in a closet?"

He felt each word like a slap. She had been so quiet when he'd found her, this girl he didn't know at all. The picture on her Missing poster had been two years out of date, showing a gangly giraffe-type preadolescent at twelve years old, all neck and long limbs that the rest of her had yet to grow into. *I'm sorry,* her mother had said at the time, *it's the most recent photo I have.* Abigail Hathaway had smiled for the camera back then. He looked around now at the ruins of her bedroom, at the strewn clothes and the glint of nails on the floor.

"I can't believe it," she said, more to herself than to him. "You think I'm insane. That I'm like *him.*"

"I thought . . ." He paused, gathering himself. "If you were insane, it would be understandable."

She blinked at him slowly. "It would?"

The simple question made embarrassment wash over him. "No," he admitted after a beat. "Not really." Psychologists and law enforcement had been studying serial murderers for years and still they had no idea where they came from, what was the switch that turned them from people into monsters. Ted Bundy had blamed his killings on the fact that he liked pornography and that his girlfriend in college broke up with him. Yet if viewing skin flicks and getting dumped in college could turn a person into a homicidal maniac, the country would be strung with bodies like paper dolls, lined up from end to end. No, when you got right down to it, they still didn't understand a damn thing about these men. Coben's parents had been distant but not outright abusive. No one had seen him coming.

Reed cleared his throat and moved to pick up one of her T-shirts that he had dropped on the floor in his frantic search for . . . what?

Body parts? Birthday cards? Whatever clues or proof he had sought, he clearly wasn't going to find them here.

"Don't," she said as he bent to touch her clothes. "Just . . . don't."

He withdrew his hand. She hadn't put the gun away, but at least she wasn't pointing it at him anymore. "You went behind my back and halted the analysis on the beer bottle," he said, sounding a trifle defensive even to himself. "You have to admit that was suspicious."

"And that gives you the right to break in here and search my house?"

"It tells me there are things you are hiding."

"My whole life is hiding, or hadn't you noticed?" She looked at the dark cave of the closet and was quiet for a long moment. "Go ahead and run the bottle if you think it's so damn important," she said at last. "See if I care."

She turned her eyes to his and held his gaze steady, letting him know she meant it. Whomever or whatever she had been protecting, all bets were off now. Her cell phone buzzed from inside her pocket, and Ellery dug it out with one hand to check the message. She digested it without any change of expression, but when she turned the phone to show it to him, his blood went cold.

You'll get what's coming to you.

"Still think I'm making it all up?" she asked tightly.

"Who sent that to you?"

She shrugged. "I don't know. The number is untraceable."

"The number—you mean you've checked it already?" Realization dawned. "This isn't the first message you've received."

"There was one last night too." She called it up and showed it to him. *I know it's you.* "I guess maybe it's more than just you who suspects me, huh?" she said with dark humor.

He stared down at the phone in his hands. "Why didn't you show me this last night?"

"Why didn't you just ask me about the birthday cards rather than break into my house?"

He flushed at the rebuke, because of course she was right, and he was starting to realize that maybe she didn't fully trust him either. The phone buzzed again and he juggled it in surprise, nearly dropping it, but Ellery snatched it from him in midair. It wasn't a text this time but an actual caller on the line.

"What?" Her eyes went wide in horror as she listened to the person on the other end. "When? Okay, I'm on my way there now."

"What is it?" Reed asked when she hung up.

"Units are responding to shooting on Larkspur Lane," she replied as she holstered her gun and left the room with the cell phone still in her hands. He followed her.

"A shooting? What happened?"

"I don't know, but I can guess," she said.

They went into the humid, sticky night. A weak breeze ruffled the trees and thin gray clouds stretched across a full moon. Reed trailed Ellie down the long driveway to where her truck was parked near the end. Speed Bump started wagging and prancing from foot to foot at their approach. "Here," she said, grabbing the leash and handing it to Reed. "You can stay with Bump. Lord knows you've made yourself at home by now."

"Oh, no," he said, even as he accepted the leash. "The dog can stay, but I'm coming with you."

"The hell you are."

"Ellery." He took her arm, the one still holding her phone. "Someone is threatening you now, remember? I don't know who's sending you those texts, but the one person you can be sure isn't sending them is me, because I was standing there practically at gunpoint when you got it. So please pardon me if I don't feel delighted about you heading off into the night by yourself, not five minutes after someone threatens your life."

She looked furious, maybe because she knew he was right. She jerked her arm free from his grasp and boosted herself into the truck. "Fine," she called down to him. "You can get in—both of you."

Reed frowned down at the dog, who gazed back adoringly and thumped his tail on the ground. "Can't we leave him here at the house?"

"Nope," Ellery said as she started the engine. "Got nails all over the floor."

Reed had no good reply to that, so he did as he was told and rode shotgun with Bump's paws digging into his legs the whole time. Ellery took the corners so hard, Reed and the dog ended up smashed together against the passenger-side windows. "Would you care to share where we're headed?" Reed asked as he pushed in vain at the dead-weight sack of fur planted in his lap.

"I'm afraid it's the Franklin place," was all she said.

They arrived at Larkspur Lane in under ten minutes, but Reed saw they were still late to the party. The street was lit up like the Las Vegas Strip, every house ablaze with light despite the fact that it was near midnight on Sunday. Neighbors had stumbled out onto the lawns in their pajamas to gawk at all the action—which was easy to spot given the presence of all three squad cars plus a fire truck. Ellery stopped her truck at the first available spot along the side of the road and leapt out practically before the thing was in Park. Bump barked after her, clambering into the driver's seat, and Reed seized this moment of freedom to get out. Ellery was already halfway across the lawn, and Reed had to jog to catch up with her.

"Sam?" she called when Chief Parker emerged from the house. "Sam, what happened?"

"Ellie?" He frowned at the sight of her, and the frown turned to a glower when he spotted Reed with her. "What are you doing here? Who called you in?"

"Joe called me. He said there'd been a shooting."

Parker gave a short nod. "Rosalie Franklin," he said with regret. "She took one shot to the leg and one to the chest. They're taking her to Bay State now, but it doesn't look good."

"No," Ellery said, shaking her head. "No. What about Anna?"

"The girl appears to be unhurt."

"Can I see her?"

Parker tilted his head at her, as if he hadn't expected this level of investment. "She's already been removed from the premises. We've got a social worker with her and they're having her checked out at the hospital, just in case."

Ellery's face was a naked mix of pain and anger. "And Darryl?" she demanded. "Where's he?"

Parker nodded with his chin toward one of the squad cars. "Don't worry. He's not going anywhere for a very, very long time."

Ellery didn't seem to hear him. She charged toward the car and the burly officer standing in front of it. "Are you happy now?" she screamed at the car. She kicked it hard, denting the side and making the big man in the back jump in surprise. "You feel like a real man, do you, shooting your wife like that?"

"Easy," said the officer guarding the car. He grabbed her with both hands, but she struggled against him. "You got to chill out, Ellie. We got him."

"Don't touch me!" She wrested free and resumed her ire at the shooter. "What's the matter? Did she cook the wrong dinner? Wear the wrong clothes?"

"That's enough!" Chief Parker strode across the lawn to

intervene. "Hathaway, this isn't your scene and you're not on duty. You should leave now."

"How dare you?" Ellie whirled on Parker now, her anger like lightning in search of the most convenient target. "How dare you send me out here, time after time to answer the disturbance calls, telling me, *Oh, there's nothing we can hold him on, Ellie. We just have to wait it out, Ellie.* Now you say it isn't my scene?"

"Look, I understand you're upset. We all are."

"Fuck upset!" She tore at her hair with both hands. "He beat Rosalie like a stray dog, and you knew it. I knew it. Hell, everyone on this block knew it! No one did a damn thing to stop him. Now Anna may lose her mother, and Rosalie may lose her life." She drew a shuddering breath, tears glimmering in her eyes. "If that happens . . . if she dies, it's on you. It's on all of us."

She kicked the squad car one more time but dodged the officer before he could grab her. She fled across the lawn, past the cars, past her own truck with Bump looking on, and off into the dark. Reed hurried after her, relieved when she came in sight again. She was striding quickly along the side of the road, muttering words he could not make out and swiping periodically at her face. He matched her pace but hung back a few steps, unsure what to say. It had become clear to him that this shooting was unlikely to be related to the ongoing abductions; it appeared to be a routine domestic abuse case, which, he gathered, probably wasn't so routine in Woodbury, Massachusetts.

They continued on this way, Ellery walking, and Reed following, until they had disappeared entirely from the neighborhood of the crime scene. It was black as coal under the trees and Reed did not see any nearby houses. "Are you going to just keep following me?" she said finally, without slowing down.

"Yes," he admitted. "I have to. I haven't the slightest idea where I am right now."

She halted when he said that and allowed him to catch all the way up with her, but she looked at the ground and did not meet his eyes.

"That was an intense scene back there," he offered finally. "I gather you knew the family?"

She nodded. "They've been on our radar for a couple of years now. Long enough that we should have seen this coming. We should've found some way to stop it."

Mosquitoes buzzed around them. Nearby, he could smell some small body of water—a creek, maybe—with its damp vegetation and earthy mud. Frogs were croaking out a late-night song. "The law doesn't always work that way," he said.

"Then screw the law! If the law can't find a way to protect a woman from getting shot in her own home, then it isn't worth the tinder it's printed on." She pulled off her shield and hurled it into the dark. "What good is this? What power does it have at all? I joined up thinking I could be the one to make a difference, that I wouldn't let this sort of thing happen, not on my watch. I went over to that house a dozen times. I begged. I pleaded. I did everything I could to get Rosalie to press charges, but obviously it wasn't enough. Whatever it was—whatever the one thing was that could have stopped this—I didn't see it. I didn't do it. The law can do its thing now, sure. But that won't save Rosalie. It won't help Anna. The law . . ." She said it like the word caused a foul taste her in mouth. "The law is just one person too late."

She stalked a few feet away from him so that he could just barely make out her silhouette in the darkness, but her words burned inside his head. *One person too late.* All these years, he'd been congratulating himself on being the person to save her, for snatching this one girl back from bloody grip of Francis Coben—a narrow but clear and joyous victory. He hadn't really stopped to consider that if they had caught Coben just a few weeks earlier, Ellie would never have been taken at all. From her perspective, he was one person too late. "You're right," he told her, feeling his way cautiously toward her in the inky shadows. Long grasses tickled at his legs, rustled under his feet. "Sometimes the law is about as useful as tits on a bull. Good people end up hurt. It's probably the worst part of the job, but you can't blame yourself for this. You didn't shoot her—her husband did."

"My job was to stop him. I didn't. I can surely blame myself for that."

Reed dropped his chin to his chest. "You can," he conceded. "It just won't help anything. It won't help this woman—Rosalie?—and it won't help the next one who needs you either."

"Right. That's really rich, coming from you."

"What do you mean?"

"One bad case and you up and quit the FBI. I don't think you're cut out for motivational speeches right now, Agent Markham."

"I . . . I didn't quit. I'm on leave."

"Same difference."

He was trying to form a protest, to illustrate how their situations were different, when he heard a powerful engine roar to life. They were standing by the edge of a road, so an engine sound might be expected, but Reed felt fear immediately, sensing danger before he could even identify why he felt threatened. This car appeared at full force out of nowhere, indicating it had sneaked up at low speed with its lights off. "Look out!" he hollered at Ellie, just as the bright lights came toward them.

They both dove toward the trees, branches crackling under the force of the sudden attack, as a large vehicle came sideways at them, veering right off the road. It clipped something because Reed heard the thump just before he hit the ground. The awkward landing knocked the wind out of him for a moment. He lay disoriented and struggling for breath as the SUV/truck that had hit them sped off into the night. "El—Ellie?" They'd rolled down into a ditch of some sort, he discovered as he sat up. He tasted blood in his mouth, and branches scratched as his face. He batted them aside and tried to find Ellie amid the skinny trees. "Ellie, are you okay?"

"I'm here," she said, and he turned toward the sound of her voice perhaps ten feet away. "I'm okay."

They crawled out of the ditch and walked back toward the road, and he could see she was limping. "What happened?"

"I don't know. My hip. I think I got hit on the left side."

He peered down at her, trying to assess. "Your arm is bleeding."

"Is it?" she asked with some surprise. "I guess it is."

"You should see a doctor." He looked around, trying to guess which way was back to the truck.

"No, it's not that bad." She took a few steps to prove it. "See? I'm fine."

It was difficult to determine the extent of her injuries in the dark, but he wasn't convinced by her show of bravery. "I think you should get checked out at a hospital."

"No," she said sharply. "I'm not going to a hospital."

"Just to make sure you're all right. I'll go with you." He could imagine she might have negative associations of hospitals and doctors, given her extended stay after Coben had brutalized her.

"I said no hospital," she snapped at him.

He folded his arms. "I'm afraid I insist."

"Yeah?" she said, her breathing unsteady. "We go to the hospital together and when they ask me how we're related, I'll say you're the guy who broke into my house earlier tonight."

Reed considered this for a long moment. "Okay, then. No hospital."

They located her shield by feeling around blindly among the grasses and then retraced their steps back to her truck, which was sitting where she left it, half over the curb outside the Franklin home. Reed insisted on driving, partly because the cut on her forearm was bleeding heavily and partly so that he didn't have to ride with the dog on his lap. Bump seemed to sense the change in mood because he curled his body close to his owner and licked her chin. At the house, Reed followed her into the black-and-white bathroom to survey the damage, genuinely worried that he might have to stitch her up himself. Under the bright light now, he saw the scrapes on his own arms and one on the side of his face, but Ellie had taken the worst of it: she had a deep laceration on her arm about two inches in length. "You should really get that looked at," he said as she washed it off. He found bandages and tape inside her medicine cabinet.

"It's fine," she said dismissively. She took some gauze and held it to the wound to try to stop the bleeding.

"It'll leave a scar."

"Then it will match the others."

"You could get tetanus."

"My shots are up to date," she replied, eyeing him. "Why do you care so much, anyway?"

He spread his hands, feeling helpless. "I don't want anything bad to happen to you."

"Oh," she said after a moment. "It's much too late for that."

She pushed past him out of the bathroom, and he stood alone, studying his exhausted reflection for a few minutes. He splashed water on his face and watched as it dripped down like tears. Elsewhere in the house, he could hear Ellery picking up nails from the floor. He wiped the last of the water from his chin and went in search of her. She froze when he arrived at the doorway, and he stood there for a moment, uncertain what to say. "I want you to know . . ." he began. "I want you to know I'm sorry for breaking in here and disturbing your things. I was . . . I was wrong." He forced a wry smile. "I've had a lot of practice being wrong lately. One could say I'm beginning to be something of an expert at it."

Ellery said nothing. She simply resumed plucking nails from the floor and placing them in her palm. It hurt just to watch her.

"Ellie . . ." He still hadn't conveyed what he wanted to say. He waited until she stood up and turned around to look at him, her expression unblinking. "I wish there were some way to change what happened to you. I wish we could have stopped him sooner." He said it sincerely, with feeling, but there was no way for her to know all that was contained inside that wish—his fame would be gone, certainly, but without it, he would never have met Sarit and there would be no Tula. His heart lanced at the thought of a world that was missing his precious gap-toothed little daughter. But the world was missing sixteen daughters already, those dead at the hands of Francis Coben, and maybe in some ways, Reed was beginning to see, maybe the loss included one more: a girl called Abigail Hathaway, who was rescued but never really came home.

"Yeah? That's nice and all." The woman now called Ellery shrugged at his words and did not appear eager to grant him any grace. "If wishes were horses . . ." She set the loose nails on her dresser and dusted off her hands. "I'm going to make tea. You can have some if you like."

"Okay, sure. That would be nice, thank you." He supposed

this was as much of an acceptance as he was likely to get, and perhaps more than he deserved.

They drank the tea in her living room—the front room, she called it. With the windows opened, the cooler night air could circulate and the atmosphere wasn't so oppressive. *If you don't look toward the black woods outside, it's almost pleasant,* Reed thought, although it was difficult not to imagine a figure lurking amid the trees. He propped himself up in an armchair and tried to stay awake, although his face was cracking with fatigue. Ellie curled far away from him, at one end of the sofa. He could see purple shadows under her eyes as well. "Do you mind if I put on some music?" she asked.

"It's your house," he said solicitously, and she shot him a withering look.

"How kind of you to notice at last."

She got up and slipped a CD into the stereo. He expected something soothing, perhaps jazz or classical, something instrumental that did not jangle one's nerves. Instead, he got loud, lurching chords and some male singer who sounded British wailing away. The man was going on about the temperature rising, something about daffodils, and then he got to the chorus: "I'm going slightly mad . . . it finally happened."

Reed looked over at Ellery, who was deliberately not making eye contact with him. He almost smiled. Damn the woman, she was tweaking him with music now. *Well, touché, my dear,* he thought. Aloud, he ventured, "Pink Floyd?"

She looked askance. "Queen."

"Ah." He paused. "Fitting selection."

"I thought you would like it."

He sighed and set aside the tea. "I could apologize again if you thought it would help."

"It wouldn't, though, would it?" She put down her cup as well.

"Why would someone use my DNA on the birthday cards? What would be the point?"

He ran a hand through his hair, trying to rub his brain into function. "Could be a message to you of some sort. Or possibly it was for this kind of contingency—so that if the DNA analysis was run, it would implicate you in these disappearances."

"So someone is setting me up."

"It's possible."

"If I'm supposed to be the fall guy, then why run me off the road tonight?"

"You have a point. It doesn't make sense from our vantage point."

She considered. "Maybe they were aiming for you."

Reed sat forward, suddenly more alert. "Why would you think that?"

"I don't know." She squinted at the wall. "But if this guy knows Coben, then he certainly knows you. He's been sending me these cards all these years, but I don't believe he's favored you with any special correspondence, right?"

"Uh, no."

She nodded. "So maybe he doesn't like the fact that you're here. Maybe you're messing with his plans somehow."

Reed had, of course, considered that the killer might recognize him, but he hadn't fully appreciated that he could be a target. Normally he flitted in and out of cases, dropping in midway to dispense advice and then leaving before the investigation was resolved. This one did feel rather more personal. "Well," he said, trying to put a positive spin on it, "maybe, then, my arrival could drive him out of his comfort zone—force him to make a mistake."

"Hmm," she said, sounding skeptical. "As long as the mistake doesn't get us both killed."

The stereo switched to a new song, this one more recognizably

Queen, at least to Reed: "Can anybody find me somebody to love?" Ellery curled in on herself, a million miles away from him despite being in the same room. He sat back in his chair and closed his eyes. He thought of Sarit, and the way her dark hair spread across the pillow like strands of silk. He heard Tula's effervescent giggle as he swung her around and around in the air. He drifted in memory all the way back to them, the people he loved.

When Reed opened his eyes, it was morning, although still early, with the weak light of dawn shafting in on the floor. He rubbed his scratchy face with one hand and looked over at the couch. Ellery lay curled asleep in the same spot she'd chosen the previous night. Reed sat forward and used this unguarded moment to study her. Strands of her hair had come loose in the night, curling over her cheek. She had lovely long lashes and her soft mouth was parted in sleep. He noted, with a guilty flush, that Coben had been right about her hands: they were beautiful, with perfect, tapered fingers. Reed could also see the scars because he knew where to look for them, and he saw they had faded with time. You would have to get close to her to notice them. Ellery, however, would see them constantly, and he supposed this was just one more difference between them: he could pick and choose when he engaged with the Coben case. A lecture here. An interview there. Ellie wore it on her body every moment of every day.

Still, as he looked at her sleeping, took in the gentle rise and fall of her body, he felt a stirring of hope. He remembered the panic, the certainty among the law officers that she was already dead. They'd had no right at all to expect any kind of happy ending, and yet here she was. Abigail Ellery Hathaway had fought for her life and won. He couldn't see this as anything less than a victory.

Maybe it was this sliver of renewed faith, this idea that sometimes you can come back from the brink, that made him rise, cover her gently with a blanket, and then step into the kitchen to phone home. He and Sarit had not signed any papers yet. Nothing that couldn't be undone. Maybe he could convince her to wait, to put off the lawyer's meeting on Thursday, and they could talk together, just the two of them. They used to be so good at talking. That first night together, they'd talked until his voice was hoarse and his throat was raw. The next night, there'd been less talking, and so different parts of him went home sore.

He was smiling at the memory when the line rang through. It was early on Sunday morning, but Sarit was usually up and getting ready for church by now. "Hello?" A man answered on the other end.

"Sarit?" Reed said, although clearly it was not she who answered.

"Sorry, one moment." He heard footsteps and murmuring and then his wife came on the line.

"Reed," she said, and the emotion in her voice—regret, apology, pity—told him everything he needed to know. "How are you?"

"Who was that?"

She took her time with her answer. "His name is Randy. Randy Cummings. His daughter Amanda goes to school with Tula."

Randy Cummings? Reed thought. That's not a real person's name. That's a porn star.

"I'm sorry," Sarit continued, "I've been meaning to mention him, but it just never seemed like the right time."

"Yes, I can understand where it might be awkward, telling your husband that you're fornicating with Randy Cummings."

Sarit's silence was icy. "For the sake of our future relationship, I am going to pretend you did not say that. Now, what can I do for you? Why are you calling?"

There were so many possible answers to this, a veritable tableau of replies, all of which had the power to strike out at her and bring the kind of pain he was himself enduring right that moment. *I was just calling to say I love you. That I wanted to be a family again. Oh, by the way, someone tried to kill me last night. Not that you'd care.* "I, ah, I think with the developments in the case, I am going to need to stay on here awhile longer. I was wondering if we could postpone the mediation on Thursday."

He supposed he should be grateful for Randy Cummings answering the phone because it had the effect of making Sarit very cooperative. "Sure, that's no problem," she said smoothly. "Do you want to pick a new date now, or shall we reschedule when you are back in D.C.?"

Back to his empty one-bedroom apartment with the blank walls. Reed leaned against the wall and shut his eyes. "I'll call you when I get back. Is Tula there? Can I talk to her?" He desperately needed a friendly voice.

"I'm sorry, she's in the bath." Sarit really did sound apologetic. "I can have her call you later?"

"Sure." He swallowed. "Yeah, okay."

"Good-bye then, Reed," she said gently, and clicked off before he had the chance to reply.

He was standing there, shattered but still somehow upright, when Ellery appeared in the doorway of the kitchen. She was yawning, and she had the blanket he'd given her wrapped around her like a cape. "Were you on the phone?" she asked.

He waved his cell weakly. "Just checking in at home."

"Oh. Nothing bad, I hope?"

"No, everything's fine." *Especially if your name was Randy Cummings.* "Maybe I could wash up and make us some breakfast," he suggested, trying to shake off the conversation with Sarit.

"The French toast yesterday was really good," Ellery admitted with a rare smile.

"Done. Just let me freshen up so I don't add my own personal grime to the mix." He still wore yesterday's clothing, which had bits of dried mud stuck to it from their hasty foray into the ditch.

Before he could head for the bathroom, someone knocked smartly on Ellie's front door. He looked to her and her eyes were wide. "I take it you're not expecting anyone?"

"I'm never expecting anyone."

They both went to the door and took turns looking through the peephole. On the other side stood a woman in an expensive pink suit, matching heels, and a head full of coiffed hair. "Who is that?" Reed asked in a whisper.

"Reporter," Ellery whispered back. "TV news. She's popular."

As they were whispering, the knock came again, more forceful this time. "Ms. Hathaway? It's Monica Jenkins from Fox News. I'd like to speak to you about a piece we're running today."

Ellery looked horrified, so Reed held up one finger to her. "I've got this," he said. "Years of experience handling the press. You stand back, okay?"

He straightened his shoulders and opened the door. Monica Jenkins greeted him with a perfunctory smile as she extended her hand. "Agent Reed Markham," she said. "What a pleasant surprise! I didn't expect to find you here, but it's so fortunate that I did. You were next on my list of people to interview."

"I'm afraid we're not granting any interviews, ma'am," Reed said. "It's per policy of the Woodbury Police Department. All media requests have to go through Chief Parker." He was firm but polite, with just a bit of a shrug, as if to say, *I'd like to cooperate, but what can you do?*

Ms. Jenkins appeared unfazed and unmoved, not budging from Ellie's porch. "I will definitely want to speak to Chief Parker too, but since you are the focus of my story, I think it's best to start with you—don't you agree?"

"Me? Why would I be the focus?" He stumbled a bit as Bump surged between his legs, eager to slobber all over the woman's expensive, pointy shoes. Ellery yanked Bump back inside the house.

"Well, you and Officer Hathaway. I confess I just love true-crime stories—let me say I loved your book—so I recognized you straightaway yesterday at the police station. What a coincidence, I said to myself, that Reed Markham would be here in Woodbury at the same time that the local police discover a severed hand. It's just like the Coben case all over again."

"With all due respect, ma'am, if you've read my book, you'd know this is nothing like the Coben case." Reed's thin, pleasant smile was still in place, but the hairs on his neck rose at the mention of Coben's name.

"I know!" she exclaimed, too loud to be sincere. "That's what I found out when I went to research the case—you know, to refresh my memory. I had my interns do some Internet sleuthing. It's amazing what you can find on the Net these days." She opened her briefcase and started sifting through the contents. "Anyway, I just couldn't believe it, because it has to be a huge coincidence, right? You arrive just as the severed hand is found." She glanced up. "No, wait. You were here already, isn't that right? It's like you even knew it was going to happen."

"I can assure you, I did not." He could feel the conversation slipping away from him.

"So then I found out it was Officer Hathaway who called you, and I thought, well, that's just another fascinating coincidence because look what we found . . ." She withdrew a facsimile of the Missing poster created fourteen years ago. "That young girl you rescued from Coben's closet, her name was Abigail Hathaway."

Reed felt the blood drain from his face. Next to him, Ellie pushed into the doorway to peer out at their visitor. Monica greeted her with a wide, bright smile, as though she were some long-lost relative. "Officer Hathaway!" she said, pushing forward so that Ellie shrank away. "Monica Jenkins from Fox News." Reed wanted to grab Ellie up like he had years ago and run like hell, but he had no choice but to stand there and take it. The story was out now. The media maggots would spread thick and fast.

Monica held up the poster so Ellie could see it, glancing back and forth from one to the other, as if to affirm the likeness. "Lovely to meet you," she said. "I understand you go by Ellery now."

9

The woman standing on her porch called to Ellie's mind a thoroughbred—lean and toned, sporting an expensively styled dark mane, and evolved beyond the rest of her species. Ellie was conscious of her own ratty college T-shirt and her paint-spattered sweatpants, of her bare feet and the visible scars on her arms. She hung back behind the door, fingers white-knuckled against the frame so that she dug her own elbows into her ribs. It was worth the awkward position not to put herself on display. For his part, Reed remained firmly planted between Monica Jenkins and Ellie's house. The reporter could not even glimpse the inside from her vantage point, but Ellie anticipated that moment when she would push her way in, maybe bringing her cameras with her, and the closets with the nails in them would say more than Ellie ever could.

These past few days, with Bea's hand turning up on her doorstep and someone creeping around in her woods, and last night, getting run off the road by a maniac, Ellery had mostly been fearing for her physical safety—sleeping with her gun, imagining footsteps behind her every place she walked—and yet here stood this woman who was calmly tearing Ellie's life to pieces using only words.

". . . your thoughts on the fact that the only surviving victim of Francis Coben received a gift-wrapped severed hand?" Monica was saying to Reed.

Reed's jaw clenched, but he was polite. "I really have no comment."

"Bea Nesbit seems like she might have fit the general description of the girls Coben abducted fourteen years ago," Monica said.

"Francis Coben is in prison, on death row," Reed replied.

"Do you think this might be a copycat?"

"I really can't comment."

Monica turned her attention to Ellery. "Ms. Hathaway, I understand you've been pushing the Woodbury Police Department for years to investigate a connection between the disappearances of Bea Nesbit, Shannon Blessing, and Mark Roy. What made you convinced that the three cases were related?"

Ellie licked her lips. The woman was good. She knew all three names of the missing persons without having to refer to any notes. Ellie tried to speak, but no sound came out, so she cleared her throat and tried again. "No comment."

Monica sighed and shook her head with a trace of impatience, disappointed, maybe, in their naïveté. "I realize you would prefer not to talk to me, and believe me, I sympathize with that response," she said, looking to Ellie rather than Reed. "I am here because I happened to recognize Agent Markham yesterday, but if you send me away, it won't stop the story. The rest of my colleagues are going to put two and two together soon." She paused and tried again. "Something about these disappearances must have reminded you of Francis Coben even before Bea Nesbit's hand was discovered on your porch." She cast a look down at her fancy heels, inches away from where the macabre gift had stood. "This is your chance to get your story out," Monica urged her. "What I am saying is—use me! Let me tell your side."

"I have a side?" Ellie wondered aloud. She barely had a home to herself anymore.

"You're at the center of this whole thing."

"You don't know that," Reed said sharply. "You can't just throw around statements like that when you don't understand the situation."

"Please explain it to me, then," Monica replied. "I'm here to listen."

Ellie exchanged a look with Reed, but neither of them said anything. Where would she even start?

"Fine," Monica said after a long stretch of silence. "Let me give you a snapshot of how the story is going to air without any context from you. Abigail Hathaway, now Officer Ellery Hathaway, was living a peaceful life in the small town of Woodbury, Massachusetts, until three summers ago when local college student Bea Nesbit disappeared. A year later, Shannon Blessing also disappeared, and Officer Hathaway immediately pressed for an investigation into a possible link between the two cases, although no one else seemed to agree with her theory. Last summer, when postman Mark Roy disappeared, Officer Hathaway claimed that he, too, was a victim of the same perpetrator—an apparent serial killer. This assertion, despite any evidence linking the cases, and despite plausible alternative explanations for the second and third disappearances. Then a few days ago she called in Agent Reed Markham, the man who caught Francis Coben—just in time for Bea Nesbit's hand to arrive, wrapped up like a birthday present, on her doorstep. People are going to ask themselves: How did Officer Hathaway seem to know this was coming?"

"Just what are you implying?" Reed asked, as if he didn't know, as if he hadn't made the very same accusations about her guilt himself just the night before. Only Reed had said the words with harrowed eyes and fevered skin, sweating bullets down the barrel of her gun, because Ellie knew he'd understood the enormity of the question. Monica Jenkins might have read Reed's book, but she clearly hadn't absorbed the vicious reality of Francis Coben or she wouldn't be so calm and collected, standing on the porch where Ellie supposedly gift-wrapped a severed hand. *If you're going to insinuate I'm a monster,* Ellie thought, *you'd damn well better look afraid.*

"I'm not implying anything in particular. I'm laying out the facts as they appear."

"Here's a fact," Ellery said, pushing past Reed and into the open air. "Coben's eighth victim, Renee Higgins? She bit off her own finger, the tip of the left pinkie." Ellie took a step forward, forcing Monica to step back. "Can you imagine how insane with fear she must have been to do make herself do that? How desperate? She thought if she destroyed her hands then Coben wouldn't want her anymore, and he'd let her go. Well, he got rid of her, all right. He took all her fingers, one by one, and she was alive when he started cutting."

Ellie had pushed Monica backward to the edge of the uneven wooden steps. Ellie's heart was hammering in her throat, but she felt the bitter taste of triumph because now, at last, the woman was pale with fright. "That's horrible," Monica stammered. The papers in her hand rustled as she fumbled, then recovered. "You could come to the studio, tell your story. People will want to know."

"Trust me, they don't."

"Those young women who died, they no longer have a voice. You can speak for all of them." Monica was pleading with her now, desperate to keep Ellery talking, but she'd unknowingly said exactly the wrong thing.

"No one can speak for them." This was the point, the thing Monica and her viewers were never going to understand, that Coben didn't just fancy pretty girls with delicate hands. He wanted to keep them and devour them, to erase them from the world forever so they would be his alone, and so he had. Sixteen young women—this one maybe had a chipped front tooth, that one, perhaps she had a talent for singing—Ellie didn't know them, but she'd imagined them through the years, pondering their possible hopes and dreams. All of them were dead now, their voices lost to the ages, their names reduced to a footnote in Coben's story. Who the hell was she to presume to speak for any of them?

Ellie left Monica teetering by the steps, her mouth open in silent protest, and stalked back into the house, making sure to bang the screen door shut behind her. She braced her back against the wall and covered her face with shaking hands. Outside, she heard Reed taking up the good fight: "I think you need to leave now, Ms. Jenkins. This is private property, and you've overstayed your welcome."

"You're making a mistake," Monica replied. "Both of you."

"Good day to you, ma'am."

There was a scraping sound, the soft cry of the old hinges on the screen door, followed by the heavy wooden door sliding firmly shut. She heard Reed's footsteps, familiar to her now, and took her hands down from her face. She was done hiding. He searched her with a sober, probing gaze. "We never found Renee Higgins's body or her hands," he said after a moment. "Coben wouldn't say what he did with her."

"Well, he damn sure told me," she replied wearily. Reed wrote the book on Coben, but there were certain things he could never know. Maybe it didn't matter now, what Reed wrote and what he didn't. Maybe they were all just different parts of the same story.

"Did he tell you? Did he tell you what he did with her body?" The intensity of Reed's gaze was too much, and Ellie turned her head away from him. She knew he must still feel the pressure, even after all these years, to bring Renee home.

"I don't know anything about her," she said finally. "Except what he wanted me to know." Reed looked to the floor, frowning as he absorbed this idea, and she felt a stab of sympathy for him, this man who had saved just one girl out of seventeen. He'd locked up the monster but failed to notice: the monster had already won.

In her bedroom, Ellie struggled momentarily with the decision about whether to close and lock the door. She could shut Reed out, but that left her alone with the gaping closet. She rested her hand on the knob as she considered the dilemma and ultimately compromised by shutting the door but leaving it unlocked. She could hear Reed moving around in the kitchen, preparing the breakfast he'd meant to start before Monica Jenkins arrived. Ellie took a few tentative steps toward the closet, which she had not confronted since the day she'd taken ownership of the house and promptly nailed every single closet shut. She approached it on silent feet, drifting toward the dark open maw.

The closet was steeped in shadow and gave off a musty smell of wood and dust and dead air that had sat undisturbed by humans for years. Ellie screwed her eyes shut and stuck her hand out, inching it over the threshold. *It can't hurt you,* she coached herself. *It's just a closet.* Her fingers trembled and she waved them blindly in the empty space. *Nothing, nothing,* she said inside her head. *There's nothing there.*

She gasped when her fingertips brushed the wooden planks that lined the wall. His closet had been made of wood, too, swollen and warped by tears and blood, gouged by desperate women trying to carve their way to freedom. Ellie yanked her hand back and all but ran to her dresser, where she grabbed the first clothes she touched and fled to the bathroom. Once there, she turned on the shower to almost scalding hot, but she had to stand under the spray a long time before she felt all the way clean.

After a tense breakfast, Ellery and Reed set out into the sticky, humid morning. Gray clouds hung low and thick, pregnant with the coming storm; the only way to break the heat was to crack it open, thunder-style, and the air nearly quivered with anticipation. *Après moi, le déluge,* Ellie thought darkly as she climbed into her truck and gunned the engine, adding some noise of her own. Reed was quiet in the passenger seat, and she couldn't guess where his thoughts might be. At least he seemed convinced for now that she was not the killer.

The town rolled past like something out of an 8mm historical film, with cedar-shingled homes and winding roads and ten-story pines waving in the breeze. Woodbury's citizens had gathered at their separate places of worship, with half the cars lining Main Street by the white-steepled church and the other half crammed into the tiny Dunkin' Donuts lot on the corner. The two sides were united by their faded Red Sox bumper stickers—a higher power that everyone could get behind. She saw the Goldberg sisters, seventy-five if they were a day, sitting in plastic chairs outside the Friendly Suds laundry, drinking their coffee and trading sections of the Sunday *Globe* as they did every week at this time. One twin looked up at the sight of Ellery's truck and waved to her, but Ellie pretended not to see. No one would be waving once the story got out.

Reed straightened up when he realized she'd driven right on past the station house. "You know, Monica Jenkins is right about one thing," he said. "You want to get out in front of the story at least a little bit. You're going to have to tell Sam."

"I know it." Ellie didn't take her eyes from the road. "There's someone else I want to talk to first."

She came to a hard stop outside the Parker home, where the big weeping willow tree bowed and swayed, and the rows of red and white impatiens trembled in their beds. The house itself sat dark and silent under the rumbling sky. Ellie twisted in her seat as she searched the place for signs of life and wondered, not for the first time, what life was like on the inside. *Julia and me have more of a transactional relationship these days,* Sam had told her one night in bed at the motel. *We each do just enough to keep the other one's reality intact. I don't ask what she does with her money. She doesn't ask me what I do with my time.* Ellie hadn't really cared one way or another about Julia Parker; she was Sam's concern, and Sam never seemed too worried. Maybe, in hindsight, he should have been.

"Are we watching for something in particular?" Reed asked finally.

Ellie stroked the steering wheel in silence for a long moment. "When Julia said the other day that Shannon Blessing only had one OUI on her record, that didn't make sense to me. I knew she had been cited multiple times. But I looked it up, and Julia is right—there is only one official OUI in Shannon's file."

"So someone made the other citations disappear," Reed said, catching on, "and you think Julia knows who it was."

"I think if she knows, then there's only one person it could have been. I just want to hear her say it out loud."

Ellery climbed out of the truck and Reed followed. The air was so wet that the black tar of the driveway was already slick, despite the lack of rain. Wind slapped at her face and whipped her hair into her eyes. As they walked up toward the house, Ellery abruptly changed course to the garage. Julia's black SUV normally sat parked outside in the summer months, and it wasn't in the drive, so it was possible she was not at home. Ellery cupped her hands around her eyes and peered in the window of the garage. There sat Julia's Lexus, and something about the shape of it up close made Ellery shift to a different window for another perspective. Again, she put face up to the glass, which was coated in a light film of dirt and pollen. "Oh, my God," she murmured when she saw the dent in the right front panel. The damage lined up perfectly with Ellie's sore hip. *You'll get what's coming to you.*

"What? What is it?" Reed crowded in behind her so that he could look too. "Well," he said when he drew back, "do you suppose that's an imprint of our backsides there on the side panel, or is this just an astounding coincidence?"

Before Ellie could say anything, the front door opened and Julia Parker emerged, her pale pink cardigan flapping in the breeze. She shouted at them over the whoosh of the wind. "What are you doing? Get away from there!"

"Your car looks as though it's been in a recent accident, ma'am," Reed hollered back. "You might want to get that looked at."

"You're not supposed to be here! He told me you would not come back!"

Ellie found her voice at last. "It was Sam who made those arrests go away, wasn't it? He erased Shannon's record."

"Shannon Blessing was a whore."

Ellie could hear the unspoken tagline: *She got what she deserved*. Her heart started pounding as the truth became clear. "She slept with him and he fixed her problems for her. That's what happened, right?" Lonely Shannon Blessing, with her sad, smoky eyes and her large breasts and poor judgment. She'd been ripe for the picking. Ellie felt sick, for Shannon and for herself. She thought she'd been using Sam to get what she wanted, but maybe it was the other way around.

"You would know," Julia shot back. "You want to know what a whore looks like, you can just look in the mirror."

Ellie ignored the insult and pushed for the information she'd come for: "Did you see Shannon that day? The day she disappeared?"

"I went out of my way not to see her. She was trash! She was nothing." Her cry was an equal mix of anger and anguish. A distant crack of thunder split the air and fat raindrops began to fall, melting the summer heat.

Reed advanced closer to where Julia stood on the porch, hugging herself. Ellie hung back, leaving the storm to fill the space between her and Sam's wife. "How do you know? How do you know your husband was involved with Shannon?"

Julia tilted her face to the sky and the rain fell like tears. When she finally answered, her reply was for Ellery, not for Reed. "Oh, that's always the best part for Sam. That I know. He leaves a paper trail a mile long and a mile wide."

Thunder rolled the clouds around, closer this time to bowling them over, and the sky flickered with white flame. Ellery's shoes were filling up with water. "We should go," she said, nudging Reed.

Water flattened his hair to his face, accentuating his high cheekbones and hawk-like eyes. "We need the proof," he said urgently. Rain dripped from his chin. "We leave now and she could destroy everything."

On the stoop, Julia seemed to be dissolving under the weight of the water. "She's not going anywhere." If Julia Parker hadn't left Sam by now, she never would.

"She may have tried to kill us," Reed insisted, his back to Julia.

"And who are we going to call to arrest her—her husband?" Ellery shook her head. "Let's get out of here before we get hit by lightning." On cue, the sky cracked in half again, split by a bolt of electricity.

Reed was reluctant but eventually trailed Ellery back to the truck. The leather seats squeaked as they climbed inside with their sodden clothes. They sat there dripping, rain pounding like bullets on the roof, but Ellie did not start the engine. Julia had known the whole time, she realized, reeling with this shift in her universe. The little voice in her head was ironic and unamused: *You should have known you couldn't try to be someone else and get away with it.*

"I hesitate to grant any weight to the ravings of an angry wife harboring homicidal intentions," Reed began tentatively, but Ellery cut him off.

"I was sleeping with him," she said. "Sam. Not for very long. Not many times. But it happened."

"Ah." Reed leaned his wet head back against the seat. "That does explain some things—for example, the sizable bruise on my posterior."

Ellie felt her face go hot. "You have to understand. There are certain ways to get Sam's attention, and so I picked the one I thought would have the most success. He wasn't listening to me otherwise."

"And apparently Shannon Blessing reached the same conclusion," he said, but there was no judgment in his tone.

Ellery looked to the house, where Julia was still standing in the rain, staring out at Ellery's truck. The sheets of falling water obscured Julia's expression, but Ellie could feel her presence in a way she had not allowed herself to consider before. "Why won't she just go back inside?" she muttered as she clawed a hank of wet hair from her cheek.

Reed gave a ghost of a smile. "Because then you would win."

Ellery glanced over at him with a frown. "You sound like you speak from experience."

Reed seemed to contemplate this for a long minute. "I did not cheat on my wife with any live women," he replied at last as he plucked several tissues from the box between them and blotted his face and neck.

"That's a creepy way to put it," Ellery answered.

He grimaced and shook his head. "Oh, I didn't cheat on her with any dead women either, not in the biblical sense. But I was away from home for weeks at a time working cases, and I guess you could say I saved the best parts of myself for the job. I cheated my family by giving them only the scraps I had left available after another exhausting case. Sarit is strong and smart and fully capable of running her own life. She didn't need me in the same way the victims did, or at least that's what I told myself."

"And what did she tell you?"

His eyes crinkled with his rueful reply. "She told me to pack my things and move out. No, that's not fair. She said other things before that, but I didn't stop long enough to listen."

Ellery looked beyond him into the rain and saw that Julia had disappeared from the porch. "Sam said she'd long since stopped caring what he did with his time, but I guess maybe he said a lot of things that weren't true."

"That beer bottle you found in the woods behind your house—did it by chance belong to Sam Parker?"

Ellery answered with a short nod and then hung her head. "He told me to make it go away, that our affair coming to light would hurt me as much as it hurt him."

"I reckon he's incorrect on that assumption," Reed said dryly.

Ellery shivered, suddenly cold as well as wet. Her relationship with Sam was now the least of the secrets coming to light. "I suppose we have to go tell him the truth."

"Maybe he already knows." Reed turned his head slowly to look at her. "Have you thought about that? He's seen your scars up close and might have had occasion to wonder, especially if he was familiar with the cursory details of the Coben case. As Ms. Jenkins so ably proved to us this morning, the connections are obvious when you know where to look."

"No," Ellery said swiftly. She started the engine with shaking fingers and turned up the heater to warm the inside cabin. Outside, the storm battered the truck with gusts of wet rain, turning the streets around them into shallow, rushing rivers. "No, not Sam."

"I can't help but notice we keep ending up here," Reed continued. "First Mark Roy disappears from the area, and now we find out Shannon Blessing may have had an intimate relationship with Sam Parker. Plus, he certainly had a relationship with you, one where you weren't giving him everything he wanted. If he somehow figured out your connection to Coben . . ."

"No," Ellery said, more certain this time. "He didn't know."

"You can't be sure of that."

"You heard Julia. The best part for Sam is that she knows. If he figured out this huge thing about me, he would've made sure I knew that he knew."

"The birthday cards," Reed pointed out. "Those texts. Someone is definitely sending you a message, Ellie."

Happy birthday. I know it's you. Ellery held her hands up to the heater to try to put some feeling back in her fingers. "Maybe," she conceded after a moment, the word barely more than a whisper. Someone had to get close enough to take her DNA to put on those cards. "But what are you really saying? That you think Sam is behind the abductions?" Surely he must realize how insane that sounded.

"It's not a perfect fit," Reed agreed. "From what I can tell, Sam Parker enjoys power as far as it goes but isn't interested in fighting too hard to achieve or maintain it. He took a chief's job in a small town where he gets to be the boss with no daily challenges to his authority. He probably resents the money his wife brings to their relationship but enjoys its benefits, so instead of ending the marriage, he demonstrates his anger through serial infidelity. But he's lazy about it. He doesn't pursue his extramarital partners but takes advantage of the women who come his way. This suggests a man who is willing to abuse his bully pulpit when he has the opportunity but doesn't go out of his way to seek new subordinates. Abducting three healthy adults is a lot of work, when you get down to it, and that's the piece of the puzzle that doesn't quite fit here."

Ellie blinked, awed and a bit rattled by Reed's incisive commentary. "Can you do that for just anyone?" she asked, wondering what he would have to say about her.

Reed was still concentrating on his own thoughts and did not seem to hear her. "But we can't discard his obvious connections to two of the three victims—and to you—and I have to say: if we're wondering why Bea Nesbit might have pulled over late at night, other than for someone she knew, you could imagine that flashing blue lights might have done the trick."

Ellery said nothing to this. She shifted the truck into gear, and it practically floated down the road into the flash floods. The storm had reached a climax over Woodbury, pounding the earth like a prizefighter delivering the knockout blows, as the trees bent in tremulous submission. She wondered which of them would be left standing when it was finally over.

By the time they reached the station, the storm had lessened to a steady rain, with just occasional gusts of wind, and so Ellery and Reed still had to run a gauntlet of reporters with microphones and umbrellas. They shouted questions at her that Ellie did not let herself hear. She hummed under her breath to block out the noise and then gasped with relief as she made it inside the building. Their wet sneakers squeaked across the linoleum floor of the entryway as Ellie used her ID to open the door to the inner bullpen. She stopped short on the threshold when she met the charged atmosphere on the other side.

The men were all there—Sam, Jimmy Tipton, Chuck Taylor, and the others—watching the old TV set mounted in the corner. "Fox News Special Report," the screen read across the bottom, and Ellie recognized immediately the Missing poster Monica Jenkins had shown her this morning. They all turned their heads in unison to stare at Ellery, and maybe at Reed too, as he was standing behind her, his breathing heightened as he realized what was going on. No one said anything, so Monica's voice from the TV filled the silence. "Abigail Hathaway switched to her middle name, Ellery, when she was in college at Williams, where she majored in history and is remembered as a quiet but serious student."

Ellie's mouth dropped open as she saw her freshman-year roommate, Orla Boone, come onto the screen. "She was more of a loner, I would say. I never knew anything about her past. Ellery barely spoke to any of us. She was the only one who didn't put up pictures from home or anything like that."

"Is it true?" Sam's eyes were dark, his jaw set.

Ellie lifted her chin a fraction and stood her ground. "Yes, I decorated my side of the room with posters of the Clash."

"Don't get cute with me," he snapped. "I mean the rest of it."

Ellie saw this was going to be her punishment, having this conversation out in the open in front of everyone. "Yes," she said quietly. "It's true."

"Someone drops off a severed hand on your doorstep, and you don't think to mention maybe there's a reason for that?" Sam seemed both angry and flabbergasted, as though he didn't have the tools to consider such a breach of protocol. He looked behind her to Reed. "And, you, Agent Markham, you kept all this to yourself, even as I had to go over and tell the Nesbits that someone carved up their daughter?"

"We didn't know there was a connection at first," Ellery began.

"Oh, that's a load of horseshit, Ellie, so don't even try. You go around for years peddling this theory about how there is a murderer in town, abducting people off our streets, and you never once mentioned that you have some relevant experience in this area. Maybe if you explained exactly what was going on, we all might have listened a little harder."

"Chief, if I may," Reed cut in. "You must understand that Ellery was in a very vulnerable position here."

"All the more reason she should have opened her mouth and said something!" Sam replied, his voice growing bigger, until it seemed to cover everything. "You said these people were dying, Ellie, but you didn't tell me that they were all going missing the same time you were abducted! When Bea's hand showed up, even then you didn't mention that *oh, by the way* this was a coded message from some deranged psychopath who might be aping one of the sickest, most famous serial killers the country has ever seen. We could've been way out ahead of him by now. Maybe we could've caught him. If this son of a bitch takes another victim, it's on you, Ellie. It's on you and your silence."

She stiffened as if he'd slapped her. Reed's hand clenched into a fist. "Now hold on, that's not fair," he said.

"I'll tell you what's not fair! I've got three people missing, probably dead, and it turns out the key to figuring out this mess might be one of my own officers, and I'm about the last person to find out about it. My ass is hanging in the breeze on national television. How the hell am I supposed to convince anyone I can run these investigations when I don't even know what's going on in my own unit? Jesus Christ." He held his head with both hands and then shook it as if to clear his thoughts. "You," he said, pointing to Reed, "you come in here and tell me absolutely everything about the Francis Coben case. Leave nothing out this time, not one goddamn detail."

Ellery felt the tension radiating from Reed, that he wanted to fight the order, but he stepped forward anyway. "Yes, sir. Happy to answer any questions," he said tersely.

Ellie moved to follow him, but Sam held up a hand to her. "Not you. You stay out here and go over the reports from the abductions, starting with Bea Nesbit and leading up to the discovery of her hand, and you add anything—I mean *anything*—that you left out the first time. You sit right there at your desk and you don't leave the building without my say-so. You definitely do not talk to the press. Do you understand?"

Ellie froze, acutely aware that everyone was still watching and that she was standing on Sam's turf. She was not without ammunition—the beer bottle, the odd suppression of Shannon's records, and Julia's attempt to kill her the night before—but it was mostly supposition without hard evidence at this point, and revealing it out in the open would tip off Sam and probably make her look like a lunatic to everyone else. So she forced a curt nod to Sam and went to her desk, watching as Reed disappeared into the chief's office. When the door shut, it was like air returned to the room, and the other officers resumed their work. All except Jimmy Tipton, who ambled over to her.

"Holy shit, Hathaway," he said as he planted his ass on the corner of her desk. "That is some story you've been hiding. You know, I saw one of Coben's photos when I visited my cousin out in Chicago a few years ago. Must've been around the tenth anniversary of the case. One of the museums had a big spread dedicated to the story, with news clippings and pictures and interviews. There wasn't anything in there about you."

"My name was kept out of it," she said, not looking at him. She had pulled out Bea's file to go over it again, as the chief had ordered. Only this time, she was going to be looking for any evidence that a cop might be involved.

"They said he nailed his victims into the closet. Is that why you've got all those nails at your place?"

The words made her freeze, long enough to forget about her current task, long enough to hear his previous statement echo inside her head. *I visited my cousin out in Chicago*. Ellie looked up and fixed him with a hard stare. "I didn't know you were from Chicago," she said.

"I'm from Philly, born and raised. But I got some family out in Chi-town. They aren't going to believe it when I tell them about you." Tipton slid off her desk, but he didn't move away. He loomed over her, casting a shadow across her desk. He clapped a hand on her shoulder, making her jump. "Good on you, Ellie, taking Coben down like that. You're a lot tougher than you look. Who knows? Maybe you'll get the next one too."

After more than an hour, Reed emerged from the chief's office, pink cheeked and grim, looking like a boy who'd just escaped the principal. He dragged a chair over to Ellie's desk and sat next to her. "Well," he said, taking a deep breath, "if Sam Parker knew the whole story before this, he's putting on an excellent show to the contrary. He is well and truly pissed off right now."

Ellery tightened her hold on her pen, scratching in the margins of the notes she'd been making. She could only imagine the questions Sam had asked. "I've been through Bea Nesbit's file again," she said, "and there is nothing new here that I can see. There's nothing I can add. Believe me, if I thought I had direct knowledge that would help this case, I would have outed myself to Sam long ago."

"I know." Reed looked distracted. "He's on the phone with the state investigators now. They're probably going to want to go another round with you. With me, too, for that matter."

"Great." Ellie threw down her pen in disgust. "What a waste of everyone's time that will be." She folded her arms and sat back in her chair, regarding the pile of folders on her desk. "You know, back when I was a kid, after it happened, I used to wonder how it took everyone so long to find him. It was on the news all the time. The whole city was looking for this guy—the entire Chicago Police Department on high alert, and yet Coben kept taking girls off the street like he was invisible. Now I think I get it: he was hiding behind all this paperwork." She shoved at it halfheartedly for good measure, sending a cascade of folders across the desk.

Reed looked at the mess for a moment and then pulled his

chair closer to hers. "Back in the early 1970s," he said in a low voice that was just between the two of them, "detectives in Santa Cruz, California, were confronted by a series of brutal murders. Some victims were college girls, hitchhiking. One was a homeless man beaten to death with a baseball bat. At one particularly gruesome scene, officers found an entire family shot and stabbed in their own home. There seemed to be no pattern, no rhyme or reason to the victims. The killer used different methods, and police could decipher no motive beyond a simple desire to kill. Only in hindsight, when one was caught and the other turned himself in to authorities, did everyone see the truth: Santa Cruz had been the hunting ground for two serial offenders who happened to be active at the same time."

Ellery sat forward, intrigued. "You think there is more than one killer at work here?"

Reed shook his head. "Odds are against it. My point is that you can be nearly sure that the answer is in that paperwork somewhere, but it may be difficult to see unless you can guess the right angle. Just to add to the stack, I've requested all the old files from the Coben case. Some I can review electronically; copies of the rest of them should be couriered over this afternoon."

"What are you looking for?"

Reed sighed. "I don't honestly know. I only hope I recognize it when I find it."

They passed hours this way, with Ellie dutifully writing up the reports on the birthday cards and combing through the missing persons reports for any bit of information that had been overlooked. There was none. Reed hunched over his laptop at one end of her desk, scrolling through old information from the Francis Coben investigation. They took turns getting grilled in Sam's office by the state investigators, who were frustrated both by their withholding of the Coben connection and by their inability to substantially add to the case.

Reed and Ellie remained chained to the Woodbury station house while the rest of the department churned around them. Ellie could feel the men trying not to stare at her as they trooped in and out from their work attending to the damage done by the storm and minding the crime scene over at the Franklin household. At one point, Chuck Taylor stopped by with bottled water and sandwiches for her and Reed. He dropped off the food and then loomed over her, as if there was more he wanted to say, and Ellie steeled herself for another round of intrusive questions. Chuck waited a beat longer and then he set a small package wrapped in tinfoil on the edge of her desk. "It's banana bread," he said, sounding sheepish. "Yolanda made it for you when she saw the news. I tried to tell her this wasn't 'zactly a bread-baking occasion, but she insisted you have it."

Ellie looked at it and found herself suddenly blinking back tears. "Tell her thank you," she managed after a beat.

Chuck nodded at her. "You hang in there," he said, and then strolled away.

At that moment, Sam stuck his head out of his office. "Ellery, can I see you, please?" The request was reasoned and free from the acid that had characterized all their earlier interactions, so Ellie rose and slowly walked across the room.

"Chief?" she said from the door.

"Come in and shut the door behind you."

Ellie shut the door as asked but did not sit down. "Before you say anything, I wanted to ask if I could please leave briefly to tend to my dog. I can leave him with a friend, but he needs walking and fresh water."

Sam nodded wearily and sank into his chair. "Sure, fine." He didn't say anything else for a long time, and Ellie shifted uncomfortably from one foot to the other. He looked her over, squinting at the bandage on her arm as if seeing it for the first time. "What happened to you?"

She considered a few replies. "Better ask your wife."

"What?"

"Never mind. What did you want to see me for?"

"I, uh, I wanted to apologize for jumping all over you like I did this morning. You should've told me what was going on, but I lost my temper and I said some things I shouldn't have." He cleared his throat and shifted some papers around on his desk, not looking at her. "Agent Markham told me a little bit about what you went through, and I looked up some old reports on the Internet . . ."

Her face burned and her vision swam as she realized he was feeling sorry for her. She swallowed twice in quick succession. "I don't really want to talk about it." Ellie clasped her hands behind her back, hiding her scars from his vision and her own. "Apology accepted, okay? Now if I can just run out—"

"Rosalie Franklin died an hour ago."

Ellie stopped short. Sam's eyes were large with sympathy.

"Her mother has come down from New Hampshire to take Anna, and we'll be filing murder charges against Darryl tomorrow morning." He took a deep, shuddering breath. "I just thought you ought to know."

"Thanks," she said tightly, which seemed like a terrible reply to news of someone's death, especially a murder, but it was all she could force out before fleeing the office, the station, and pack of frenzied reporters who ran with her to her truck. They surrounded her on all sides, shouting questions, shoving cameras in her windows so that she could move forward only inches at a time for fear of running them over. "Ellery! Ellie! How does it feel to be the only one who survived Francis Coben? How did you know

Bea Nesbit was dead?" They were a force that pulled her harder the more she struggled to escape, like quicksand, keeping her stuck in the parking lot and mired in her past. When at last, finally, she hit the road, she peeled away as fast as she could, her head down and her wheels kicking up a wave of water. She knew if she checked her rearview mirror she would still find the reporters there, too close behind.

Dogs are the cure for whatever ails you, Ellie thought as she pulled into the Angelman Animal Shelter with Speed Bump panting happily at her side. Bump had let her hug him and pet his soft, floppy ears and bury her face in his short, silky fur. He didn't care what had happened to her in the past or who knew her secrets now. He lived in the moment, and at that moment, he was tail-up, tongue-hanging, delighted to be trotting in to see some of his favorite people. The feeling was obviously mutual as the older woman at the front desk came out from behind the counter to greet them. "Is that Mr. Bump, I see?" She knelt down and rubbed his ears as he pranced around in appreciation.

"Hi, Kiki. It's been awhile. How are you and Carmen doing these days?" Carmen was the director of the shelter, and Kiki sometimes lent a hand as free labor. The fact that she was on site now, on a Sunday, suggested there was some sort of crisis afoot.

"Oh, we're good," the woman said, still focused on lavishing attention on the dog. "If you're looking for Brady, he's actually out with Carmen now. They had to go over to Worcester to bail out the Third Street Shelter. The storm knocked their power out and they have an overflow of animals, so we're taking in a few since we have the room at the moment. Do you mind if I give this handsome devil a cookie?"

At the word "cookie," Bump offered an enthusiastic woof, and

Ellie couldn't suppress a smile. "I think he's already made his opinion clear. It's okay by me." Kiki went to the counter to fetch a dog biscuit from the jar, Bump wagging after her. "You're easy," Ellie called after her dog. "You know that, right?"

The front door swept open on a gust of wind, and Carmen and Brady entered, armed with several animal carriers. Bump immediately went to sniff at the new arrivals, and Ellie had to hold him back as the cats and dogs in the crates hissed and barked through the slats. "Ellery," Carmen said warmly, "how nice to see you—and the Bump, too, of course. Will you please excuse us while we get these new guys settled in back?"

They wrestled the menagerie through the door, and Ellery waited a few minutes before wandering back in search of Brady. She found him securing a last water bottle in place while the resident black cat lurked in the back, giving him the evil eye. Brady's hair was wet and his sneakers were covered in mud and wet grass. He looked even younger than usual, which was pretty young in the first place, given that Ellie had a few years on him. "Hey," he said, grinning at her. "Check out my new shirt."

He swiveled so she could read his T-shirt. It depicted an old oil painting of some long-haired man from the nineteenth century, and over it sat the words YOU MAY DANCE, IF YOU FANCY IT. YOU MAY ALSO TAKE LEAVE OF YOUR COMPANIONS. FOR IF YOUR COMPANIONS DO NOT DANCE, THEY SHAN'T BE COMPANIONS OF MINE.

Brady spread his arms. "Pretty sweet, eh?"

"You're the worst," she said, rolling her eyes.

"You say that, and yet I feel like you're here to ask me a favor."

"Yeah, could you watch Bump for me for a while? I have some stuff going on at work."

Brady sobered and scratched the back of his neck with one hand. "I heard." There was an awkward silence. "You never said anything."

She scuffed at the cement floor with one shoe. "I wanted to put it behind me. I didn't want everyone to look at me and see Francis Coben, to think about what he did. To think about me like I'm a victim."

"I suppose I can see that. You still could have told me, though."

"Maybe," she said, feeling guilty because she didn't really mean it. To tell even one person was to keep the story alive. "It doesn't matter now anyway. Everyone knows."

Brady tugged up his shirt with one hand, and she could see several small, round scars on his abdomen. "My mother did this to me," he said. "I was three years old."

"Oh, my God," Ellery said. "Brady, I'm so—"

"We're the same, you and me." There was a fervent, purposeful look in his eye, one she had never seen before. "I knew it when I met you, and now I understand why. We're survivors. So fuck 'em. Anyone who wants to judge you over this? Fuck. Them." He blinked several times, and suddenly the grin was back. He gestured at his shirt. "If your friends don't dance, Ellie, they're no friends of mine."

That night, Reed tried to convince Ellie to stay at the motel with him, but she insisted on returning to her house, where the press sat camped at the end of her long driveway, tangling traffic on Burning Tree Road. Thanks to the trees, she would not be able to see them from her windows. Reed refused to let her stay alone, so he picked up groceries and another change of clothes and joined her back at the house. He took over the kitchen, and soon the air was filled with the scent of sautéed garlic and spicy tomato sauce. Ellie left him to his work and went to her bedroom, where she took up the hammer and the nails and pounded the door back into place. The noise and the violence felt liberating as she used her anger to bang each nail into submission. She was sweating and breathing hard, her hair in her eyes, by the time she was finished.

Reed appeared in the doorway. "Supper's on," he said, and they looked at each other. His gaze flickered to the closet and back to her. "Sorry for that."

There was regret and sorrow in the words, layers of meaning that were almost too much for her to bear. Sorry for trespassing. Sorry for the fact that she still felt the need to nail her demons in the closet. Sorry for what happened to her in another closet, years ago. Ellie let the hammer slip from her hands to the floor. "Let's eat, then."

Over pasta puttanesca, she told him that she'd looked up the cases in Santa Cruz that he had referenced earlier. "Herbert Mullin was just plain crazy," she said. "Killing people to try to prevent an earthquake. It makes no sense."

"It rarely does. They have their reasons for killing, but they typically aren't rational reasons. This is why catching them can be so difficult."

"Yeah, well, that other guy, Edmund Kemper, it seems like he was tortured by his mother until he just snapped. He killed a bunch of people and then after he killed his mother, he pretty much stopped. He called the cops and turned himself in. Makes you think it was his mother who he wanted dead all along—everyone else was just collateral damage."

"You wouldn't be the first one to reach that conclusion," Reed agreed as he reached for his water.

"Which one do you think is our guy? The crazy one or the one who just keeps going until he gets the right victim?"

"We might not know that until we catch him."

"I had an idea today," she said slowly, "while I was going through the three missing persons files. The only concrete bit of new information we've had in three years is that Shannon Blessing was at the gas station with Bea Nesbit the night she disappeared—meaning she was potentially some sort of witness, but of course we didn't know that, so no one ever interviewed her."

"Right."

"But I was thinking about that, and Shannon might not just be any old witness—she could have been the last person to see Bea alive that night. If you read the file on Shannon's disappearance, Mark Roy was not only the guy who reported her missing, he was also the last person to see her. She signed for that package, remember? No one is on record of having seen her after that."

"So Shannon was the last living witness for Bea, and Mark was the last witness for Shannon." Reed had put down his fork and his brow was wrinkled in concentration. "Interesting, but I'm not sure what it means."

"I don't know either, except maybe Julia Parker should watch herself. She was the last person to see Mark Roy before he disappeared last year."

Reed opened his mouth to say something, but she never found out what it was, because they both heard the sound of a car rolling up outside. *Please no reporters,* she thought as she rubbed her head. But the frantic banging on her front door a moment later did not sound like it came from the press.

Reed and Ellie's eyes met in shared recognition and unease. If you worked in law enforcement, you knew trouble when you heard it, especially when it came knock-knocking on your front door. They went to answer it, and Ellie found Sam standing on the other side, looking wild-eyed and panicked. "Julia's gone," he said. "Her car's in the garage but I can't find her anywhere. She isn't answering her phone. It's like . . . it's like she just vanished."

10

Reed rode along with Ellery in her truck to the Parkers' house, where they parked in the exact spot they had occupied earlier in the day, when Julia had stood in the rain and watched them. They took their industrial-strength flashlights and followed Sam across the darkened yard. The ground beneath their feet was sodden from the storm, redolent of wet earth and grass, and a passing breeze shook water from the trees. The house itself was lit up like a birthday cake, every single window ablaze with light. Reed could envision Sam going room by room in search of Julia, his steps quickening as each flick of the switch failed to turn up any sign of his wife. Reed did not typically participate in the early frantic searches; by the time he showed up at a scene, everyone already feared the worst.

"She usually prepares dinner starting around six," Sam was saying as he let them in through the front door, "but the salmon is still marinating in the fridge. At first I thought maybe she had run out to the store, but then I saw her purse here in the kitchen, and when I checked the garage, her car was still there."

Reed put aside the fact that Julia had likely used the car to try to, at best, scare the pants off him and Ellie the other night, and at worst, send them to an early grave. In fact, under typical situations, he would dismiss Sam Parker's concerns as premature. Julia Parker was angry, possibly unstable, and wounded by the knowledge that Sam was cheating on her—again. She could very well have run off to drink herself into oblivion, or have gone to vent to a friend about what a prize jackass her husband turned out to be. Maybe she had wanted to send Sam a message, shake him up a little.

Except the town had already seen three people go missing, and given the current circumstances, it seemed wiser to presume that anyone who disappeared from Woodbury might be returned to the town in pieces. "No sign of forced entry?" Reed asked as they walked through the kitchen. "Nothing out of place?"

"Nothing," Sam said, spreading his arms helplessly. "It's like she just walked out the door and didn't come back."

"Maybe she did," Ellie said tartly, echoing Reed's thoughts.

Reed glanced around at the large kitchen and had to agree it seemed undisturbed. Julia Parker either cared a lot about appearances or she loved to cook, because the space reminded Reed of home. It was done up gourmet style, with an extensive knife block, a wide wooden cutting board, a dual oven, and a deep, farmhouse sink. The pots and pans hung over the expansive granite-topped island. The only sign that Julia had been there at all was an overturned coffee mug with the Daughters of the American Revolution insignia on it sitting in the drying rack by the sink.

"She called me around midday," Sam said, his voice tight. "I told her I couldn't talk then and that I'd see her at home for dinner."

"Does she have friends in the area she might have gone to

see?" Reed asked. "Family? Someone could have stopped by to pick her up."

"I made some calls. No one has seen her. But she barely goes to the mailbox without her purse."

They walked the house, the three of them, although Ellery hung back and seemed reluctant to touch anything. She trod so lightly that the floorboards made almost no noise under her feet. Sam opened and closed the closets, as though Julia might be playing some cruel children's trick, and Ellery flinched visibly as he flung open each door. "She's not here," Sam said, his expression strained, his voice taking on a note of desperation. "I've searched from top to bottom already. We've got to figure out what happened to her. If someone . . . if someone took her, where did they go?"

Reed looked to Ellie, and she looked at the floor.

"Well, come on, tell me!" Sam demanded. "I know the two of you have been working on your own theories about these disappearances. You must have something you're not sharing!"

There was a tense moment of silence, and then Ellery cleared her throat. "We think it's possible that the kidnapper is repeating a pattern of sorts." She explained her observation that each subsequent victim appeared to be the last living witness to the previous year's disappearance. "If that's true, and if Julia is part of that pattern," she continued, "then her abduction had been planned for a while."

"For a year," Sam said, both horrified and amazed. "You knew this was coming and you never said anything?"

He advanced on Ellie, who stiffened and took a step back. Reed put himself bodily between them. "It's just a theory," he said. "And one we only determined a few hours ago."

Sam's nostrils flared, his face flushed with fury, and for a second, Reed thought he might take a fist to the teeth. "Well, screw your theory," Sam spat out. "He's not going to get away with it this time, you understand me? I'll call in the damn National Guard if I have to, but I'm going house to house until I find her."

Sam stalked off to use the phone, leaving Reed and Ellery standing in his wife's living room, with her carefully chosen paisley sofa and coordinated forest green armchairs. There was a floral arrangement on the coffee table, roses and lilies that were just beginning to fade around the edges. Reed picked up a book sitting on the end table next to a delicate porcelain lamp. It was not a title he recognized, but the stamp on the front said it had been endorsed by Oprah once upon a time. Reed fingered the bookmark stuck roughly one-third from the end, the place where Julia had stopped. "What do you think happened?" Ellery asked him softly.

In the other room, Sam was hollering into the phone. Reed set Julia's book down where she had left it and drifted toward the windows, where the panes only reflected his image back to him. "They don't see him coming," he said, because he felt sure now their offender was a male. "He doesn't seem dangerous at first, possibly because they know him, possibly because he has created a situation that feels normal to them—maybe he's a deliveryman or a repairman, or, as we were theorizing earlier, someone in law enforcement." He turned to look at her, and she was listening, wide-eyed. "They let him in, and now he has the element of surprise on his side. They're relaxed, on their own turf. They don't suspect he is there to do them harm."

He began walking toward the front door, and Ellie followed.

"Maybe he overpowers and incapacitates them, but I tend not to think so."

"Why?"

Reed kept walking, retracing the path Julia and her captor likely took. "He's abducted several people during daylight hours.

Even if he has the physical strength to carry them away from the scene, he risks calling attention to himself. More likely he convinces them to leave under their own power, either by forcing them to cooperate by use of a weapon or some other direct threat, or by creating a ruse to get them to come quickly." At these words, Reed opened the front door and stepped out into the thick humid air. He stood where Julia had watched them from the porch and surveyed the shadowed lawn. Frogs and bugs chattered back and forth at each other in the trees.

"Eventually, though, they're going to realize something isn't right," Reed said as he started down the driveway. "They'll see through the trick. But by then it's too late and they've progressed too far into the trap to be able to work free—it's his turf now, his fantasy. He's had a year to plan out all the details."

They walked down the rain-slicked driveway to the edge of the street, which was dark and quiet in both directions. Ellery shone her flashlight first one way and then the other. "And we have no idea where he's taking them," she said.

"Someplace where they can be alone. Somewhere no one is watching or listening."

Ellery shivered and switched off her flashlight, enveloping them in darkness once more. "It's been three years so far, and we haven't found him yet."

"True." Reed cast a look back at the house, where Sam was visible through the windows, pacing in the kitchen as he talked on the phone. "But at least this time, you aren't the only one looking."

True to his word, Sam Parker pulled out all the stops in his search for his wife. Law enforcement officers from neighboring communities poured into Woodbury, swarming the streets and overwhelming the local coffee shop. Paper cups piled up around the station, stacked three deep on desks and ledges, and flowing like a waterfall out of every wastebasket. Reed had switched to bottled water an hour ago because he feared his blood was now fifty percent caffeine. He punched a few keys in his laptop and brought up another blank-faced mug shot of a guy busted six years ago for sexual assault in Springfield, Massachusetts. The victim said she had met the offender at a local bar, where they spent a few hours together, after which she agreed to go back to his apartment for another round. Once there, he pulled out a switchblade and threatened to rape her, but a neighbor heard her screaming and called 911. The reason Reed was looking at the case at all had to do with a single line in the woman's statement: *He threatened to cut off my hands if I didn't cooperate.*

Across the room, Ellery was on the phone, fielding tips from the general public. She had chewed off the end of her pen in the process, and Reed knew she wasn't pleased with the assignment or his role in suggesting it for her, but the truth was they had a killer out there somewhere who was eager for her attention. If the guy wanted to make contact with her, Reed would prefer that he have to come down to the police station to do it. Ellery had reluctantly agreed with this logic, but she did not look happy about it. "You don't know how this looks," she told him earlier, as the rest of her unit trooped in and out, reporting back on their futile searches. "Everyone else is out there looking for Julia, and I'm stuck behind my desk."

"I'm not really concerned with the optics," he'd told her. "The rest of them didn't have a human hand special delivered to their doorstep. Besides, we practically have front-row seats right here." He gestured up at the television, which was on mute but playing what looked like live footage of the ongoing helicopter search.

The press had doubled seemingly overnight, as the New York reporters rolled in with their bigger budgets and wider audiences. The story was now national news.

Midafternoon, the door swept open with a burst of noise from the reporters outside, all of them clamoring after Chief Parker himself. Parker looked grim and haggard, dressed in yesterday's clothes, skin sagging on his face. "Anything?" he asked Ellery.

She blinked twice and shook her head. "We've sent out units on a couple of leads—your neighbor Barbara Winter said she heard a prowler last night—but nothing has panned out. Chuck says it looks like a raccoon was after her garbage."

Parker nodded dumbly and shuffled over to where Reed was sitting with his notepad and laptop. "I thought you FBI types could read these guys' minds by now. Don't they make whole television shows about that? You should be able to whip up a personality profile and think like him long enough to figure out where he took Julia."

"I wish it worked like that."

Parker rubbed his face with both hands. "I keep thinking— what's he doing to her? What's happening to her right now?"

Reed saw Ellie look away, as if removing herself from the conversation. He wished he could do the same. "We're going to keep looking," he told the chief, because it was the one thing he could promise. "Don't give up."

"'Course not." Parker scoffed as he looked down at him. He rapped his hand on the edge of Reed's desk. "Ellie had been gone for three days when you found her, right? We've still got time."

He stalked away, and Reed risked a glance at Ellery. Her gaze remained trained on the wall, but he saw her shake her head, almost imperceptibly, because she could have told Parker the truth: if they were counting on her eleventh-hour rescue for their salvation, then they were already damned.

As the day wore on, amber light shafting in from the high narrow windows of the station was the only sign of the passing hours, as inside, the atmosphere remained unchanged. Phones rang. Men and women from law enforcement came and went. Jimmy Tipton was coordinating a new search team to investigate the nearby Wendell Forest. Crime scene investigators scoured the Parkers' home for a second time. The only thing they found was Julia's cell phone, steeped in a dirty puddle halfway down the street—a clue that led precisely nowhere.

Reed's face was so tight from fatigue he felt like it might crack in half if he yawned. He turned bleary eyes to Ellery and saw she had her head down on her desk next to the phone. They had been awake for more than twenty-four hours straight. He was about to suggest they go back to her place to get a few hours of rest, a possibly foolish plan in some senses, seeing as how her property was one of the few places that they could be sure the killer had visited, but between the horde of reporters now following their every move and the throng of men and women in blue spread out around the town, Reed felt reasonably sure it would be safe. He powered down his computer and was about to gather his notes when the station house door opened again, and Russ McGreevy stepped inside.

Reed sank back in his seat as Russell "Puss" McGreevy approached. "Puss," he said by way of greeting. "Guess you must have seen the news."

Reed had always thought that if Puss McGreevy had been an actual cat, he would be an Abyssinian; he was fastidious, with close-cropped silver hair, an alert, assessing gaze, and above-average intellect. But the nickname did not have to do with

McGreevy's appearance or his attitude; rather, it dated to a story from fifteen years ago, when McGreevy had participated in the rescue of a teenage girl who had been kidnapped by her neighbor. The man had murdered the girl's parents but for some reason took the family cat with him as he fled with the child toward Mexico. The standoff in a border town had ended in a hail of gunfire that left the abductor dead and two agents wounded. The girl was miraculously unharmed, and when the smoke cleared, legend had it, there was McGreevy, holding the cat. He had taken some friendly ribbing about it over the years, but everyone who knew the whole story understood McGreevy's critical contribution. The girl had been terrorized and assaulted, and her parents were dead. Puss couldn't fix a damn bit of that mess, but he could give her back her cat.

McGreevy's mouth was a thin line as he took in Reed's rumpled clothes and day-old stubble. "You're supposed to be on leave," he said finally.

Reed, punch-drunk from exhaustion, spread his hands expansively. "I did leave. I left the whole damn state."

"You know, a phone call would have been nice. A simple heads-up."

"I was here on my own time."

"That's crap and you know it." The others in the room, who had not been paying much attention to the latest arrival, snapped to attention at McGreevy's angry tone. "You come up here and go flashing your federal ID around town, you damn well better let us know what the hell you're up to—especially if you're going to invoke a name like Francis Coben."

Maybe it was habit by now, but Reed stood up the instant McGreevy said the name, planting himself between his boss and Ellie Hathaway. "Special circumstances in this case," he said. "It's rapidly evolving."

"So I gather. You know how I found out about it? I found out when Warden Mike Driscoll from Terre Haute called us to say Coben tried to sneak an unauthorized letter into his outgoing mail this morning. Guess where it was addressed? Right here."

"What? Coben tried to make contact?"

Ellie materialized from behind Reed. "What did it say? The letter."

McGreevy jerked his attention toward Ellie as if seeing her for the first time. Reed said, "Puss, allow me to introduce Officer Ellery Hathaway. You may remember her as Abigail. Ellie, this is my boss, Agent Russell McGreevy."

"Oh, right. Yes, of course." McGreevy looked surprised, although surely he must have expected her. Maybe he was still seeing that fourteen-year-old girl from the closet. "How do you do, Ms. Hathaway? It's wonderful to see you looking so well."

Ellie ignored his pleasantries. "What did the letter say?"

McGreevy checked nonverbally with Reed, who kept his gaze neutral. "Maybe we should discuss this privately first," McGreevy suggested to Reed. "The two of us."

"I want to see it," Ellie insisted.

"I can appreciate that, but I'm afraid the letter is currently classified."

"It's from Coben? Then I think I've got a right to see it."

Reed held up a hand. "Ellie, could you excuse us for just one moment? Thank you." He nudged McGreevy over to the far wall, where the two men turned their backs on the rest of the station. "What is the deal here with this letter?"

"Probably nothing. You know how these guys operate. Coben saw the news reports and seized any opportunity he could to make himself part of the story."

"Looks to me like it worked." He gestured at the folders McGreevy had in his hands. "What did he have to say?"

"Nothing of obvious evidentiary value, but given the circumstances here in Woodbury, the warden felt he had to flag it up for us." McGreevy hesitated. "The original's still in Terre Haute," he said as he pulled out a standard envelope from one of the folders. He handed it to Reed, who opened it to reveal three folded sheets of paper. The top one was a photocopy of the envelope with the Woodbury PD address on the front, and one important additional detail: it was addressed to Ellery Hathaway.

"It's got Ellie's name on it."

"Yes, she's the intended recipient."

"Well, then, we're the ones tampering with her mail, aren't we? That's a federal crime, if I recollect correctly."

McGreevy scowled. "It never entered the U.S. postal system so there's no crime being committed here. Jesus Christ, Reed, you've talked to Coben how many times? You know him as well as anyone, and you really want her to read this thing?"

Reed closed his eyes briefly. None of this was anything he ever wanted. "I think," he said at last, "it isn't up to me." He walked back to where Ellery was standing, arms folded and pissed about not being included in the federal tête-à-tête. "This is the letter," he told her quietly, his eyes locked on hers. "It's addressed to you and so you've a right to read it if you choose to. But before you do, I think you should consider that it's unlikely to be anything other than Coben looking for any small way he can to get back into your life. Into your head. And you can choose to say no."

Ellie searched his face as she digested this information. "Did you read it?" she asked finally.

"No, not yet."

She waited another beat, her gaze shifting to the papers in his hand. "But you will."

There was a time when he would have seized upon the letter with intellectual zeal, hoping for a chance to see into Coben's mind to understand just a bit better where he had come from and how those like him might be discovered in the future. But McGreevy was right: Coben wasn't using this letter for any kind of deep personal insight or communication. It was a mindfuck, through and through. Still, someone had to read it, and who was more suited than Francis Coben's unofficial biographer? "Yes," he allowed finally. "I'll read it."

"Then so will I."

Resigned, Reed waved over McGreevy, and the trio sought out the privacy of the small interrogation room. It had white concrete walls and garish fluorescent overhead lighting. No fancy two-way mirror or intercom technology. There was a tripod with a video camera in the corner and a table with four chairs in the center. McGreevy took one side of the table and Ellie took the other. Reed paused only for a moment before siding with Ellery. He put down the sheaf of papers in front of her and waited for her next move.

Ellery looked at the replication of the envelope for a long time. "He knows my name now," she said eventually. "My new one."

McGreevy coughed to clear his throat. "You've been on the news," he explained, as if somehow Ellie might not have noticed the TV playing her face all day long inside the station house.

She moved the top sheet aside to reveal the letter itself. It was short and written in Coben's heavy, dark printing:

Dear Abigail,
I see you have a new name now but I shall still call you Abigail. That's how I always think of you, and I think of you always. Imagine how surprised I was to see you on television today, just across the room from where I was sitting. You looked real enough to touch. You certainly touched me, didn't you? You changed my life. Now I spend

my days and nights locked up in a place not much bigger than a closet.

I see you have a new friend. A mutual admirer of ours. Please remember that he only wants you because I had you first, but he will never be me, no matter how much he believes otherwise. Don't let him get too close, will you? I've always thought we'll meet again one day, and I would hate for him to ruin that.

Yours forever, F. M. Coben

Ellie's eyes glittered as she finished reading. "Could've been worse," she said, her voice rough with emotion. "The things he's said before . . .

"There's also something on the back," McGreevy said with a frown. "It's copied onto the next page."

Reed reached over and tugged the top sheet of paper to the side, revealing the image underneath. Ellie gasped and pushed back from the table. On the page was a handprint, presumably Coben's, rendered in black ink in exquisite detail. The sicko had even signed his initials in the corner like it was a piece of art. Reed scrambled to gather up all the pages and shove them back in the folder. Ellie was bent over at the waist, one hand braced on the table, looking like she might be sick.

"I'm sorry," McGreevy told her. "I promise he's no threat to you. This was just some desperate, ill-considered attempt to get the FBI's attention—something he's enjoyed precious little of in the past few years."

Ellie sat up and looked hard across the table. "With all due respect, Agent McGreevy, he addressed the letter to me, not the FBI."

"Coben's been locked up fourteen years. He knew damn well that letter was never going to make it past inspection, let alone in the mail to you."

A humorless smile twitched at Reed's lips. "And yet here it is in front of her, Puss, hand-delivered by the FBI itself." Probably just like Coben anticipated when he scribbled the damn thing in the first place.

McGreevy shifted uncomfortably at this idea. "Yes, well. There's nothing in there he couldn't have learned from the news reports, but obviously we are following up."

"Following up how?" Reed asked.

"I've got a ticket booked for Indiana, leaving in two hours. We're going to put Coben in a box and shake him to see what falls out." He paused. "There's a seat on that plane for you too if you want it."

Ellery looked quickly at Reed for his reaction, but he wasn't sure how to feel. He'd expected McGreevy to show up here and hand him his ass for working while on stress leave—in a case that just blew up national news, no less—but instead he was offering Reed an official assignment and a return to grace. "I don't know," he said finally. "I think it might be better if I stuck around here right now."

McGreevy hitched up his pants and rose from his seat. "You mind if I speak to you outside a moment?"

Ellery scowled, suspicious again at the mention of another private conversation, but Reed raised his eyebrows at her. "My turn for the doghouse, it would seem," he said lightly before he followed McGreevy out the door. His boss cornered Reed by the watercooler, blocking him in with one arm and leaning down into Reed's personal space. "What are you doing here, Markham?"

"My job, sir, amazingly enough."

McGreevy blew out a short breath in disbelief. "This isn't a job. It's a crusade."

"You don't need me to handle Coben."

"If he's going to talk to anyone, it would be you."

"Talk, yes, sure," Reed agreed. "He'll chat with me all day and jerk off to the memory at night, but he won't tell me anything useful. Meanwhile, they could use me here to work the Coben angle—everyone local is involved in the search for Julia Parker."

McGreevy backed away, looking reproachful. "*They* could use you, or *she* could use you?"

"What's that supposed to mean?"

"She grew up real pretty, I'll grant you that."

Reed cocked his head in deliberate fashion, holding a thin line on his temper. "It isn't like that."

"Oh, no?" McGreevy's eyebrows shot up. "I heard you're sleeping at her place now."

"On the couch. Someone around here is maybe out to kill her, or haven't you read that far in the reports just yet?"

McGreevy shook his head. "Let them protect her, then. You're too close to this investigation to do her any good anyway. You helped her the last time because you were following the leads, not your feelings. Look, Markham, I get that this case is personal to you—I do—but if you're right that she's in danger, about the worst thing for her is a federal agent with a bad case of Hero Syndrome. Believe it or not, I'm trying to help you."

"By getting me on a plane out of here."

"If that's what it takes, then yes."

Reed thought of Ellery, pounding each of the nails back into her closet door. "She called me for help," he said finally. "Not the FBI."

"And that's exactly why you oughtn't be here." McGreevy paced a few steps away and then back again. He held out a finger at Reed. "I can order you off the case."

"I'm not officially on it."

"Dammit, Reed. I don't want to have to make this leave permanent."

A fresh wave of exhaustion hit him, and Reed held up both hands in wordless surrender. "Do what you've got to do, Puss," he said finally, "and I'll do the same."

In the car on the way back to her place, they idled alone at a pointless red light, as no traffic was visible for miles in either direction. Woodbury residents were too scared to leave their homes. Reed gave Ellie a sideways glance. She had said almost nothing to him since they had met with McGreevy and read the letter, and Reed worried it had rattled her. "You know," he said softly, "Coben wrote that letter to try to make himself important again. That doesn't mean you have to let him."

She gave an ironic smile but didn't look at him. "You're not going to feed me some bullshit about how I'm in charge, and I decide what kind of power he has over me, are you?"

Reed winced inwardly. *Jeez, when she put it like that . . .* He ducked his head, glad for the cover of darkness. "Uh, no?"

"Good," she said with a nod as she drove forward again. "I had a shrink try that line on me after it happened. She worked for the school, and looking back on it, I should probably feel sorry for her. She was totally out of her depth with me. She was there to help kids whose parents were getting divorced or maybe to counsel some pipsqueak who was getting bullied on the playground. Francis Coben was way out of her league." She paused, considering. "You know what's funny? She wanted me to write a letter to him, to Coben. Not to send it or anything. Just 'to get your feelings out,' she told me. 'Write them down and make them go away.'"

"Did you do it?"

"Ha, as if. Instead I wrote two thousand words on why forced interaction with school-based social workers was a violation of human rights." She shook her head, bemused. "I didn't have to go see her again after that."

He gave a wry grin. "No, I would expect not."

Ellery was quiet for a moment, her eyes on the shadowed roads. "Coben's in my head for good. I accepted that a long time ago because I don't see any way I could really change it. There isn't a way to remove him without a lobotomy or some soap-opera kind of amnesia. I could write him a thousand letters and it wouldn't make a damn bit of difference. The funny thing is, though, I didn't realize until I saw his letter that it goes both ways. I'm in his head forever too. He's rotting away inside those concrete walls and what's he got to think about? Me, and how I helped put him there. A bunch of letters aren't going to change that fact either, so let him write as many as he wants."

Reed felt the truth of this immediately, down to his very bones. Coben and Ellie lived within him too. She had changed and shaped him in a way that was both ineffable and unalterable. They were linked together for always. Reed looked at her profile and swallowed back a surge of emotion, of tenderness and pride and a flicker of something baser, a sudden heat at his center that tinged his thoughts with shame. He'd rescued her as a girl when he'd known nothing more about her than the statistics listed on the missing persons poster. Now she was a grown woman, insightful and infuriating, with just a bunch of nails keeping the worst of her past at bay, and suddenly he was fiercely grateful for her. He wished she could see how remarkable she really was. "There's something maybe you don't know," he said, wondering even as he said it whether his two cents would be helpful or not. After all, she had deliberately avoided knowing the details for years.

"Don't know about what?"

He hesitated again. "The other young women Coben abducted . . . evidence suggests they probably didn't live longer than a day or so afterward. Two at most." Ellie had survived three days in the closet, almost four. They had theorized at the time that Coben was losing focus and becoming more disorganized as the investigation closed in on him. Reed wasn't a big believer in destiny, but he wondered now if the man had simply met his match.

Ellie absorbed this news in silence for a moment but ultimately shook her head. "Don't," she said. "Don't try to tell me I'm special or that this happened for a reason, because I don't believe that either. I'm not a hero. I lived just long enough for it to be over."

She stopped talking to him after that, and Reed turned without argument to look out at the passing trees. *He only wants you because I had you first,* Coben had written, and Reed feared this was the truth. So it wasn't quite over. Maybe what Ellie was trying to tell him was that it never really would be.

Reed startled awake in the middle of the night to the sound of nearby footsteps. He jerked upright on the couch and squinted at the shadowy figure in the doorway. "It's just me," she said in the darkness. She switched on a flashlight, and he flinched as the beam caught him across the eyes. "Bump has to go out."

Okay, yes, he heard it now that he was more awake: the faint sound of panting and toenails scratching on the wooden floor. He groped for his trousers and tugged them on. At the front door, Ellie paused in a pool of silver moonlight. "You don't have to come. We'll just be in the yard for a few minutes."

"I'm coming," he said, taking his gun and smothering a yawn on his forearm. Outside, the storm had cleared away the heat and the night was almost chilly. The crickets' song had gone silent and the only noise was Bump's dog tags and the whispering of the trees. Reed and Ellie stood in their shirtsleeves on the dewy grass while Bump hurled himself enthusiastically at the bushes. "This isn't going to a take long, is it?" he asked her.

"Depends. He can be . . . particular."

"Remind him I'm armed and dangerous," Reed groused. "He could lose a tail."

"No one holds a gun to your head when you're in the bath-room."

"I don't wake the entire household just to take a piss at two o'clock in the morning."

The jingle of Bump's collar grew fainter as he moved deeper into the woods. "Bump, no!" Ellie called, starting across the lawn after him. "Come back here!" But instead of complying, the col-lar picked up speed, running away from them into the trees.

"Aw, hell," Reed muttered as he jogged after them.

"Bump? Bump, stop it. Come back here now!"

Reed held up one arm to protect his face from the slapping branches as he followed the sound of Ellie's voice and Bump's dog tags. "Where the hell is he going?" he called out.

"Looks like the Ingram house," she yelled back. "They have a poodle."

"Great," Reed said under his breath. "I'm going to get my eye poked out because some grungy mutt thinks he's got a starring role in *Lady and the Tramp*." He forged onward, unable to see much until a clearing appeared ahead. Ellie was still in hot pur-suit of the dog.

"They're not even home, you silly animal," she called out to Bump.

Reed caught up with her where the woods thinned out into someone else's backyard. There was a rickety old swing set and an empty patio. Bump was snuffling around eagerly, his outline just visible in the silver moonlight. Ellie hugged herself as if to warm up. "You see? They're not here. They went to the Cape for the Fourth of July, same as always."

Not surprisingly, the dog ignored this bit of information and continued his in-depth exploration of the yard. It was when he stopped suddenly that Reed got curious. "What's he got there?" he said, fearing some dead rodent.

"I don't know." Ellie walked closer and trained the flashlight down to where Bump was snuffling. "Oh, my God!"

The alarm in her voice made Reed race across the lawn so he could see too. There, on the patio, were two hands raised beseechingly to the sky, as though their owner was standing underground. The spotlight on them shook as Ellie's own hand trembled, and Reed gently took the flashlight from her for a closer observation. The severed hands looked to be real and human, belonging to a middle-aged female with a neat French manicure. They had been stuck to the spot with some sort of putty. "That's Julia Parker," Ellie said, covering her mouth. "Those are her hands."

From his crouch, Reed turned to look up at her. "You're sure?"

Ellie nodded, her eyes so wide he could see the whites even in the low light. "She's still wearing her wedding band."

Pandemonium reigned for the next few hours. They couldn't very well report the discovery to Sam Parker, so Ellie called Jimmy Tipton instead—at home, using his private line so as not to alert the whole department. "Jesus, Mary, Mother of God," he said when he heard. "This is going to kill him." Tipton knew his role was just to babysit the scene until State Investigators Matthew Tovar and Tracy Grigsby arrived, but with the press tracking Woodbury PD's every move, there was no hope of keeping the discovery entirely quiet. By the time Sam Parker showed up at the house, the news vans had their lights and cameras rolling.

Reed hung back out of the way with Ellery, as Tipton intercepted his boss. "Chief, you can't go back there."

Parker shoved Tipton out of the way. "The hell I can't. This is my town and I'm in charge here."

"Not this time," Tipton said firmly, stepping in front of him again. Sam grabbed him by the shirt front and the two started to struggle. They grappled for a minute and Tipton tried to plead his case again. "Chief, listen—you don't want to see, okay? You don't want to."

"Don't tell me what I want!" Parker seemed to have the strength of ten men as he threw his deputy to the ground. He went storming around the back of the house, and there was a terrible moment of silence followed by his howl, a guttural wounded sound that made even the veteran reporters turn away. Ellie covered her face with her hands, and Reed recalled Parker's words: *I keep wondering: what's he doing to her?* Everyone would know the truth now. Reed scanned the line of cameras and their unblinking eyes that were taking in every moment so later they could beam it back out into the world for popular consumption, horror-cum-cinéma vérité.

Tipton and another deputy escorted the chief back around to the front of the house, and he put up no resistance this time. He was a shell of the person he was only minutes before, smaller somehow, and broken in a way that could never be made whole. The camera shutters *click-clicked* away, but the reporters said nothing, standing in a hush as Parker walked on past them like they were not even there.

"Sam!" Ellery called, a desperate edge in her voice. Parker didn't seem to hear.

When she started after him, Reed grabbed her elbow lightly to pull her back. "Let him go."

"I should tell him."

"Tell him what?" Reed asked gently.

She faltered, opening and closing her mouth several times. There would come a day when perhaps she could tell Sam lots of things, stories and difficult truths that few others could share, like how to walk around with this kind of crime inside you, but the chief would never be able to hear her now. "I'm so sorry," she whispered.

"I know. But you did not do this. You are not responsible."

"I didn't do this," she agreed, squinting at the crime tape circling the yard. "But I didn't stop it either."

"It's not up to you to stop it, not by yourself. You're just one person, Ellie."

She shuddered and wrapped her arms around herself. "Yeah, but I'm the one he wants."

Dawn arrived in a scant few hours, streaking watercolor pink across the empty sky. Reed and Ellery dropped Bump off with Brady before heading into town. They had to use a circuitous alternate way to the shelter because the press was even stalking the dog now that he had discovered Julia Parker's remains. Brady looked tired and wan himself as he accepted the leash. "No problem, he can hang out here as long as he wants. We'll just tell them 'no comment,' right, Bump? If they won't take the hint, I'll send him to pee on their legs."

"Thanks," Ellie said with obvious relief. "I'll text you when things calm down."

The Woodbury station had undergone a personality transplant, seized as it was by outside law enforcement and missing its usual leader. Parker's office sat in shadow with the door closed; the investigating officers used the interrogation room to conduct their interviews. Tovar and Grigsby were back again, this time with more bite to their questions. They grilled Ellery for at least an hour, and when it was Reed's turn, they marched him perfunctorily through the facts of the case before getting down to their real questions. "We know you have a background in behavioral analysis," Matthew Tovar said as he leaned across the table.

"And you caught Francis Coben," Tracy Grigsby added.

Reed sat back wearily, anticipating the request to perform another miracle. Surely by now everyone could see how limited his powers were.

"We need to know what we're dealing with," Tovar said. "Who we should be looking for."

"Is this a straight-up Coben copycat we're looking at?" Grigsby added, leaning in.

"No," Reed replied, glancing at the door. He hoped Ellie was on the other side of it, safe inside the station. "Coben kept his victims' hands, while this offender uses them for displays. Coben avoided the authorities and did not otherwise engage with the investigation. This offender wants attention."

"He wants us to catch him."

Reed looked at Tovar sharply. "Oh, no. He wants us to admire him. Ellery in particular. He's obviously taken great pains to get her to notice him."

At the mention of Ellie's name, Tracy Grigsby frowned. "Officer Hathaway didn't provide much insight into why someone might be abducting people and chopping off their hands simply to gain her attention."

"And I can't tell you that either," Reed said flatly.

"So what can you tell us?" Tovar was irritated now too.

Reed had revised some of his earlier profile based on the

latest developments. A killer this practiced would have to be older, more experienced. "He's most likely a white male who lives in Woodbury or the surrounding area. He's on the older end of the spectrum, maybe forty to forty-five—still physically strong but developed enough in his technique that he can abduct healthy adults in the middle of the day. He belongs here. He fits in. There are probably witnesses who have seen him just before or after his crimes who have no idea what they're looking at because he seems so ordinary. That's part of the excitement for him, that he knows something about himself that they don't know. He likes secrets—you can tell this from the way he's taunted Ellery about her past. Knowledge, as they say, is power, and this guy gets off on power. He probably has a job that permits him to wield that power in other ways, which is one reason he can be so disciplined in his crimes."

"What kind of job are we talking about?" Grigsby was taking notes.

"Anything where he gets to push around people smaller or weaker. Could be anything from issuing or denying building permits right up to law enforcement."

"Law enforcement?" Tovar looked alarmed. "This guy could be a cop?"

"A cop. A meter reader. President of his home owners' association. You get the idea."

"Is he married, or does he live in his parents' basement?" Grisby wanted to know.

"I think he most likely lives alone or at least he has a separate space where he can be alone with the victims."

"Whom he picks out the year before, based on whether they witnessed his last abduction?" Grigsby had been paying attention when Reed laid out his theory, but she still sounded skeptical.

"That is the only detectable pattern right now, yes."

Grisby blew out a long breath that flapped her lips like a horse. "Well," she said, "we can print out a list of guys in the area who are age forty to forty-five and living alone and start going through them. Or we can just wait a year and set up surveillance on the current target and hope we catch him in the act."

She wasn't being serious, but a queer feeling passed through Reed.

"Yeah," Tovar agreed, leaning over to peer at her notes. "If you're right, this guy already has his next victim picked out, right? Who was the last Woodbury citizen to see Julia Parker before she was abducted?"

Reed looked at the door again, this time with more alarm. "That would be Ellery," he said.

He did not let Ellery out of his sight for the rest of the day. When she heard his latest concerns, she went pale for a few seconds but then squared her shoulders. "Sure, maybe, but we've got a year before I have to worry about that, right? We just need to find this asshole before next summer."

"Right, sure," he agreed, hoping he sounded convincing. Privately, he resolved to keep up his personal surveillance. The killer needed his victims to be alone for the abduction, so it stood to reason that if Ellery wasn't alone, she would remain safe. He trailed her everywhere but the ladies' room.

At the end of the day, they picked up a pizza for dinner and took it back to her house. Reed wasn't especially hungry, and what appetite he did have disappeared entirely when he saw Ellery take the day's mail from her mailbox. On top was a plain white envelope with her name and address in square black printing. "Is that—?"

"A birthday card." She held it so he could see. "To go with Julia Parker's abduction. You see? I told you I was not making any of this up."

"I'm not doubting you," he replied as he set the pizza down on the coffee table. "It looks the same as the others."

She went to the kitchen to fetch a pair of gloves, which she used for handling the envelope. "Wouldn't want to get any more of my DNA on it," she said darkly.

Reed looked at the postmark and saw it was from Worcester, stamped two days ago. Ellie took a knife to one end of the envelope and slit it open. When she tipped it to one side, the familiar clown card slid out. She opened it with one gloved finger and started in surprise when a folded piece of paper fell out. "This is new," she murmured as she picked it up.

Reed peeked at the writing on the interior of card and saw it was identical to the previous ones: HAPPY BIRTHDAY ELLERY. "What does the paper say?"

Carefully, she unfolded it so they could both see the inside. "Oh, wow," she breathed when she saw the drawing it contained. It was a pen-and-ink piece that showed a city street at night. There was a dark car stopped in the road with a man inside it. A girl with a long ponytail and a bicycle was talking to the man. The scene was entirely black and white except for the red tie holding back the girl's hair. "This is me," she whispered. "This is what it looked like the night Coben abducted me."

"I know." He had heard the story enough times to recognize the players. Ellie was wearing her brother's old soccer jersey with the number 6 on the back. Coben was driving a black Acura sedan. The viewpoint was of someone standing perhaps thirty feet away on the sidewalk.

"I don't understand," she said. "What does this mean?"

"I'm not sure. Coben's name has been in the news these past

few days, what with everyone going on about the possibility of a copycat. Maybe this guy is needling Coben, pointing out the place he went wrong."

Ellie shuddered and put the paper down on the coffee table. "It's creepy."

"Very," he agreed as they took seats next to one another on the sofa. "We should get this to a lab and have it tested." The kidnapper had been very careful thus far, even perhaps planting DNA evidence to obscure his identity, so Reed didn't hold out a lot of hope that a fresh analysis would reveal any clues, but one small mistake could be enough to nail him.

"Yes," Ellie replied, but she sounded distracted. She bent over so that she could look at the picture some more. "The level of detail is impressive," she said after a moment. "He's got a vivid imagination." She tilted her head for another angle. "Reed . . ."

"Hmm?"

"Do you have a copy of that poster Monica Jenkins showed us the other day? The one made up of me when I went missing?"

"I can print one from my laptop," he said, moving to grab the computer. It didn't take more than a few minutes before he had a copy of the flyer in his hands. Ellie was right that the artist had an eye for detail. He had captured roundness of her face, the last vestige of childhood, and her beat-up secondhand bicycle.

Ellie grabbed the paper from his hands and scanned it quickly. "'Last seen wearing a green soccer jersey that says HORNETS on the front and the number 6 on the back. Jean cutoff shorts and white sneakers.'"

Check and check, Reed noted as he looked at the drawing. Ellie raised her eyes to his.

"There's nothing here about the scrunchie," she said.

"The what?"

"The red ponytail holder. It's not on the flyer. It fell out in

Coben's car when I was struggling to get free. Reed, this guy didn't draw my kidnapping from his imagination. He watched it happen. That's what he's telling me with this drawing."

Reed snatched the flyer back from Ellie to check the physical description for himself, even though he already knew she had to be correct. "Well, then," he said, a hum of excitement in his veins at last, "we finally know where to start looking for him."

Two hours later, they sat surrounded by printouts in her living room. Reed had somehow managed to eat half a pizza without even tasting it. All his attention was focused on poring over the witness statements from the night Ellery was abducted. Beside him, Ellie sat on one end of the sofa, holding her half of the pages to a nearby light. "I didn't realize how many there would be," she said, sounding discouraged.

"The entire city was looking for you," he replied. "Cops went door-to-door asking everyone if they had seen anything."

"What a waste of time that turned out to be," she said. "Listen to this one, from Angela D'Arby: 'I sleep with earplugs on account of the traffic noise outside. I didn't hear nothing.' Or this one, from Ken Collins and Israel Riley, who were playing basketball down the street. 'We saw a lady on her bike but she was black, not white.'"

Reed had similar problems with his reports. "Dick Butkus," he said. "A guy gives that as his name and no one in Chicago thinks to question it?"

Ellie looked over at him. "What did Dick see?"

"A whole lot of nothing. He claims he was watching the late-late show."

Ellie returned her attention to the printouts, shuffling papers until she found a fresh page. "Here's something. A guy named

Peter Gonzalez says he remembers a dark-colored car parked on the street."

"Flag it," Reed replied without looking up.

"Virginia Willett says there was a pervert in the park two days beforehand. He exposed himself to her nephew and his ten-year-old friend."

"That doesn't sound like Coben to me," Reed said. "But this rather does: a man named Martin Macon saw a black Acura circling the block at around ten that night. He thought the guy was either lost or looking to score drugs. Didn't get a license plate."

Ellie's papers sagged a bit at this news. "Ten," she murmured. "I didn't go out there until past midnight. It's like he was out there waiting for me and I didn't even know it." She put the reports aside and curled a bit tighter in on herself. "I was thinking about the drawing. And about what you said—that maybe I'm next."

"Ellie." Reed turned to her and kept his tone gentle. "We aren't going to let that happen."

"What if the drawing is meant to say something else? What if he means to finish what Coben started? You know, like you were saying before how sometimes there is one intended victim and the rest of them are collateral damage."

"If that were the case, he probably would have targeted you to begin with," Reed said, hoping this was reassuring.

"Unless he was waiting."

"Waiting for what?"

"Waiting for it to be my turn."

"It's not your turn," Reed said firmly. "It's his turn, and we will find him."

The following day, Reed started running down the names of witnesses to Ellie's abduction to determine what they were up to now. Ellie was helping him with this herculean task initially, but Tovar and Grigsby showed up with a new round of questions for her. "We've subpoenaed Sam Parker's cell phone records, including his text messages," Grigsby told her. "He had some really interesting things to say about you—and to you."

Reed saw Ellie's face flush as the evidence of her affair came to light. "It didn't mean anything," she said.

"Why don't you come tell us all about it anyway?" Tovar suggested, and Ellie had little choice but to comply. Reed alternated between his background searches and watching the clock as the hours ticked by and Ellery did not appear.

Late in the afternoon, they finally kicked her loose, and she returned to her desk looking tired and drained. "I think I've managed to convince them that I didn't kill Julia," she said. "But I'm not to leave the area without letting them know about it."

Reed blinked. "You were with me. I'll vouch for you."

"Oh, the way they're going in there, they'll probably just think we were in on it together," she said, disgusted. "Plus, I went off alone that day to take Bump over to Brady's. That's apparently my 'my window of opportunity.' Shoot, speaking of Brady . . . I should go pick up Bump before he wears out his welcome over there." She fished out her cell phone and began texting.

The door to the station swung open and Jimmy Tipton stepped in. Reed couldn't help but notice the man was now wearing the chief's hat. "There she is," Tipton said of Ellery. "I've been looking for you."

Ellie set down her cell phone. "What's up?"

"Now that the chaos has settled down somewhat, I want you to come over to the Ingram place with me and walk through what happened the night you found Julia Parker's hands."

"Is that necessary? I've given a complete statement."

"It would be helpful, yes. I want to see it through your eyes."

"It was dark," Ellie said flatly. "We didn't see much."

"All the same." Tipton gave a tight smile. "I'd be much obliged."

"Fine," Ellie said, heaving a sigh as she pushed back from her desk. "Let me just pick up my dog, okay?"

"I'd like to do this first," Tipton said. "I've been waiting all day as it is. Won't take long."

Reed closed his laptop and prepared to go with her, but Tipton held up a hand. "No need for both of you to come," he said. "Ellie's account will be enough."

"It's no trouble for me," Reed protested. "After all, I was there that night too. Surely two witness statements would be better than one." He didn't particularly see the point of this little exercise, but he wasn't keen on the idea of Ellery going off unattended.

"You're of better use staying here, doing . . . whatever it is you're doing," Tipton said with a small frown. "We might need you in some other capacity. Don't worry about Ellie. I'll take good care of her."

He gave an exaggerated wink and Reed wanted to punch him in the mouth. "Ellery?" Reed said, looking toward her. "I'll come if you want."

"It's okay," she said, clearly feeling the strain of the day. "We'll be there and back in no time. If you want to do me a favor, you could go pick up Bump for me and take him home. I already told Brady I was coming to the shelter to get him."

"You want me to fetch the animal? On my own?"

"Would you? Please? He likes you."

Reed raised his eyes to the heavens. "I know I will regret this," he said, "but okay." He held out his hands for her keys.

"Thanks, you're a lifesaver," she said, and then stopped as she heard the words come out of her mouth. She smiled slightly and ducked her head. "My lifesaver," she added, touching his arm quickly—the first time she had initiated any physical contact. Reed looked down at his elbow in wonder and then glanced back to the door, seeking her out again, but Ellery had already disappeared from sight.

Reed drove Ellery's truck to the animal shelter, where he parked in the empty lot and headed inside in search of her canine companion. There was no one at the front window and the place seemed deserted. "Hello?" he called, leaning over the counter. The only reply was the dinging of his cell phone, signaling a new message. He pulled it out, hoping it was Ellie. Instead, it was an e-mail from his friend Alfred at the gas station, the alias Oil Can Boy. "Dear Mr. Agent Markham," the message read. "I went through all my files and this was the only other video I have from that night. Bea Nesbit isn't on it, and neither is that other woman. Sorry I can't help you.—Alfred."

Reed called up the attached video anyway and started it playing as he began to wander the halls, looking for Brady or Bump. The video showed surveillance footage from inside the convenience mart, people waiting in line to pay for their purchases. Reed paused to watch some bald guy with a hefty paunch buy a six-pack and a carton of Marlboros. "Hello?" he called again, and this time he heard Brady's answer.

"Back here!"

He found Brady in the rear of the building, cleaning out stainless steel cages. When Reed set foot in the room, Bump lumbered to his feet and came running over for a snuffly greeting. "Yes, yes, I've missed you too," Reed said, sidestepping the worst of the slobber. He peeked at the video again. This time it was a woman in a tube top buying what looked like six bags of chips.

"Where's Ellie?" Brady said. "I thought she was coming by."

"She had work to do," Reed told him. "I'm here to take custody of the furry beast."

"Suit yourself," Brady said. He turned with a smile, and Reed noted he was wearing an AC/DC concert T-shirt, complete with the shaggy-haired band and a guitar that appeared to be on fire. *Some people have no musical taste at all*, he thought, and glanced at his phone again. A man buying lottery tickets. Taking his sweet time about it too. Reed turned his attention back to Brady.

"Thanks for watching the dog." Reed looked vaguely around for a leash, lest he have to drive back to the station with Bump riding square in his lap.

"No problem. I told Ellie he could stay as long as she needed."

"That's kind of you, but I think she rather misses the creature." He gave up looking for the leash momentarily as the video switched to a new person, and this time the shape was immediately familiar: Brady Archer. Reed stopped the video and double-checked the image against the man standing three feet away from him, his brow furrowed in concentration. It was definitely Brady on the screen. They were even wearing the same damn shirt.

"What kind of work is Ellie doing?" Brady asked, yanking Reed's attention back to the present. He was moving around again as he put away a cage.

"Oh, you know, reports related to the discovery of Julia Parker's hands last night. I bet she'd like to tell you about it." Reed tucked his phone away so the other man couldn't see it. "You could come back to the station with me. I bet she's there now."

Brady froze for a moment at the invitation. Reed forced himself to appear relaxed and calm, to give nothing away as his mind raced on ahead with this new discovery. It didn't make a lick of sense. This kid was maybe twenty-four years old. He'd have been in grammar school the night Ellie was abducted. It didn't seem possible he could be practiced enough to be their killer. "Yeah?"

Brady asked. "The station? That would be cool. Ellie's never given me the grand tour."

"Then we should go," Reed said, hoping he didn't sound too eager. He wanted to get Brady in the box and find out what he knew.

"Sure. Let me just wash my hands and then I can lock up."

Reed stepped back to allow Brady to pass in front of him to the sink. But as he did so, there was an impossibly fast flash of movement from Brady, a man used to capturing fleeing animals, and Reed felt a sharp jab of a needle go straight into his neck. His vision went starry white, the ground rushing up to meet him as he fell down, down, down, past a relentless barking animal. *Ellery,* he thought with a last gasp of desperation. Then he thought nothing at all.

11

The sun was a blood orange, a fiery orb just visible in between the dense trees as Ellery and Jimmy Tipton retraced her steps the night she had found Julia Parker's hands. "Your dog sure can pick 'em," Tipton grumbled as he pushed aside some brambles. Branches hung down around them, snapped off by the force of the recent storm. "He couldn't just have used the sidewalk?"

"He usually sticks to the trail, but this is a more direct route. Guess he was in a hurry." The ground was soft beneath her feet, a blanket of wet leaves and pine needles. She called up a vision of Bump in the moonlight, forging on ahead with his tail held high and his nose to the ground, like he'd been scenting something. She followed his ghost through the woods and into the clearing that marked the Ingrams' backyard. "This is where we came out," she told Tipton as he came to stand next to her. "It took a couple of minutes before we saw the hands."

Tipton walked over to the place where the grass met the cement patio. "Her hands were here," he said, nodding down at the ground. "What else did you see?"

"What else? Nothing. It was dark. No one was home."

"I know that," he replied, sounding irritated. "I mean did you see or hear anything on your way over here, or while you were standing here—anything else that seemed out of place?"

She stared at him. "I don't know, Tipton. Once we saw the hands we pretty much focused in on those. There wasn't any other obvious disturbance, if that's what you're asking. Why?"

Tipton cocked his head a moment and then scanned the tree line at the back of the yard. The fading light cast deep shadows across the grass. "We found a footprint over there near the edge of the woods—a man's boot print size eleven. It had to be fresh, with all the rain we just had, and your buddy Agent Markham was wearing loafers that night. It obviously didn't come from the Ingrams since they weren't at home. On top of that, the putty used to hold up the hands on the pavement was still wet. They can't have been sitting here very long before you stumbled on 'em."

"You're saying we just missed him. That he might have been here that night in the woods, watching the whole thing."

Tipton squinted into the trees. "It seems possible, yeah. You're sure you didn't hear anything?"

"No," she murmured, feeling suddenly exposed in front of the thick wall of trees. "There was nothing." But as they tramped back through the woods, she considered that maybe Bump hadn't been scenting his favorite poodle or Julia's hands at all; perhaps he had been on the trail of the killer.

Back at her house, Tipton seemed reluctant to get into his squad car and drive away. "I don't like you out here by yourself with the possibility that someone is creeping around in these woods," he said. "We already know this guy takes an unhealthy interest in you. Maybe I should stick around just in case."

It might have been a sincere offer, but what Ellie heard was the note of hope in his voice. *I'll stick around and maybe bust a serial killer in the process.* "No thanks," she told him firmly. "I'll be just fine. Besides, Reed should be coming back any minute now." In fact, Reed should have beaten them to the house, and she was a little confused about where he could have gone.

"Well, all right," Tipton said with a last look at her house. "You know the number to call if he comes back around again."

"I've got his number right here," she replied, patting her sidearm.

Tipton snorted in appreciation of her bravado. "Don't try to be some kind of hero, Hathaway." The implication, of course, was, *as if you really could.* "You don't know the kind of dangerous animal you're dealing with here."

"I know exactly what he is," she replied tartly. "I met his mentor—you know, the original—and I lived to tell about it."

Tipton frowned at the reminder that her knowledge in this area soundly trumped his own. "Yeah, well, just watch yourself," he mumbled as he drew out his keys and walked to his car. "I'd hate to be finding your hands chopped off next."

Ellie stood at the bottom of her front porch and watched him drive off, the red taillights growing smaller in the distance as the sound of his engine grew fainter and fainter, until at last it was quiet again. Her yard looked particularly empty without her truck sitting in it, and she took out her phone as she mounted the steps to her house. No messages from Reed, so she dialed his number as she fiddled with the lock. The phone rang straight through to voice mail. She left a brief message to call her and went to the kitchen for a drink. The back of the house looked out toward the black woods, but Ellie saw only her own tired reflection in the windowpane. She downed two straight glasses of water and took out her phone again. This time, she called Brady at the shelter.

"Hey," she said when she reached him. "Is Reed there?"

"Reed? Haven't seen him. Why?"

"He was supposed to pick up Bump like an hour ago now."
She checked the clock on her wall. "Actually, more like two. You're
saying he hasn't been by?"

"No, and I have Bump right here with me. Say hello, dog
breath."

Ellery heard snuffling and a soft whine on the other end. "I
don't understand. He should've been there and back by now."

"Did you call him? Maybe he had car trouble."

"He's got my truck," she replied. "And he's not answering his
phone."

"Beats me, then. Maybe he had some hot lead he needed to
follow up right away. That's a thing you guys do, right? Follow
hot leads?"

"I guess. Maybe." Ellery paced the house, looking out the
front windows now in case Reed was coming up the driveway.
"Listen, I'd come get Bump myself, but like I said, Reed has my
truck."

"No problem," Brady said easily. "I'll just swing by and drop
him off. Say in a half hour?"

"That would be great," Ellie said with relief. "Thank you."
She was still watching out the windows. The long expanse of
driveway and the thicket of trees hiding her house from the road
normally felt cozy and reassuring, but at that moment, they
seemed dark and isolating. She hung up with Brady and went to
sit on the couch in front of all the notes she and Reed had made
the night before from the Coben files. He had taken the most
promising names to track down today, leaving behind statements
from people who were too young or too female to be their current perpetrator. Ellery picked through the pages. A few names
she recognized as neighbors from the apartment building where
she'd grown up and where her mother still resided.

I seen that girl out riding her bike at night all the time, Mariela Hernandez's statement read. *Too dangerous for a young girl like that. Where was her mother?*

Another neighbor: *Shame what happened to that family. The father takes off, then the boy got sick. Now this. Some people are just cursed, I guess.*

Ellery didn't believe much in curses, but she had seen tragedy beget tragedy enough times to know it wasn't a simple matter of bad luck either. When your whole world blew apart, the shrapnel sprayed far and wide, taking out anyone in its path. She rubbed her tired eyes and tried to focus on the concrete details in the statements rather than any editorializing. The sheer volume of the material made it hard to parse. One woman saw a red car. Another woman reported a suspicious Asian-looking man hanging around on the corner. None of it was remotely helpful, and Ellery plucked up another sheet with a sigh. This one was Virginia Willett again, dutifully recounting "the pervert" who harassed her young nephew and his friends in the neighborhood park. "Maybe the pervert saw something useful," Ellie muttered as she tossed the paper aside.

She tried Reed on her cell phone once more but got his outgoing message in reply. It had been only a few hours since she'd seen him, but under the circumstances she felt right to be concerned. If he still hadn't checked in by the time Brady dropped by with Bump, Ellie resolved to call in the troops to help look for him. In the meantime, she decided to take a quick shower to rinse off the grime and sweat she had accumulated from traipsing about in woods. It was hot in the house, but she didn't dare unlock the windows to air it out. She shut the blinds and stripped her grubby clothes to the floor, leaving her gun in its holster on her dresser. She took clean shorts and a T-shirt with her to the bathroom, where she ducked under and out of the hot spray in less than five minutes. Even still, she barely had time to redress and towel-dry her hair before she heard a knock at her front door. A quick check of her peephole told her it was Brady and Bump on the other side.

The heavy wooden door had to be yanked open from where it had swollen up with the humidity. "Hi," she said, feeling somewhat self-conscious because Brady had never been to her home before. Bump surged through the open door and into the house, prancing about and snuffling her legs. Brady, on the other end of the leash, had little choice but to follow. "Please excuse the mess right now," Ellery said as she accepted the lead from Brady.

"Hey, don't worry about it. You should see my place."

She realized suddenly she never had and that maybe this was weird. Brady was drinking in this new opportunity, though, looking around at her walls and the chair that was half covered in Reed's clothing. His gaze went to the coffee table and the piles of paper scattered across it. "That's about Coben?" he asked, perking up in interest at the black-and-white picture of the killer that graced the top of one stack.

"Old files, yeah," she said as she ran a hand through her damp hair and then moved to shut the folder. "I can't really discuss it." At her feet, Bump was twining figure eights in and out of her legs, tangling her in the leash, so she bent down to unhook him. Bump whined and pawed at her as she rubbed his ears. "You missed me, huh?" she asked. "I hope he wasn't too much trouble."

"The Bumpmeister? Nah." Brady had made a slow circle around her front room, pausing to study the art on her walls and the porcelain hedgehog figurine that she kept on her mantel. It had been a housewarming gift from her mother, one of the few presents from her mom that she ever really liked. She hadn't talked to her mother in weeks, not since this whole thing began, she realized, and then Ellery had to swallow back the sudden lump in her throat. "You don't keep family pictures around, huh?" Brady asked, jerking her attention back to him. "Me either."

"Not even your aunt?" Ellie asked. She searched her memory for the name of the woman who had taken over raising Brady. "Ginny?" Bump pawed at her again, whining and nudging her leg with his soft muzzle. "What is up with you this evening?" she asked him as she tried to put a few inches of space between her and the dog. She cast an anxious glance toward the window but saw no sign that Reed was on his way up the drive.

"Still nothing from Reed?" Brady asked, following her gaze.

"No, and I'm starting to worry. He should have called by now."

There was an awkward pause. "I'm sure he'll turn up," Brady said finally.

She supposed she should be a good hostess and offer him a drink or something, but mostly she wanted him to be on his way so she could go look for Reed. Still, he had watched her dog for the better part of two days. One beer wouldn't make a difference. "Can I get you something? Iced tea? Beer?"

"Glass of ice water would be great," he said, flashing her a smile. "Mind if I use your washroom?"

"Sure, that's fine," Ellie said, distracted by her worry for Reed as she headed for the kitchen to fetch the water. Bump followed her, whimpering and pawing at the floor. She heard Brady's footsteps disappear into the back of the house and it was then she realized she'd never told him where the bathroom was. He just seemed to know.

Fear broke out like a rash on the back of her neck, and Ellery froze at the sink with the water still running. *You're being ridiculous,* she told her reflection in the window. *You're just suspecting everyone now.*

But the fear kept going now that it had its hooks into her,

pricking her memory, opening it up in new directions. Brady could draw—really well. Reed had gone to see Brady earlier and had not returned. Bump, in pursuit through the woods the other night, had his eager tail held high, as though he was off to find a friend. She had felt familiar with Brady even when they first met, in part because they spoke the same vocabulary. *Pop for soda. What a Grabowski! Can I use your washroom?*

A horrible thought struck her and she raced to the coffee table to find that statement from Virginia Willett about her nine-year-old nephew. Brady would have been around nine back then. *Aunt Ginny,* he called her. Virginia. Her heart raced as she sifted through the papers until she found the right one. She scanned it quickly but found no mention of the boy's name. Maybe it wasn't true.

She heard a noise from the other side of the house and realized with a start that she did not have her gun. It was in her bedroom on the dresser. Slowly, she started for the hall, listening for his presence. "Brady . . . ?"

"Yeah?" His voice was coming from inside the washroom.

Her heart lurched in her chest and she forced herself to sound casual. "Your aunt Ginny . . . did she live in Texas like your mom?"

Ellery crept along the hall but Bump was following her, his nails scratching all the way. "Why do you ask?" Brady called back. She heard water running in the sink.

"Just curious!" She turned her head when she spoke so that it didn't sound like she was edging past the bathroom door. When she reached the other side, she picked up her pace and ran to her bedroom to fetch her holster. She picked it up with shaking fingers and found that it was empty. Her stomach dropped even before Brady appeared in the doorway behind her.

"Ginny lived in Chicago," he said, his voice still friendly.

She turned around and saw him holding her gun.

He smiled as he weighed the weapon in his hands. "But I'm guessing you've finally figured that out."

Bump sat directly on her feet and growled. "What are you doing, Brady?" she asked, struggling to keep calm.

"My name's not Brady," he told her flatly, all the light gone from his eyes. "It's William. William Willett. And you, of course, are Abigail. Finally we can tell each other the whole truth, huh? God, you don't know how long I've waited for you to figure it out."

She searched his face and her memory for any trace of recognition. "I knew you before?" she asked finally.

"No. No, you never looked at me back then. Nobody did. That's why no one noticed me on the street that night when Coben grabbed you."

"You saw it happen," she whispered, remembering the drawing. She was careful to hide her revulsion, and he nodded.

"I was standing just across the street near some steps and you never even knew it. I thought that stuff was made up, like on TV or in the movies, but there he was, getting out of his car and just taking another person like it was his right. It was amazing—the most exciting thing I'd ever seen."

Her stomach quivered. "Brady," she said, "where is Reed?"

"Somewhere safe," he replied, looking her up and down. "I kept waiting for you to recognize me. For you to feel the connection we made back then. He looked at me, you know. He saw me when he took you, and we shared this look, like it was our secret . . . like you belonged to both of us now."

"He," she repeated, her gaze alternating between his face and the gun. "You mean Coben saw you."

"Yeah, he looked over and he saw me watching, and he just went like this . . ." Brady raised a finger to his lips. "He knew.

He knew I would never tell. So I've been trying to find other ways to let you know I was here, sending you signals about that night, but you never seemed to pick up on them." He was petulant and irritated with her now.

"You sent me the birthday cards," she said suddenly, and he shot her a glare. She felt stupid at how obvious it was now. He was one of the few people close enough to steal her DNA. "Right, of course you sent them. I realized they were connected to the disappearances, but I didn't realize it was you." She swallowed hard. "You should have just told me."

"Weren't you listening to what I just said?" He waved the gun at her angrily. "I promised not to tell."

"I don't understand. You've been following me since that night?"

He looked at her like she was an idiot. "Of course not. I was a little kid back then. I watched all the TV coverage, though— watched when they took over Coben's farm where he killed the girls, watched the cops give updates on your condition. After you were released, I used to walk past your apartment building, figuring I would get to see you, but you didn't come outside anymore."

Ellie's hand went to her throat as she remembered the rest of that awful summer, stuck inside the stifling apartment as her mother made trips back and forth to the hospital to see Daniel.

"Then my mom's boyfriend of the month dumped her, and she decided she wanted me back in Texas, so Aunt Ginny had to ship me back down there. I didn't see you again for years."

She licked her dry lips. "How? How did you find me?" It didn't matter much at the moment, but as long as he was talking to her she had more time to think. *Reed. Where was Reed?* She'd un-wittingly sent him off to rendezvous with a serial killer. Maybe he was still alive, but she bet he wasn't in great shape if Brady felt confident enough to leave him. She had a flash of Julia's severed hands, raised as if in surrender, and barely held back a dry heave.

Brady was watching her face intently, a hint of amusement in his eyes. "It wasn't that difficult since you didn't bother changing your last name," he told her. "But your friend Agent Markham helped a lot. That book of his was super informative, particularly the update at the end when he mentioned you had switched schools but your basketball team won a state championship. Once he pointed me where to look, it was easy as pie to track you down." He gave her a sardonic smile. "Then it was just a matter of waiting for us to get reacquainted."

Her head swam and the floor felt like it was sucking her under. How long had he been watching her? "So you found me," she said, her voice barely above a whisper. "But why involve the rest of them? What about Bea and Shannon and Mark? What did they have to do with any of this?"

He shrugged. "Why not them? Seriously. What did they really have going for them, anyway? Bea was fucking some weirdo instead of paying attention to her studies. Shannon was a loser drunk, and Mark just moped around over his dead son. They weren't living lives that mattered to anyone."

"That isn't your decision to make," she said, more hotly than she intended.

Brady went cold again. "Yes," he replied, "it absolutely is." He waved the gun at her. "Let's go."

"Go where?" she asked without moving an inch.

"You want to know where Reed is, I'll show you. I'll show you everything."

She considered her options. Brady clearly didn't want to shoot her where she stood; this wasn't his endgame. If she resisted, she might throw him off and gain a psychological edge.

He tapped his foot impatiently. "You better hurry. Reed doesn't have much time."

So she shuffled Speed Bump off her feet and moved slowly to the door, woefully underdressed for her doom in flip-flops and jean cut-offs. It was, she realized as she looked down at her T-shirt, almost the same as the clothes she had worn fourteen years ago when she'd encountered Francis Coben. Bump trotted along after them to the front door, whining and wagging pitifully. "Easy," she told him, not wanting him to be afraid.

Bump replied with a series of short barks. "Shut up," Brady hissed at him. "Shut up or I will shut you up!"

"Leave him alone," Ellie said, even as Bump began barking louder.

Brady tossed the keys out onto the porch. "You're driving," he said over Bump's raucous complaints. "Let's go."

Ellery went outside and bent over, fumbling in the semidarkness to pick up the keys. Her own harsh breathing rasped in her ears and her thoughts raced as she tried to make sense of this new reality.

Behind her, Brady cast a deep shadow. "Get the fuck back in there," she heard him say, followed by a thump and then Bump's painful whimpering. She stood up but did not turn around. She heard the door creak, saw the light in front of her disappearing as if in slow motion as Brady moved to close the front door. She held her breath, waiting for the snick of the lock, for his next command, but instead a gunshot split the night like thunder. She convulsed at the sound, believing herself to be hit, but Brady shoved her roughly forward to the steps and the searing pain did not arrive. "Move it!"

She stumbled forward, realizing then that he'd fired inside the house, at the dog, and bile rose up in her throat. She went weak at the knees and Brady jabbed the gun between her shoulder blades. "Get in," he said as they reached his car. Pain and horror combined to scald her eyes with tears. Blindly, she climbed behind the wheel of his hatchback and started the engine. Brady was looking around frantically to see if anyone had heard the shot. "Go, go," he urged her. "What're you waiting for?

She wiped at her face. "Go where?"

"Go out to the road and head north. Don't try anything stupid, okay? Not if you want to see Reed again in this lifetime."

She backed the car up and started slowly down her long driveway, loath to leave Bump behind. Maybe a news van would be parked at the end, someone she could signal for help, someone who maybe had heard the gunshot. But when she reached Burning Tree Road, her heart sank when she saw no traffic in either direction. The reporters were all with Sam Parker and the search teams; they'd moved on to a different part of the story.

"You didn't have to shoot him, you know," she murmured as she drove down the silent street.

Brady was staring out the windshield and did not answer.

"He loved you," she said, unable to keep the emotion from her voice. "He loved you."

Brady glanced at her with something that almost looked like curiosity. "He didn't love me," he said after a moment. "He didn't even know me." His gaze returned to the road, as if he was still searching for their destiny. "Now drive."

She drove. The tiny engine on his hybrid car made almost no noise as they ghosted out of town, away from civilization and down the long, empty roads filled on either side with thick cornstalks or dark empty pastures. In one field, she saw the distant, bobbing flashlights of the search team as they fanned out in the tall grass looking for Julia Parker's body. She observed Brady in her peripheral vision to see if he had noticed the crew, and his attention was riveted. "Look at them all," he murmured with awe. "This whole town is crawling with cops right now, and it's all because of me."

"Because they want to stop you."

His gaze didn't move from the far-off dancing lights. "Yeah, but they won't," he said, so matter-of-fact that it gave her a chill in the warm summer night. "Not until it's over."

She thought of leaning on the horn, of driving straight into the field at them to get their attention. Brady might well shoot her but the manhunt would be on. He couldn't outrun all of them.

"Don't even think about it," he told her, reading her thoughts. "You'll end up dead, and then what would happen to Reed?"

She clutched the wheel tighter. "How do I know he's even still alive?"

Brady's smile was thin in the dim light. "I guess you'll just have to trust me. Make a right up here."

She did as he ordered her and watched in the rearview mirror as the lights from the search team grew smaller and smaller in the distance, until they winked out for good. He directed her to an edge of town she hadn't even known existed, out beyond the McGregor farmland and past the silent cornfields to a dirt road not unlike her own. The house that appeared out of the mist at the end of it was at once both unfamiliar and straight out of her nightmares. The headlights on the car illuminated the front of the house, with its rickety steps and shingled overhang. But it was the dark metal weather vane on the roof, forged in the shape of a human hand and spinning lazily in the spotlight of the moon, that made her jam on the brakes and stare aghast at what he had done.

The hand with its index finger pointed to show the direction of the wind bobbed and settled on east. Coben's house had featured a weather vane just like it. In fact, the whole property seemed to be fashioned after Coben's old farmhouse, from the wood-post fence to the rocking chair on the porch. "Do you like it?" Brady asked. "I did it all myself."

"They tore down that old farm," she said, wide-eyed at her memory come to life. It was the only thing that had let her sleep at night after she came home, the knowledge that Coben's closets had been obliterated by a wrecking ball.

"I know. I had to work from memory, from what they showed on TV. No one thought to keep any pictures." He waved the gun at her midsection. "Get out."

Somehow she forced herself to get out of the car, but she couldn't look at the house. Time had slowed. Her ears rang with the force of all the screams she kept inside, while overhead the stars seemed to spark without cadence. She would almost rather he kill her than make her go inside the farmhouse. "What do you even want from me?" she asked, her voice raw and strained. "Why are you doing this?"

"You know."

"No, I don't. I don't know! This doesn't make sense to me at all."

"You were there, Abigail, the same as I was. I saw him take you. I saw you go down in his arms like a rag doll. You were dead—I saw you were!—but then suddenly on TV there you were alive again. You were supposed to be dead!"

He flung the hard words like an angry accusation. Like she had cheated him somehow. "You're sick," she told him. "You need help."

Even as she said it, she didn't believe it was true; he was beyond help. He didn't seem to hear her anyway. He appeared caught up in the memory of her abduction, his eyes hazy. "It's an amazing thing, watching the life go out of someone. One minute they're here and then the next they're gone for good."

"Where is Reed?" She looked around at the desolate yard, which was steeped in shadow and smelled sickly sweet due to the decaying sunburned grass.

"I'll show you," Brady said, nudging her toward the front porch. The steps groaned under her weight. She could practically feel Brady's breath on her neck. He reached around her with one hand and shoved open the unlocked door. "Go on, then." He pushed her forward and she staggered over the threshold into a dark room.

"Reed?" she called out into the blackness.

Brady kicked her hard in the back of her knee, sending her sprawling to the floor. "Shut up," he ordered as he loomed over her. "I'm the one who talks now."

She crawled as far away from him as she dared and got to her feet again. He flicked on the switch for the light, and she gasped to find herself standing next to a huge black-and-white portrait of Francis Coben. The room was otherwise bare—no furniture at all, just a scuffed wooden floor and some faded red gingham curtains left over from a happier time. The paint had peeled in several places, and water damage leaked in from the roofline. The ash-coated fireplace hadn't been touched in years. "You live here?" she asked him.

"No, this is where I work. Upstairs now." He directed her to another rickety wooden staircase that had a loose railing and a broken tread. She climbed slowly, weighted down by the dread in her stomach, and halfway up, she smelled it: the unmistakable scent of death. It had crawled up inside her during her days in the closet, so deep in her pores she didn't think she would ever get free. She halted and squeezed her eyes shut.

"I said *move*." He jabbed her with the gun again, and somehow she forced her trembling legs up to the top of the stairs. "Thataway."

The stench got stronger as they went to a room at the back of the house, where he turned on another light, this one just a pair of naked bulbs up against the ceiling. Ellie saw bloodstains on the floor and a bucket and hacksaw in the corner, and she realized the downstairs walls had not been damaged by water. He had turned the whole house into an abattoir.

There were two doors at the back of the room. Closets. "Please," she said, "don't do this."

"Your hero, Agent Markham, he's behind one of those two doors. Probably not in the best shape, but he's alive. Did you read his book?" Brady waited, apparently sincerely interested in her answer. She shook her head. "Too bad. It was pretty good. He wrote about how he would never know what you and the other girls went through in Coben's closet. Sounded like regret to me." He shook his head and eyed the doors. "You know now, though, don't you, FBI man?" he hollered at the closets. There was silence on the other side.

"Let him go," Ellie said. "He's got nothing to do with this."

"He has everything to do with this! If it wasn't for him, you'd be dead by now. Let's see if you can return the favor, hmm?" He pointed with the gun at one closet, then the other. "Which should it be? Door number one or door number two?"

"Let him go," Ellie repeated.

"Choose."

"I'm not choosing. Just please let him go. This is between you and me, right? The rest of them don't mean anything. I'm the one you really want." Her heart pounded in her ears and her mouth had gone completely dry. The gun seemed to sway in his hands.

"It's a hell of a story he wrote," Brady said, sighting the closets in turn once more. "Who's going to write this story, do you think? Who's going to make us all famous this time?" He looked over at her, his face in an open sneer. "Pick a door, Abigail."

"No." The word had barely left her mouth when Brady opened fire, pumping six shots through the door on the right. Ellie screamed and put up her hands to shield herself from the noise and horror. The scent of gunpowder filled the air and Brady wiped his nose on his sleeve. Ellie's ears were ringing and her arms shaking as she made herself look at the battered door with the holes in it.

"Let's show the lady what she's won," Brady hollered as he took a couple of old keys from his pocket. He tossed one to Ellie. "Open it."

"I . . . I can't." Her hands were too unsteady. The key clattered to the floor.

"I said open it!"

She choked back a sob and stumbled to the closet. She considered turning and rushing for the gun, seeing as how he was going to kill her anyway. She fumbled twice before she could get the key into the lock. The knob stuck and she had to lean into it to open the door, which came free with a sudden cracking noise. "Oh, God," Ellie breathed as her stomach turned over. Inside, Julia Parker's body lay propped up against the back, her hands gone and her torso now littered with bullet holes. She had been dead for some time.

"Guess he must be in the other one," Brady said casually from behind her. Rage overcame reason. She took several quick steps toward him, forcing him to back up.

"Ah, ah," he said, pointing the gun at her chest. "Don't you want to see what's behind door number two?"

"You're a monster."

"I am only what you made me."

"Screw you," she spat at him. "This isn't on me. I'm not the one kidnapping people and butchering them. For what? For fun?

To make you famous? You think it'll be fun bunking next to Coben on death row?"

"Coben," he repeated, spreading his arms and waving her gun about the room. "Coben couldn't get the job done. His time is up, don't you see? No one will mention his name anymore without also talking about me."

"Yes," she said scornfully. "What a sad, lonely little loser you are. Couldn't even make up his own crimes. He had to fake someone else's."

"There is nothing fake about me!" Brady roared. In a flash, he raised the gun and Ellie barely had time to shout before he had fired seven shots through the other closet door.

"No!" Ellie shouted, her eyes blurring with tears. "No, no, no!" She whirled on Brady but he was ready for her this time, with her own gun pointed right between her eyes.

"Ask yourself," he said, breathing hard, sweat dripping down his cheek. "How many more bullets do I have? How many to make sure you're really gone this time, hmm? I can stand here and watch the light go out from behind your pretty eyes."

Ellie lunged at him, claws out, and roared a furious, fiery scream fourteen years in the making. His eyes went wide with shock. She screamed so hard it brought the roof down, or so it seemed, with a crash and a cloud of plaster. She drew up short as Brady went down inside the dust cloud as the ceiling caved in, only it wasn't the shower of paste and mortar that trapped him—it was Reed. He dropped like a paratrooper out of the sky and tackled Brady to the floor, the two of them wrestling around and grappling over the gun. Ellie circled until she saw her opportunity, and she stomped hard on Brady's hand, forcing him to release the gun and sending it skidding across the room toward the bucket and saw.

Brady yelped in pain, and his distress was enough to gain Reed the upper hand as he pinned the other man's hands behind his back. "Get the rope," he said, red faced and breathless.

Ellie had the gun trained on both of them, her arms still shaking.

"The rope!" Reed repeated, and Ellie saw there was a length of bloody rope lying near the bucket. She threw it to Reed, who bound Brady's hands. He stood up and Ellie vaguely noticed his face was streaked with dried blood. On the floor, Brady glared up at her, furious and impotent.

Dimly, Ellie could see Reed's mouth moving, but his words made no sense to her. The static inside her head was a radio with the volume turned way up. Her arms ached, but they felt locked in place and she had not lowered the gun. She had it pointed toward the floor now, right at Brady's head.

"Ellery? Ellie. Put down the gun and call for backup."

Brady might have laughed. The sound was a rattle, blood trickling out of his injured mouth. "She's not going to shoot me. We're the same, her and me. We go together or not at all."

"Shut up," Reed said, bringing his foot down hard on the back of Brady's leg. "Ellie, put the gun down."

She shook her head, unable to comply. She saw Brady's face swim in and out of focus on the other side of the gun barrel. It wavered as she trembled.

"You can. Do it now."

Do it. Her heart surged in her throat, adrenaline like electricity in her veins.

"Forever!" Brady yelled from the floor. "You and me, Abigail. Screw Coben—you belong to me now!"

He seemed to rise up as he said it, his body levitating from the floor, and her finger clamped down on the trigger. Noise exploded into the room. Brady slumped on the floor.

"No!" Reed's shout of horror bounced off the empty walls and disappeared with the reverberations from her shot.

When she could see again, she staggered forward and slowly lowered her shaking arms. Reed stood frozen somewhere to the side in her peripheral vision and she did not look at him because she did not want to see his face. Her chest heaved and her cheeks burned red hot. In front of her on the floor, Brady was still and silent at last, blood leaking out from the side of his head. "One," she whispered brokenly as the gun slipped from her fingers to the floor. "There was one bullet left." Then she covered her face with both hands and wept.

Epilogue

Reed sat with his bandaged hands resting on the table in the interrogation room of the Woodbury Police Department. The doctors at the hospital had removed one hundred and eleven splinters in all, plus sewed up a good two-inch gash on his left palm. *Coben would love me now,* he thought ironically as he admired his ravaged hands. Across from him, Puss McGreevy switched off the recorder and put down his pen. "It's just you and me in here now, Reed. You may as well give it to me straight."

"I told you what happened."

"Yes, you told me: you leapt like a tiger from the trees, whereupon you and Willett struggled for control of Officer Hathaway's weapon. The gun got loose, Hathaway retrieved it, and she fired to stop Willett from strangling you to death."

"That's right."

McGreevy squinted at him. "Your face is bruised all down one side. You've got a nice shiner and a real lump on your head. Your hands look like they've been through a meat grinder."

"You can see then why I was losing the fight."

"But I don't see any markings on your neck," McGreevy finished, fixing Reed with a hard look.

Self-conscious, Reed put a gauzy hand to his throat. "It was more of a crushing feeling than a squeeze . . ."

"Willett also had ligature marks on his wrists." McGreevy paused to indicate the spot on his own hands. "Here and here. And there was rope found at the scene."

"Maybe he liked to tie himself up," Reed said coolly. He held McGreevy's gaze. "He was one sick bastard—or didn't you notice?"

"Oh, we noticed," McGreevy said heartily as he shifted in his chair. "We noticed so much that probably no one is going to look too closely at these little discrepancies in your story. Because you know very well it is a story. I'd file it under 'f' for 'fiction.'"

Reed knew that discretion was the better part of valor in this case, so he said nothing.

McGreevy sighed again and tugged at his chin. "They finally found Shannon Blessing about an hour ago. She'd been buried far out in the backyard, little more than a skeleton now, but dental records are a match."

"That's all of them, then," Reed murmured. Julia Parker was in the closet. Bea Nesbit's remains had been discovered packed away in a heavy-duty freezer in the basement of the house. Mark Roy had been dug up the day before. His hands had not yet been found.

"I'll give her this: Ellery saved the taxpayers a ton of money on a trial and spared the families the trauma of having to relive it."

Reed had already considered this and wondered whether Ellery had been thinking of it when she pulled the trigger. Or maybe she just hadn't wanted to spend the rest of her days living inside some other serial murderer's head. Brady couldn't touch her now. Couldn't even breathe her name.

"Of course," McGreevy continued, "her shooting him in the head means we'll never be able to question him. We'll never understand why he did it."

Reed bowed his head at this essential truth. "No," he agreed, "we never will." He hadn't been able to see Ellery in the past couple of days because they had been kept separate until their statements could be recorded. From what McGreevy said, it sounded like Ellery had stuck to the narrative. "What's going to happen now?" he asked his boss. "To Ellery."

McGreevy's frown softened a bit and he cleared his throat. "That isn't up to me. Or you either, for that matter. She's on mandatory leave at the moment, but I think she'll be cleared in the shooting. After that? Well, shit, Reed, you know how these things go. Four people are dead. Ellery held some things back early in the game that might have broken the investigation sooner. I can't promise you she emerges clean from all of this."

"She's the only one who saw this coming," Reed protested. "She tried for years to draw attention to these cases, but Chief Parker wouldn't listen."

"Yes. I'd say he paid the price for that, wouldn't you?" The two men eyed each other through a tense beat of silence. McGreevy broke first, with a heavy sigh. "You've seen how this breaks down in big cases, Markham—there's what actually happened, and then there's the story that gets told about it afterward. My advice to Ellery Hathaway is to get herself a lawyer and try to seize control of the narrative. Hell, maybe she can write a book that will outsell yours."

Reed thought of Ellery's stricken face as she stood over the body, the dead quiet that had filled the room. "Ellery would never go public on her own," he told McGreevy.

His boss shrugged and shook his head, dismissing the whole case into history. "Nothing more you can do for her, then. Tell her good-bye and come on home." He pushed aside the legal pad and rubbed the back of his neck with one hand. "I don't know about you, but I could use a drink or six. Somewhere dark and quiet. What do you say?"

Reed had three empty water bottles lined up on the table in front of him, the product of his new, unslakable thirst. The hours he'd spent in the dirty, sweltering closet leached half the sweat from his body. McGreevy's offer, and the thought of cold hard alcohol, made his mouth tingle. A few quick drinks and maybe he'd no longer see Julia Parker's handless corpse, or hear the ringing shot from Ellery's gun.

His palms itched and stung like hell under the bandages. He held them out loosely for inspection, pondering their significance. Alcohol would numb this pain, too, if he wanted. He could forget how desperately he'd clawed his way out of Brady Archer's makeshift coffin. Or he could embrace the sting like a slap across the face. The life he'd fought so hard to reclaim, it could still be lost. He carefully laid his hands on the table and looked McGreevy in the eye. "No, thanks. I've got to go."

It was dark when Reed left the station house, but reporters swarmed him like pickpockets, eager to steal whatever bit of him they could pry free. He put up his injured hands as a shield. "No comment. No comment." He ducked away from the cameras and the lights and the microphones, wanting no part of the dog-and-pony show. He had already seen enough of the reports on TV, the coverage endless on all the news channels. CNN played it on a loop now: Brady's picture taken from his social-media accounts; the footage of law enforcement traipsing in and out of Brady's bloody lair; the breathless accounts from neighbors who'd heard the gruesome details and could not wait to share them with the world. Reed had participated with pride in the media circus fourteen years ago, but now, knowing young Brady had been taking it all in with hungry eyes, it mostly turned Reed's stomach. As the infamy machine went to work on Brady Archer, Reed had to admit there might be another little boy out there watching the news and imagining his future.

The next day, Reed made a last trip out to Ellery's house on Burning Tree Road. He had a plane ticket home at four that afternoon, and Sarit promised to be at the airport with Tula. He ached at the thought of holding them again, that they would be a family for a few minutes, at least until he picked up his baggage.

He stood on Ellery's porch with a paper sack clutched awkwardly in one bandaged hand, wondering how he was supposed to knock in his condition. He hadn't actually formulated a plan when the door swung open and Ellie leaned against it, looking solemn. He smiled at her and held up his hands in surrender. "You saved me from knocking," he said. "I can't bend my hands yet."

She said nothing.

"Can I come in?" he asked, and she hesitated a moment before stepping back and allowing him inside. As he crossed the threshold, Speed Bump came limping toward him, tongue slobbering everywhere, but this time, Reed grinned at the sight. "I see the beast is recovering well."

"Searchers out in the woods heard the shot that night," Ellery said. "They got here pretty quick, and the bullet went clean through. The vet said Bump should be chasing squirrels again in no time." She leaned down and scratched him on the head.

"Just not any poodles—right?"

Ellery gave a small smile, humoring him. "Right."

They stood in awkward silence for a moment and then he thrust the bag at her. "Here, I wanted to give you this."

"What is it?" She accepted the paper sack and peered in at the pink frosted cupcake he had purchased from the bakery in town.

"It's your birthday today," Reed explained. "Everyone should have cake on their birthday."

She just stood there, her eyes welling up, and he felt guilty regret wash over him. He'd been presumptuous. "Ellie, I didn't mean to—"

"I haven't celebrated my birthday in years," she cut in, holding the sack to her middle.

Reed bit his lip. "Maybe it's time you start," he suggested gently. She looked away, shaking her head. "Hey," he said, shifting so that he was in her line of sight again. "If it weren't for you, I wouldn't be here."

She snorted a protest. "I think you have that backward."

"No, if you hadn't kept him talking, I wouldn't have had time to get through the ceiling to the attic. I would be full of holes right now."

"Don't," she said swiftly. "Don't even say that."

He looked her over searchingly, willing her to look at him, to truly see him and how he had changed. "You saved me," he told her seriously. "More than you know."

She sniffed and scuffed at the floor with one shoe. Bump raised his large nose to sniff at the paper bag in her hands. "You didn't have to cover for me about what happened. I don't want . . . I don't want you to have to lie. To live with secrets. It's harder than you might think."

Reed considered this with a tilt of his head. "He's dead. We can't change that, and I can't say I'm sorry. Can you?"

"No," she admitted slowly.

"He wanted us to keep talking about him, to keep telling his story. You and I were supposed to be the ticket to his immortality."

Reed paused for effect. "So I propose we don't ever mention the little bastard's name again. What do you say?"

She looked at the floor for a long moment, and when she raised her head, he saw her eyes were clear. "I say . . . this cupcake looks too big to eat by myself, and Bump isn't allowed to have chocolate. Do you want half?"

"That's the best offer I've had all day." He followed her into the kitchen, where she took down two small plates and fetched a knife. "Wait," he blurted out before she could divide the cupcake in half. "Do you have any candles?"

"Let's not push it," she replied, eyeing him. "I'm rusty at this, remember?"

He straightened up and nodded. "Right. Of course. Got it."

She set his half on the plate and gave him a fork. They ate together as the sun slanted in through the kitchen window, the dog thumping his tail between them, ever hopeful. Then Ellie informed Reed that he looked like a mummy as he fumbled to hold the fork with his bandaged hands, pink icing smearing across the gauze. He licked it off anyway. Her gray eyes went wide in shock at his indecency before she broke into a surprised, genuine laugh—a clear crystal sound that harkened back to the fourteen-year-old girl she might have been. Reed smiled, savoring every last bite on his plate, because it was very sweet indeed.